Coon Dogs And Outhouses

Volume 3

Tales From Tennessee

I0587265

Luke Boyd

TotalRecall Publications, Inc.

TotalRecall Publications, Inc.
1103 Middlecreek
Friendswood, Texas 77546
281-992-3131 281-482-5390 Fax

Printed in the United States of America with simultaneous
printings in Australia, Canada, and United Kingdom.

FIRST EDITION
1   2   3   4   5   6   7   8   9   10

This is a work of fiction. The characters, names, events, views, and
subject matter of this book are either the author's imagination or are
used fictitiously. Any similarity or resemblance to any real people,
real situations or actual events is purely coincidental and not intended
to portray any person, place, or event in a false, disparaging or
negative light.

FOR ALEX AND ABBY
THE THIRD GENERATION

About the Author

Dr. Lucas G. "Luke" Boyd first saw the light of day in a three-room shotgun house on Jabe Dunaway's place near Anguilla, Mississippi. It was the depths of the Depression. His father had lost everything and had returned to the land to feed his family. However, within a few years he was managing one of those sprawling, 2,000-plus acre cotton plantations the Delta was known for. This plantation culture of his early years left an indelible mark on young Luke.

A stroke of good fortune and a good scholarship allowed him to attend The University of Mississippi, where he earned a B.S. degree. During his career he attended a total of five universities, three of which saw fit to grant him degrees: Middle Tennessee State University (M.S.), The University of Tennessee (Ph.D. in English History). Stints at The University of North Carolina and The University of Chattanooga were for special study in Economics and Far Eastern History, respectively.

He entered the Army through the ROTC program and served for two years as a lst Lt. in an armored unit.

After leaving the service, he began a career in education which spanned 48 years both at the secondary and college levels. He retired after serving for 19 years as Principal of Battle Ground Academy, a private, college preparatory school in Franklin, Tennessee.

His publishing credits include: three books, Coon Dogs and Outhouses, Vol. I and II, Don't Call Me Hero (ghost writer) the story of a WW II bomber pilot; 9 short stores; 1 article in The Tennessee Encyclopedia of History and Culture. He currently writes regular columns for a local newspaper, The Williamson Herald, and for Mature Lifestyles magazine.

He and his wife, Sara, have been married for 57 years and have two children and two grandchildren. They live in Franklin, Tennessee.

About the Book

It all started back in 2004. I had grown tired of reading stories in our local newspaper whose writers had problems putting sentences together correctly. An especial egregious error was the misplacement of modifiers and modifying phrases. It was common to read a caption under a picture that "Joe Quick, star running back for the Pinecrest Panthers, signs a letter of intent of play football in the coming year for the University of Tennessee on Thursday." This, of course, would make him a <u>very</u> specialized player as he would only be playing in games scheduled for that one day of the week. Figuring these errors to be the property of the sports writers, I held my tongue until the curse of the roving modifiers began to migrate to other sections of the paper. Critical mass was reached when a local fellow was killed in a motorcycle wreck on Concord Road. A misplaced modifying phrase made it appear that the accident had occurred at Centennial Hospital.

No longer able to restrain myself, I wrote a letter to the editor, pointing out these reoccurring errors and asking that the paper try to present a correct and positive writing example for our youth. My letter was not printed. I had known the editor for a number of years and expected some response but got none. A few weeks later I ran into the editor at a Christmas open house. Her first words to me were, "You can come down to the office and read copy any time you want to." My response was that I didn't have time to be the paper's copy editor and that the paper ought to have someone to fill that role. Next she asked, "Do you think you can do any better."

"I know I can," I replied.

"Well, write me a couple of columns and let's see," she said as she obviously threw down a challenge.

I did so and soon after came the offer for me to write a

regular column. I almost panicked. What if after two or three months I found that I had nothing left to say? Crashing and burning in full view of a lot of people who knew me would be an inglorious end. But I decided to give it a whirl. That was over nine years ago and so far I've written about 250 columns and still have a writing folder full of ideas and topics that (I think) need commenting on. And in 2007 the editor of <u>Mature Lifestyles</u>, a monthly magazine for seniors, read some of my stuff and asked me to do a column for their publication. And through it all I've managed to keep my modifiers in the correct places.

As I was beginning my newspaper career, one of my good friends asked me what I was going to write about. When I replied that my editor told me that I could write about anything I wanted to, he said, "I don't believe I'd give you that much leeway." So far I've only had one piece rejected for being "too controversial." That piece is included in this book. I'll let you readers figure out which one it is.

Someone asked me if this was going to be a book of my "best" columns. The truth is I'm not real comfortable with that "best" designation. Taste tends to differ. So what I've tried to do is select a variety of topics and group them into several categories even though some pieces seem to defy categorization.

Even though the words and thoughts are mine, I owe a tremendous debt to others who actually made them come to print. Foremost is Sara, my "tech support," who did all the typing and computer work. Our marriage has survived for 57 years, four books, and numerous short literary pieces—a remarkable feat in and of itself. A grateful "thank you" has to go to Bruce Moran and all the folks at TotalRecall Publications who know how to put all the parts together.

TABLE OF CONTENTS

PART I

COON DOGS
AND OUTHOUSES

A DISCLAIMER

Volume I of this series was true to the title: it had a story about a coon dog and one about an outhouse. When I did Volume II, my publisher liked the title so much that he wanted to keep it even though there were no such stories included. I apologized for this misrepresentation in the Introduction but still felt badly about misleading the reader. Now we've come to Volume III and the time has come to make this one an "honest" book. So this first section does just that before heading off in many different directions. Both stories happen to be true.

BUYING THE COON DOG

Milton was from Kansas but had come South to go to college at Vanderbilt University in Nashville. He majored in English and upon graduation secured a teaching position at The Webb School in Bell Buckle, Tennessee. Webb was and is a small college-prep, boarding/day school in a hamlet of about 300. Milton enjoyed the rural flavor of the place and was intrigued by the local people and culture. He heard about coon dogs and decided he would be more accepted by the locals if he had one. Since there were no "coon dog stores," he set out to locate a local owner who might have one for sale. He went to Gray Vance, the town's Postmaster, who knew everyone in the area and asked him about local coon dog owners. Gray replied, "You might try 'Hired' Hatchett. He's gotta bunch." Milton thought "Hired" to be an unusual name but he didn't question it. He thought maybe he'd just found a job or maybe was often hired by local folk. Anyway, he got directions to "Hired's" house and set out.

Finding what he thought to be the right place, he parked in front of the rambling house and went to the front door. His knock was answered by a very large man wearing bib overalls. "I'm looking for Hired Hatchett," said Milton.

"I'm Hired," the man responded.

After Milton stated his business, Hired invited him in and took him through the house to several pens in the back yard. They contained a number of dogs of various ages. Milton, of course, didn't know what to look for in a coon dog so they all looked good to him. And since he wanted the dog for a pet, he didn't care if the dog ever treed a coon or not. All the dogs, especially the young ones were very friendly—good pet material.

However, when Hired began to quote some prices, Milton realized that Tennessee coon hunters and coon dog breeders thought an awful lot of their dogs. He'd seen AKC registered dogs for less. And there were no "papers" on any of Hired's dogs—just statements like, "This 'un came from Black-eyed Sue and Speedy Sam." None of this meant anything to Milton so he bowed out as gracefully as he could, telling Hired he would give some thought to which dog he might like to purchase.

On his way back to his car, Milton noted the name on the side of the mailbox and realized that he had a lot to learn about the Southern way of pronouncing words. He'd been calling his host "Hired." The letters on the mailbox plainly said, "Howard Hatchett."

John's Two-Holer

John was born in 1925 on a farm in rural East Tennessee. His was a large family and for the sake of efficiency his father had constructed a "two-holer" outhouse. John liked their outhouse mainly because he got to go to the outhouse with his father. With a number of brothers and sisters, that was about the only time John got any private time with his dad. He said they'd talk about all sorts of things and that he learned a great deal from is dad during their "outhouse sessions." One early lesson was to use the black and white pages of the Sears catalog first because they were much softer than those in color. Then he taught him how to take the colored pages and wad and unwad them several times to make them softer and easier to use.

Another lesson was how to deal with outhouse spiders, especially the poisonous black widow. This breed was drawn to dark, secluded places and the underside of the seat area near the hole made a perfect home for them. Bites on the behind by a black widow were fairly common and very painful although not usually fatal. John's father solved the spider bite problem by lighting a page of the catalog and passing the flaming paper around underneath the hole, burning away the spider webs and either killing or chasing off any lurking spiders. When this was done, the burning paper was dropped into the pit. On one of their outhouse trips, John's father had performed his fire ritual and they were sitting and talking when John began to get warm. In fact, he was getting very warm and finally said, "Papa, I'm getting hot."

"Now that you mention it, I am, too," his father replied. "Wonder what's wrong?" They both got up and looked down into the pit. The flaming page had ignited other debris in the pit. The fire was getting more intense and climbing the walls toward them. They ran to the pump and pumped several buckets of water and poured them into the pit to douse the flames. The whole family was grateful for the outcome. If word had gotten around the community that they had burned up their outhouse, they never would have lived it down.

PART II

FAMILY STUFF

MAMA

Mama did not have an easy life. But in spite of the harshness of her existence, she was basically a cheerful and optimistic person.

She was born in 1897 and grew up on a hard scrabble farm hear Grayson, Louisiana. After high school she went to the nearest good-size town, Alexandria, and got a job in a drug store. It was there that she met my father who was, at that time, a traveling man. After marrying they began traveling together throughout Louisiana and Mississippi selling cookware. With bad roads and poor accommodations during the 1920s, this was as much an adventure as it was a job.

Then came 1929 with the Stock Market crash and the ensuing depression. Folks were having enough trouble just getting food to eat. They surely did not have money to buy new pots to cook it in. With no jobs and no prospects, my parents returned to the land.

It was not an easy existence for Mama but she could cope with it since she had grown up under similar conditions—no electricity, no plumbing, hard farm work from before daylight until after dark. Daddy worked in the fields while Mama took care of the house and two small children, cooked three meals every day, raised a large garden, raised a yard full of chickens, and milked the cow.

Monday was wash day and took up most of the day. Clothes were boiled in a big black pot which sat over a wood fire in the back yard. They were then scrubbed on a wash board, rinsed, blued, and starched in tubs which sat up on a wash bench. After being wrung out they were hung on the clothes line to dry

Tuesday was ironing day and everything was ironed with flat irons which were heated on the wood cook stove in the summer and in the fireplace in the winter.

The garden provided fresh vegetables for the table as well as a source of produce to can or dry for winter food. Mama spent most of her time during warm months weeding, picking, and canning. Jars filled with beans, peas, tomatoes, etc. were cooked in a pressure cooker on the cook stove. This was a hot job. With the temperature at 100 degrees plus outside, it was probably 130 degrees plus in the kitchen.

Cooler weather did not alter the pace of raising and preserving food. The garden became a large patch of turnips and greens. Hogs were butchered when the weather got cold enough for the meat not to spoil. Mama canned sausage and pork chops; the rest was either smoked or salted.

We didn't have much money but, as one can see from the above, we never were hungry.

Mama never had a house of her own but she knew what she wanted. We'd see a house and she'd say," Wouldn't have that one. Doesn't have a porch." A porch was essential for siting and catching breezes in the evenings during the sweltering summers. Every summer morning you could count on Mama to say, "There was such a good breeze last night. So good for sleeping," or the opposite if such as the case. She appreciated the simple things. Her house would also have to have some umbrella chinaberry trees in the yard (for shade) and a silver leaf maple because "it looks so pretty when the wind blows."

As Daddy began managing large Delta plantations our houses got better eventually having electric lights and plumbing. A black woman was hired to man the wash pot on Mondays but there was still plenty of work for Mama to do.

Then, a bad heart took Daddy leaving Mama with only a small pension and two teenage sons. I'd just finished my second year of college and offered to quit and get a job. She wouldn't hear of it. She said, 'I'll get a job," and she did—driving a laundry truck and later working in a plant making athletic equipment. I was on scholarship but had to work during the summer to make spending money for the school year. She wouldn't let me give her any of it and when she'd write during the terms, there'd always be two or three dollars bills pinned to the last page "just for incidentals."

Age finally caught up with her and she had to quit work. By this time my brother and I could help her with a little money each month but not nearly enough. She lived in a small rental house with no porch but there was an air conditioner.

Mama was not an affectionate woman but we knew she loved us. She showed it in many ways. She was always proud of her sons' accomplishments and rightly so because of the lessons she taught us and the example she set.

Mama was also a stubborn woman. Fiercely independent, she refused either to live with her sons or go to a nursing home. As she began increasingly to lose touch with reality and with a nursing home looming just ahead, her heart played out. She was a couple of months past 80. She'd had her way to the end.

When we were growing up and would get a nice gift from someone, Mama would often say, "Why that's too nice to use. Put it up and save it." I suppose this feeling came from not having many nice things. As we were clearing out her little house, we found things she'd been given—scarves, handkerchiefs, gloves, and other personal items—all new, unused, and in their original boxes. They'd been too nice to use so she'd put them up and saved them. Sometimes old habits are hard to break.

FOR GRANNY ON MOTHER'S DAY

G̲ranny was my paternal grandmother. The best I can
figure, she was born about 1859, give or take a year or
two. She grew up and spent most of her adult life on a farm in
Bogue Chitto, a rural community which took its name from the
creek that ran through it. It is located near McComb in southern
Mississippi. She was not born there but, as she used to say,
"somewhere back to the East." She told of coming to the Bogue
in a wagon when she was just a little girl. She never said
whether or not it was covered.

There were three prominent families along the Bogue--
Beard, Boyd, and Dunaway. She was a Beard before she
married my grandfather, John L. Boyd. He had a farm. I don't
know how large it was but I'd guess several hundred acres since
they raised thirteen children on it.

Granny was a short woman, no more than five feet tall.
Pictures show her as a slender, young woman. I suppose
running a farmhouse and rearing all those kids kept the weight
off. But I did not know her until she was well up into her
seventies--very much overweight and walking with a cane. In
those days fatness was not considered particularly bad. She did
love to eat. I remember one night at our house we had a big
supper with hot biscuits. Granny was finishing up with hot
buttered biscuits and homemade preserves. She must have
eaten six or seven extra biscuits, trying to make them and the
preserves come out even.

One thing she prized was her long hair. It had probably
never been cut and fell to her waist in the back. She claimed

that at one time she could sit on it but that it didn't grow so long since she'd gotten older. Every morning she would take it down and brush it--a hundred strokes she always said. I never knew if this were true because I always lost count. After the brushing she would take her comb, divide it into thirds, and plait a long pigtail. If she were just going to be around the house, she'd let it hang down but if she were going someplace, she'd wind it up in a tight bun on the back of her head and hold it in place with long hairpins and some small combs.

After Granny "broke up housekeeping" (her words), she went to live with one of her daughters. However, she felt it her duty to visit each of her children at least once a year. She did not wait for an invitation. They were all her family and that was a standing invitation in and of itself. And since nobody traveled much in those days, everyone was home most of the time. Arrangements were always made by mail because most did not have phones. We'd get a letter several months in advance stating that she would make a visit in late July. Then, closer to that time a letter would come saying that she would arrive on a specific date at a certain time either by train or Greyhound bus. She never gave advance warning of the length of her stay but you could usually count on two or three weeks. Sometimes she would be on a circuit run and would hit two or three of her children before returning to home base.

My brother and I loved to have her visit because she would play cards and other games with us, tell stories, and use funny expressions. When she wanted us to hurry up, she'd say, "Make ace, now, make ace." It was long after her death that I realized she'd been saying, "Make haste."

Granny majored in snake stories, some of which were true. She told about gathering eggs as a young girl. The nests were so high along the wall of the smokehouse that she'd have to use a stool to reach in for the eggs. One day she stuck her hand in on a big chicken snake that was in a nest swallowing the eggs.

This frightened her so much that she fell backward off the stool and flat on the ground. The fall knocked the wind out of her and she could do nothing but lie there gasping for air as the snake made his escape.

One snake she liked to tell about was the coach whip, named for the long whip used to drive horse-drawn coaches. This reptile was _very_ long and _very_ fast. He would not bite you. Instead he would chase you down, wrap himself around your body to hold you in place, rear his head up and look you in the eye, and give you a good whipping with his tail.

Another of her favorites was the hoop snake. He did not bite either but had a very poisonous stinger at the end of his tail. If you tried to run from him, he would form himself into a hoop and roll after you. When he caught you, he'd sting you. Granny told one time about running from a hoop snake and jumping behind a large oak tree just as he caught her. The snake stung the tree. All its leaves immediately fell off and it was dead before sundown. We never saw any of these breeds of snakes but we just knew they existed because Granny said so.

I liked to hear her tell about when she was young. She told about riding to church in an open wagon in the hot summertime wearing all those heavy clothes women wore in those days. They'd stop at the last house before church to freshen up. They'd get a drink of water, dry off the perspiration, and use some flour from the flour bin to dab on their faces in place of face powder.

Granny was a big supporter of _anything_ her family did. In the early 1940s one of her relatives, a Dunaway, concocted a salve that he touted to cure everything from dandruff to hemorrhoids. Somehow Granny got hold of case of it and was peddling it to anyone who came walking by on the street. Her daughter nearly had a hissy fit when she found out and made her stop. After all, "What would the neighbors think?"

With all her children and grandchildren, Granny got a lot of gifts at Christmas. They mostly came in the mail and usually began arriving shortly after Thanksgiving. Sometimes she'd get two or three a day and she opened them as soon as they arrived. One year I asked her why she didn't save them until Christmas. She answered, "Why, I might die before then." She was then in her eighties and not about to put off any pleasure.

The only time I remember Granny being sick was when she went to visit one of her relatives who did not have indoor plumbing. She sat down in the outhouse and a black widow spider bit her on the butt. After a few days in the hospital, she was as good as new. We all speculated that she'd live to be a hundred. But it was not to be. She developed a bleeding ulcer and in those days the only solution was surgery. The operation was a success and they almost had her closed up when her heart gave out. She was 86.

They took her back to Bogue Chitto for the services and burial. I was a pallbearer. The large country church was filled to overflowing—a tribute to one of the community's matriarchs and to a life well lived.

TRAVELING MAN

Daddy was a traveling man—at least he was during his early years. He traveled for the Wrought Iron Range Company selling iron cook stoves and heaters to families in the rural South. This was in the early 1900s before cars were very common. He would travel by train to a small town where he would rent a horse and buggy. Weekdays would be spent riding the country roads looking for prospects. Each day he would locate some family who would put him up for the night. For fifty cents he could get a night's lodging, supper, breakfast, and a stall and feed for his horse. Weekends were spent in town at the local hotel or a boarding house. I have heard him relate many tales about happenings as he roamed the countryside as well as weekend events in town.

He told of one family who seemed almost too eager for him to spend the night. The day was growing late and he didn't have another option. They didn't look too prosperous but he was not in a position to be too choosy. He surmised that they really needed the fifty cents.

Apparently, the family had not had a good crop year overall but had raised a bountiful crop of sweet potatoes. When Daddy unhitched his horse and put him in the barn, there was no grain to feed him. Instead the farmer gave him a little hay and half a sack of sweet potatoes.

Supper was about the same except for the hay. His wife served creamed sweet potatoes, candied sweet potatoes, baked sweet potatoes, and sweet potato pie for dessert. The only variety was plenty of milk. Daddy was thankful the cow hadn't gone dry.

Sometime in the night, they were awakened by a terrible commotion in the barn. Daddy's horse was making all sorts of whinnying sounds and kicking the sides of his stall. He was having a severe gas attack from all the sweet potatoes. Daddy and his host went to the barn, turned him out, and ran him around the barn lot. Finally, the horse raised his tail and passed gas with such force that Daddy said he thought he might below the barn away.

After a breakfast of fried sweet potatoes and fatback, Daddy went on his way. He said he didn't eat sweet potatoes for a good while after that experience.

Sometimes Daddy and another salesman would travel together and work the same towns. They would go their separate ways during the week but keep each company in town on weekends. From some of Daddy's stories, it seemed like they spent a good bit of their time playing practical jokes on the local folk. It's a wonder the natives didn't do them in over some of their escapades.

The towns were always crowded on Saturdays—especially in the afternoon when all the area farmers came in to get supplies. At some point during this busy time either Daddy or his buddy would walk out into the middle of the main street and start looking up. When the local folk began to notice him, the other conspirator would join him. The first "looker" would point to what he was looking at and the two of them would stand there pointing, craning their necks, and talking about what they were seeing. They would, of course, soon be joined by others who'd start looking and asking, "What is it? What do you see?"

"Well, look right there>"

"Where?"

"Right there by that big cloud. Did you ever see anything like that?"

"I don't see anything."

"Well, it just went behind the cloud. Look close and maybe you'll see it when it comes out. (Pause) There it is! Over on the other side!"

And so the conversation would go. More would join the group. Some would point. Some would actually see something. As the crowd grew larger, the two instigators would work their way to the periphery and finally go stand on the sidewalk observing the results of their handiwork and laughing to themselves. According to Daddy, some of the crowds lasted for quite a while and every crowd would have a few who would swear that they actually saw something, although there was never a common agreement as to what it was.

On one occasion Daddy was having Saturday lunch in a diner. A local farmer and his small son, a boy who looked to be about seven or eight, came in and took stools near him at the counter. The man ordered wieners and sauerkraut for the two of them. When the counterman sat the plates down, the boy looked suspiciously at his wieners which had curled up during the boiling process. He picked one up gingerly and took a bite. As he chewed, his eyes grew wide in amazement. He elbowed his father and exclaimed in a loud whisper, "Daddy, this chicken neck ain't got no bone in it!"

No one had to guess which chicken part he was used to getting at home.

Daddy also liked to tell about the time he was in some small town one Saturday in a one-chair barbershop waiting for a haircut. There were several waiting. A sign on the wall over the mirror behind the chair said that the barber could also "draw" teeth. As he finished with one customer, he called, "Next." A fellow who was obviously from way out in the country rose to his feet and climbed into the chair. "What'll it be?" asked the barber as he spread the white cloth over him.

"Ah needa shave," the man replied. And indeed he did. He had several days' growth.

"Yes, sir," said the barber. "You want a wet shave or a dry shave?" he asked teasing the man and winking at the waiting customers.

Apparently, the fellow had never had a shave in a barbershop. He thought for a moment before replying, "Well, ah reckon uh dry shave'll be jest fine."

"Coming right up," said the barber as he laid the chair back and picked up an old straight razor from the marble shelf over the sink. He didn't even strop it but just turned the man's head to one side and began scraping the hair from one cheek. The pain had to be severe as the fellow clutched the chair arms and squirmed about. The other customers were having a hard time keeping their laughter in check. Just at that time, a mule which was tied to a hitching post a few doors down from the barbershop began braying loudly, "Hee Haw! Hee Haw!"

"Wonder what's going on out there?" asked one customer as he went to the door and looked out.

By this time the man in the chair had about figured out that he was the butt of a painful joke and answered with, "It's probably jest another jackass gittin' uh dry shave."

Yes, Daddy was a traveling man. And I'm glad that he was because one day in one of those small towns, he met my mama.

EATING OUT

When I was growing up, eating out was not common. In fact, it was practically non-existent in my family. Of course, it was all right for people who worked in town to eat dinner (at noon) at one of the local cafes. But at suppertime these establishment had few customers. The only people eating out at night were traveling men, men who had no woman to cook for them, or women of ill repute who were looking to augment those reputations.

Mama always said, "Eating out is wasteful. We've got better food at home. Why would you want to pay a bad cook to cook you bad food and give you weak tea to drink?" It was a question I never had an answer for.

Mama always had dinner ready at noon so Daddy could eat and lie down for about thirty minutes before heading back to the fields. I've seen him come running in at mid-morning on his way to town to get a part for a broken down combine or tractor. Mama would hurriedly dip him out some servings from the pots she had on the stove so he could eat and not have to spend money at a café in town. I can hear her now saying, "Now, Luke, I know you're going to be hungry before supper. These beans aren't good done yet. You'd better come back by and eat you something else before you go work on that combine. I'll keep things warm for you." Sometimes he would.

On Saturdays we'd always go to town after we'd had dinner. However, about mid-afternoon after I'd taken in an episode of Wild Bill Eliot or Hop-a-long Cassidy, I was always hungry and the eating places called me as the Sirens had Ulysses. They'd have pictures of tempting foods in the windows and I longed to sink my teeth into some of those exotic dishes we never had at home. When I'd ask if I could have a hamburger, hot dog, or barbeque sandwich, I always got the same reply from Mama. First was, "You don't need to eat anything now. It'll ruin your supper." And then, "There's no telling what they've ground up in that meat. That's how they get rid of all the tails, snouts, entrails, and all the other parts nobody'll eat. It wouldn't be good. I know you wouldn't like it." I suppose I should have been grateful to have somebody to look out for my wellbeing like that. But, even though I knew the speech by heart, I still asked.

Daddy always took a different approach. Rather than the food, he would attack the establishment. "Naw, we wouldn't want to eat in there. It's nothing but a hole-in-the-wall." That was the term he always used for businesses (of all types) which he considered shoddy, dinky, low class, and beneath patronizing. Now I was just a little boy who was very literal-minded. I knew how big a hole-in-the-wall was. We had some at home. These cafes looked normal-sized to me. They had doors, windows, and a lot of space inside. It took me quite a while to figure out what he meant.

Sometimes, when on a trip to visit relatives, we'd pass through a larger town with a fancy restaurant. My request to eat there would be denied with, "Naw, that's way too expensive. We couldn't afford that." This led me to conclude that there were only two types of eating paces: hole-in-wall or too expensive. One we couldn't eat in, the other we wouldn't eat in. It seemed to me there should be a few somewhere for folks like us. I can't remember finding one.

Even when we went somewhere on the train or bus or took a long car trip (which was rare), a lunch was always packed along with a jug of sweet tea. None of that pay-for-food for us.

One place that especially intrigued me was the Bar-B-Cutie up on the main highway. It was topped with a large sign which featured a leggy, scantily clad waitress outlined in multi-colored neon. I thought the waitresses inside looked like that. I was severely disappointed later when I got inside and found the place run by a dumpy, middle-aged woman wearing a dirty apron who had her hair rolled up in a bun on the top of her head with a pencil sticking through it.   Life had lots of disappointments.

Of course, all this was happening during the Depression and World War II. After I got a little older, I understood why we never ate out. We didn't have any money.

When I got to the ninth grade, I got a Saturday job in town at one of the grocery stores. That meant I could have lunch at one of the two cafes on the Square—Shorty Wilkes' Café or Alvin's Café. We just had cafes—no restaurants. I suspect one reason was that it took too much neon tubing to spell "restaurant."

Shorty Wilkes was the father of one of my classmates. He had a speech impediment which became more pronounced in direct proportion to his level of excitement. His place was staffed mostly by his family members.

I always ate at Alvin's place, mainly because it was next door to the poolroom. Eating took about twenty minutes. During the rest of my lunchtime, I could get in two or three games of pool before going back to the store. A plate of beef stew and a large Pepsi was forty-five cents. A meat and two and Pepsi was sixty-five cents. I usually got the stew because the twenty-cent difference represented two games of pool.

Alvin was of Syrian descent. He had a swarthy complexion and coal-black hair and in today's thinking would be profiled as an international terrorist. He was known for employing the older high school girls as waitresses. He was also known for getting them pregnant. Apparently, he was able to work out some "arrangement" with them because there never was any public scandal.

Undoubtedly, Alvin was able to turn a good profit with the

little café. A few years after I graduated, he was able to move East and build a large steak house close to the University. He became a high profile supporter of the University's athletic program and his "restaurant" prospered from the patronage of University students. I am unaware of his relationships with the waitresses in this new location.

Four years of college and a tour of duty in the Army broadened my experiences with public eating establishments — both cafes and restaurants. However, marriage and a young family coupled with the salary of a starting teacher precluded a lot of eating out. I think that's why in our retirement years, we consider it quite a treat to go out to eat. And we do it often. Honey's position is that there are a plethora of restaurants in the area and we need to do our part in seeing that they stay in business.

In another vein our extensive (albeit recent) experience with a variety of eateries has caused me to be more critical. In fact, I think I could offer some good consultation to managers in the training of their servers. For one thing, I would forbid any twenty-year old to walk up to table of greying, balding geezers and greet them with, "How're you guys doing tonight?" Another thing is iced tea served with a straw and no iced teaspoon. How are you supposed to stir with a straw? I guess you could blow into it to create a bubbling effect but this usually causes an overflow onto the table. Now, iced tea is a long-standing, traditional Southern custom. I see the straw-in-the-tea movement as an insidious Yankee intrusion.

And contrary to Mama's admonitions I've tried hamburgers, hot dogs, and barbeque not to mention pizza, Mexican, Chinese, Italian, and few others and discovered that her assessment was way off base. However, I have occasionally come across a hole-in-wall. It's nice to know that your parents were not totally wrong.

LIFE WITH A ZINGERETTE

Recently, in a moment of reflection, it dawned on me that I have lived more than the number of years promised in the Bible—three score and ten. Along the same time line, Honey and I have passed the "golden" number of wedded years.

During these years I have acquired the reputation for being quick with a quip and/or a sarcastic remark. What people don't realize is that Honey is capable of throwing in some zingers as well. I suppose she's had to have that trait to survive and to hold her own with me all these years. I offer some cases in point.

Early in our marriage we were living in Bell Buckle while I taught at Webb School. We usually drove into Shelbyville once a week for groceries and usually took Fairfield Pike, the shortest route and one that was sadly in need of repair. There was one deep pothole that I kept hitting every week. It would almost jar your teeth out and no telling what it was doing to my right front tire. It was just at the crest of a little hill in a curve which made it impossible to see until you were right on it. There were a lot of hills and turns like this on the road so I never knew upon which one it lurked.

One day we set out with the mission to "locate the pothole." I said, "I'm going to drive very slowly up all these hills until I find it and then I'm going to find a landmark at that point to locate it with." Everything seemed to be going well. Suddenly, I spied it but the late afternoon sun was in my eyes, I was meeting a big truck, and I was trying to miss the hole and truck on the narrow road. The last thing I had time to do was to look for a landmark. So I shouted to Honey, "Look for a landmark! Look for a landmark!"

She replied, "There's a goat."

"Don't tell me that!" I said as I frantically tried to keep the car out of the ditch.

"That's all I see," was her calm reply.

We had some discussion about the matter but she steadfastly maintained that there was nothing else distinctive at that location. And, sure enough, the next week I hit the hole with full force. I let out a few choice words about the hole and the lack of road maintenance and another thing or two. Honey's response: "The goat's gone."

The incident has led to a family joke. At times when we are looking for an obscure address or some place that we can't seem to locate, Honey will comment, "I guess I'd better look for a goat."

* * * * *

A number of years ago we were on a shopping trip to Nashville. The Opry was still quartered in the Ryman Auditorium. As we drove up 5th Avenue in the middle of the afternoon I noted a long line of people in front of the Ryman obviously waiting to buy tickets. I commented, "They sure love the Opry around here. Just look at that line."

"They're going to have a long wait," was Honey's reply.

"How come?" I asked.

"Because it's Tuesday," she replied nonchalantly.

* * * * *

At one time Honey worked at the Arnold Center near Tullahoma. Her supervisor was a fellow she didn't much care for. She said something to him on one occasion to which he replied, "You know, you're the most sarcastic person in the world."

Her reply, "I couldn't be; I'm married to him."

* * * * *

One day while I was Principal of BGA, one of my teachers had come over to the house to see me about a matter. Honey was sort of taking me to task about something or other. He said to her, "You're sorta giving the boss a hard time."

She came back with, "When he walks across that street, he's got thirty teachers and four hundred students who have to do what he says. My job is to keep him humble."

* * * * *

For a number of years we ate a light evening meal on Sunday at a restaurant on Baker's Bridge Road in the Cool Springs area. One evening as we were nearing the place, I noticed a beautiful sunset—bright reds and yellows in an unusual cloud formation. We were in the middle of a conversation so I did not mention it. However, the hostess seated us in the southeast corner and as we were sitting down, I noticed again the brilliant colors shining through the ferns and other plants which almost covered the windows. I commented, "Look at that beautiful sunset."

Honey glanced casually around and then leaned a little more closely and said, "Sunset? That's the neon tubing around Logan's Roadhouse."

And it was.

* * * * *

I suppose there are many things which could be said about our marriage of "more than golden length." But no one can say it's been dull.

THE '37 FLOOD

I missed the one in '27, the one that William Alexander Percy wrote about in his classic, _Lanterns_ _on_ _The_ _Levee_, the one that Delta folks say was the real bad one. But I had gotten myself born before the Big River decided ten years later again to inundate a large portion of that area of Mississippi called The Delta. And the one in '37 was bad enough for my family since we were in it.

For the uninitiated the Mississippi Delta is not a true delta which is a deposit of silt at the mouth of a river. It is the old flood plain of the Mississippi which begins south of the bluffs at Memphis and runs in an arc to the southeast and then back southwest to the bluffs at Vicksburg. It is 60-70 miles across at its widest point. The land is almost flat with only slight undulations making it very susceptible to flooding. It was the land of vast cotton plantations and the home of most of the State's slaves prior to the Civil War.

I was 4 ½ years old that spring of '37. My father had lost everything in the crash of '29 and was sharecropping a new ground farm in The Delta back toward the River. The soil was black, grainy buckshot, very rich but hard to work when damp in the spring and susceptible to large cracks when it dried out in the summer. Our house was a double-pen log house which sat up on five-foot blocks. There was no electricity, no plumbing. Our water came from a pitcher pump in the back yard. The road in front was dirt. This was land that was just being opened to cultivation. There was a large bayou across the road in front of the house and a very large bayou behind the fields. There were no other farms between us and the River.

One afternoon my father called me out into the backyard, saying he had something to show me. We walked down to the fence and he lifted me up and pointed down toward the end of the fields. "See that black line," he said. Sure enough there was a black line between the field's end and the bayou. "That's back water," he informed me. I didn't know what back water was but from the tone of his voice, I knew it couldn't be good.

Unlike the '27 flood in which the levees along the Mississippi broke in several places, the flooding in '37 came from back water—water which came down the Yazoo and other tributaries and just backed out over the land when it couldn't get into the Mississippi. Today there are four large flood control reservoirs on the upper Yazoo to hold this water back but in '37 it just inundated the land.

After having the back water shown to me, I'd go down and climb up on the back fence several times a day to check on that ominous, black line. It grew wider and wider as it moved inexorably over the fields toward our house.

One morning Mama shook me awake saying, "We've got to go. The water's over the road." After a hurried breakfast, we were loaded into the wagon along with some bundles of extra clothes. Daddy had taken our model T Ford out to the main road the afternoon before. Water was about two feet deep over the road. Ike, a black sharecropper who worked the next farm, was driving the team. The road was cut by several drainage ditches which were bridged by wooden bridges. They were just two beams laid across with planks nailed to them. Daddy had on his hip boots and carried a big pole. When we'd come to one of these ditches, he'd climb down and wade ahead, probing for the bridge to make sure it hadn't floated away. None had. I remember being frightened at first but then I became fascinated with the whole process. I'd never seen so much water. After getting us out, Daddy went back to stay with the house and livestock.

Mama, my brother who was 2 ½, and I would stay with my aunt and uncle who lived up on Highway 61. Aunt Olivia was Daddy's sister who had married a doctor. They had a nice house with an indoor bathroom, running water, and electric lights. We were there until the water receded which took about three weeks. I don't recall too much about our stay except for one incident which burned itself into my memory.

Uncle Doc was just an unassuming country doctor who loved to drink and hunt. Aunt Olivia loved to be a part of "Delta Society." One afternoon some club she was a member of met at her house. We were relegated to a back bedroom where we were to remain quiet and unseen. Imagine keeping two small kids shut up in a small room quiet and entertained for three-plus hours. Since we didn't have access to the bathroom, we had a chamber pot for emergency use. Children understand a great deal without being told. Although no one ever said it, I sensed that we were the "poor relatives" who were not good enough to mingle with the "upper crust."

During our exile Mama began to worry about the electric stove. She'd cooked lunch but couldn't remember turning the oven off. She was determined to check it although she could not go through the house without being seen by the guests. Her solution was the back window. She raised the window and unhooked the wood-framed screen. I held the screen out while she put a chair out onto the ground. She climbed out using the chair as a platform, went to the back kitchen door, and returned the same way. She had not left the stove on.

I have never forgotten that afternoon of incarceration and the humiliation I felt. However, it was a great lesson in how _not_ to treat the people you supervise or those who happen to rank lower than you on the social scale. I have endeavored never to make anyone feel the way I felt that day.

Finally, Daddy came for us. There was still a lot of water and the road was impassable so he used the boat he'd used to get around in and to tend to things. I remember floating over the garden fence and landing by the front gate. The water had not gotten into the house. There was one small spot in the backyard that had not been covered. Daddy had built a walkway to it from the chicken house so that they could get off their roosts and be fed. He'd moved the cow and mules to a rise in the pasture where he ferried in feed and milked the cow each day. He had gambled that the water wouldn't get so deep that they'd all drown. It didn't.

That was our last experience with a flood. That Fall after the crops were in, Daddy was hired by Mr. E. J. Ganier to manage his 2000 acre plantation near Percy. It was good to get to higher ground and out of the stumps, the buckshot soil, and the bayous. I was also glad we never again had to go live with relatives.

PEOPLE WHO USED TO COME AROUND

I grew up in the country—the real country—where many of the roads were dirt and a gravel road was a main artery of transportation. The "real country" lasted longer in the South than in other parts of our country and pockets of it can still be found if you look hard enough. Because of the poor roads and no means of long-distance transportation, many services had to be brought to these rural, isolated areas. Although this time was fading, there was some of this still going on in my early years.

We were always glad to see the rolling store which came around about once a week with canned goods and staples like flour, meal, sugar, and coffee. There was always a candy rack which attracted the kids. We'd beg Mama to buy us a penny piece of candy. The "store" was an old school bus with the seats stripped out and replaced by shelves and bins. The storekeeper also bought or bartered for surplus goods like potatoes, eggs, and chickens which he would sell in town. The chicken coops were strapped on the top. It was a sight to see the "store" come along, stirring up a cloud of dust mixed with chicken feathers, with the birds squawking, and with chicken poop running down the sides.

In the summer time, a visit by the ice truck was a major event. Electricity had not yet gotten much beyond the major highways and rural people were still using iceboxes. The truck was a flat bed with four-foot sides and run by the icehouse in town. It was filled with rectangular, 300-pound blocks of ice covered by a heavy tarp. The driver would deftly chip out a 25 or 50-pound piece and tie a grass cord around it so you could carry it to the house. There was always a stream of ice water running out underneath the truck bed. My brother and I loved to stick our heads under these cold fountains. And the driver would always let us gather some of the slivers to suck on. With temperatures well over 100°, the ice truck was a welcome summer time treat.

The Watkins man only came around about once a month. He came in a car with the seats, floorboards, and trunk crammed full of small boxes in various sizes with their tops open. They contained bottles, cans and tubes of kitchen spices, male and female grooming supplies, cleaning supplies, salves, liniments, patent medicine, and a host of other things. The Watkins Company had a good reputation and put out a good line of products. What amazed me was that the man could locate anything in the jumble of cartons in his car.

My brother and I were always glad to see a stranger come by especially in the summer when we were out of school—anything to add some spice to our humdrum days. However, we were taught to fear tramps and hobos. If we saw one coming down the road, we would run to the house and Mama would latch all the doors. Occasionally, one would stop and ask to do some chores for a meal. Sometimes Mama would let him do something or just give him a plate of food but she'd make him stand way out in the yard while she put the plate on the porch, scurried back into the house and latched the door. Mama always told us stories about a tramp who had done bad things to a family over in the next county. She also said they liked to kidnap little boys and make them ride freight trains with them. That sounded like great fun to me. We never knew of anyone who got harmed by a tramp. The ones who came by our house were always polite and respectful. When I got older, I was sorry we had treated them so badly.

When spray paint guns became the rage after WW II, crews

would come through the country painting barns. One came through our community and red barns began to appear all around. Apparently, red was the only color they had. They came by Honey's place. Her father, Mr. Fred, had one big barn and several smaller cribs and sheds. He was a sharp farmer who knew how to make a good bargain. The paint crew gave him a good price for all his buildings. They started on the big barn and soon the whole place was turning red. Honey's mother, Miss Mattie Lou, thought everything was gong well until they started on the house. Mr. Fred had gotten them to throw in the house for free. Miss Mattie Lou was unhappy, complaining that they had the only barn-red house in the community and that folks would think they were living in a barn. A few years later Mr. Fred built them a new house. It was still red but this one was brick.

In my father's generation, country folk really were dependent on these traveling men for sharpening knives and scissors, mending pots and pans, fixing sewing machines and clocks, and providing a host of other services. Portrait painters would come around with their wagons stocked with canvases of all sizes. With everything already painted in except the face, a portrait could be produced in short order. And with the advent of photography, the painters were replaced by traveling photographers. These "drummers," as they were called, never had to look far to find a place to stay at night. For 50 cents he got a bed, a place to wash up, supper and breakfast, and a stable and feed for his horse.

My father used to tell the story about the man who came through their community selling eyeglasses. One of his great uncles, Uncle Ben, who was up in his 90s and nearly blind, had bought a pair. Daddy said it was a couple of days later when they were working in the field that Uncle Ben wandered by wearing is new glasses. One of the men said, "Well, Uncle Ben, I see you done got yourself some new specs."

"Yep, I shore have," replied Uncle Ben, as he leaned on his cane, "and I can just see all sorts of things. Why lookie over yonder. There's a gnat flying over that fence row." Looking down at the end of the field where he was pointing, they saw a buzzard sailing along, proving that things don't always work out as planned.

HOG KILLINGS: FACT AND FANTASY

Mark Twain once observed that "One of our problems is that so many people know so much that ain't so." And that's still true today. Quite often I hear someone making authoritative statements about some historical event that have no factual foundation. Most of the time they're not trying to deceive anyone; it's just that they're speaking out of ignorance. Hitler knew that a lie spoken loud enough and often enough would become a reality. That hasn't changed and is doubly true with the written word. Too many people accept that which appears in print as gospel. That's why writers should be careful especially when they're writing about something they know little or nothing about. A case in point.

About a month ago while reading a newspaper from a large nearby city, a column on Southern cooking caught my eye. The lady was a cookbook author and, apparently, an authority on Southern cooking. That week she was writing about hog killings and pork bellies. One of her points was that the availability of certain foods followed certain cycles and that fresh pork was available in the late fall because the breeding cycle of the hogs produced offspring that were large enough by late fall to be butchered. Of course, that's totally wrong. It has to do with the weather. You have to have a stretch of weather that's cold enough to keep the meat from spoiling. To her credit she noted in her next column that several readers had corrected her on this point. A local friend of mine says that he'd lost too much meat by killing too early. Even if he kept the meat from spoiling, flies would get to it and lay eggs and he'd end up with wormy meat.

Also, you don't kill this year's hogs. If you're going to the trouble of killing a hog, you want as much meat as possible which means a hog of 500 pounds or better which translates into a 2 – 3 year old animal.

Then the cookbook lady began to wax poetic about pork bellies. She stated that bellies were almost always smoked for bacon. Wrong. Bacon comes from higher on the side of the hog. Generally speaking, the lower you go on the hog, the less desirable the meat, which I suppose gave rise to the expression "eating high on the hog" denoting good eating or a luxurious life style. The bellies were preserved by salting and used for cooking meat in vegetables. Of course, you could fry it like bacon but since it is almost totally fat, you don't have much to eat when you finish. Where I grew up it was referred to as cooking meat, salt meat, or sowbelly, although not all came from sows. On those that did, the mammary glands were very prominent and not very appetizing. In the late 1940s I worked in a grocery store where some customers would just hand you a written out list for you to fill. One day this lady had on her list "3 lbs. Salt meat—no tits, please." It took some judicious slicing to meet her request.

She goes on to describe fresh pork belly as a "hot" cut of meat that is coming onto vogue in fancy restaurants and at society events. She uses such words as "dashing" and "bold" to describe recipes using it. Who does she think she's kidding? It seems to me that all this fawning over pork bellies is just another good example of a bunch of culinary snobs "discovering" something that only the very poor ate (and only because they couldn't afford better) and elevating it to exotic status. As far as I'm concerned, she can have my share of pork belly; I'll take the pork chops and hams.

Also referred to were the "trotters." I'd never heard of this part of the hog but I figured they had to be the feet. A dictionary confirmed this but I never heard this term in Mississippi hog killings or in my meat market days. None of my Williamson County hog killing friends have heard it either. In the market I worked in we sold just about every part of the hog except the squeal: tails, ears, feet, brains, chitlins, jowl (cheek), souse, aka, hog's head cheese made from the lips, snout and other parts of the head.

This cooking lady admitted that she'd never been to a hog killing. She didn't have to tell me. It was clear by the way she wrote about it. For example, she mentioned "frying cracklin's." Of course, you don't fry cracklin's. You build a nice fire around a wash pot in which you will "render" the lard. The fat cut into small pieces goes into the pot. As the heat begins to liquefy the fat you stir it with a wooden lard paddle which has holes drilled through the stirring end. You also press the pieces against the side of the pot to squeeze all the lard out of the meat. Finally, you're left with nothing but liquid lard with the bits of "spent" fat meat floating on top. These are cracklin's which are skimmed off and allowed to drain and dry. When put in corn bread batter, the result is cracklin' bread—one of the great Southern culinary inventions. The liquid lard is drained into round tin containers called "stands" where it cools and hardens. A family would use several of these 50-pound "stands" per year in cooking.

In her second column, she waxes nostalgic about these hog killing days of old, seeing them as community social events that brought people together like a barn raising or a quilting bee. They weren't. I think this is a perfect example of someone who's never been there waxing eloquently about one of those events of the "good old days." There is some truth in this but I don't think this writer lady would enjoy a hog killing. It was always cold and it was a dirty, smelly, bloody event—not an activity for the squeamish. I doubt that she would be willing to take an ear of corn, lure a hog to the driest part of the lot, and watch him get shot between the eyes. And after he was hoisted upside down and hung from a big tree limb, the throat cutting was not a pretty sight but the blood had to be drained before the butchering began. And I never liked the smell of scalded hog hair but it was necessary to loosen the bristles so that they could be scraped off. I was glad to get the job of keeping the scalding pot filled with water and keeping a good fire going around it. At least I could stay warm.

Of course, I always enjoyed the fresh tenderloin and sausage Mama cooked in the days after the hog killing, but most of the meat was preserved by salting, canning, or smoking it. My mouth would water just seeing the hams, sausage, and sides of bacon being smoked in the smokehouse. I'm sure the USDA would not sanction any part of either the butchering or the curing but they did produce some mighty tasty eating. Even that is not enough to make me want to go back to those "good old days." I've been there and done that. I just don't have a T-shirt to prove it.

Body Art

A few years ago I began to notice the increasing popularity of body art. Apparently, that's the current correct term since "tattoo" has been relegated to "common" status. This change in nomenclature probably is a direct result of the growing number of tattoos on the bodies of females. A "nice" girl wouldn't sport a tattoo but art falls into a whole new category—an acceptable category.

One of the most popular of the female body art forms is the butterfly, especially the monarch and swallowtail. The first ones I noticed were at the base of the neck or high on the shoulder. With the present fashion of short tops and low cut pants, it has been easy to observe the butterfly's migration to the base of the spine, the upper abdomen, and around the navel. I thought the one which had a monarch lighting on a navel-centered sunflower to be especially creative. I have been told that these colorful insects have invaded the more secluded areas of the body like the buttocks and breasts but I have had no first-hand sightings in these areas. However, I did notice one time a young lady wearing a scoop-neck top which exposed a swallowtail fluttering up out of her cleavage. There's probably quite a bit of symbolism here which I will not explore at this time.

Of course, now female body art runs the gamut—flowers, animals, geometric and floral patterns, portraits of Elvis, religious symbols. You name it and it's there. And I've also noticed that this art form is not the sole property of the young. I noted this during a recent cruise. Honey was using the hot tub in the pool area and I was sitting back in the shade under the overhang reading. A woman in a skimpy swimsuit was sunning a few feet in front of me. She had a lot of wrinkles and her body sagged in most places. I mentally compared her to a carton of milk, several days past its expiration date, which could be used but a fresher one would be better over your cereal. Anyway, when she turned over, I couldn't help but observe the red jalapeno pepper at the base of her spine. Oh, for those thrilling days of yesteryear.

And males also have been caught up in the surge, covering large portions of body area with extensive patterns. This is especially true of athletes. It appears that a basketball player is not eligible for the NBA draft without body decoration.

I once asked a friend of mine who had served in the Navy if he had any tattoos. He drew himself up in Naval officer fashion and replied, " Officers do not have tattoos. Those are for the enlisted personnel. I once knew an officer who was denied a promotion because he had a tattoo." I surmised that some facets of our society are slow to change.

As time passed and I saw myself growing older, somehow this aging process came into juxtaposition with the growing popularity of tattooing. Important milestones came and went causing me to consider marking some of them in some fashion—doing something I'd never done before. I did some research and even visited one of our local tattoo establishments. I found it to be licensed, regularly inspected, and sanitary. They also had a section devoted to body piercing which I avoided. That's another ball game entirely. After some careful thought, one day I announced, "If I make seventy, I'm gonna get a tattoo." My family and friends just laughed and looked at me as if I'd gone into my dotage. Little did they know—or suspect

And then it happened. I did make seventy and Honey was out of town for a week. I called for an appointment. The fellow asked me what type tattoo I had in mind. "A name with a flower under it," I answered.

There was a pause before he replied, "We discourage people

from getting names on their bodies. They break up and they're stuck with a name they don't like or may even hate."

"Well, she's my wife," I replied.

"How long have you been married?" he asked.

"Forty-eight years," I replied. I guess I don't sound old over the telephone.

After another pause he said, "Well, I guess it'll probably be okay. Looks like you're in this for the long haul."

"It sure looks that way," I agreed as he gave me an appointment.

The whole process took about an hour. The entire operation was fascinating. Alex worked up the design I wanted and got it to the right size before cutting a stencil of it. I showed him where I wanted it and he stenciled it on. He had me take a long look at it to make sure it was in the exact position I wanted pointing out that there was no going back once he began with the needle. Only when he was satisfied that I was satisfied did he begin the permanent work. The needle hurt a little every once in a while but it wasn't really painful. After finishing Alex taped a patch over his work, gave me some salve and written instructions on the care and feeding of my new tattoo, and sent me on my way.

Honey was quite surprised when she returned. "I can't believe you'd do something like that!"

"Why not? I've been telling you for two or three years I was going to."

"I know. But I didn't believe you."

After about a year, she has come to accept it. But she still shakes her head from time to time.

Our daughter was equally amazed and somewhat concerned when I told her I was in the process of considering what I might do if I make eighty. After thinking about the latter possibility for a minute or two, she said, "I think at your age you should go in increments of five."

STANDING ON THE SHOULDERS OF A GIANT

Early in the 18th century when he was complimented on his great accomplishments in math and science, Sir Isaac Newton replied, "If I have seen farther than others it is because I have stood on the shoulders of giants." Newton understood the importance of the platform built by others from which he launched his great works. And so it is with us all.

I once heard a fellow say that if you ever saw a turtle on top of a fence post, you'd know he didn't get up there by himself. It is my observation that anyone who accomplishes anything in this life does so by "standing on the shoulders of giants."

I hope you readers will indulge me a little today as I pay tribute to one of the giants on whose shoulders I have stood. I call her "Honey" when I refer to her in this column. Her real name is Sara and come the 20th of this month we will mark 50 years of marriage. And it hasn't been like some couples say today, "We've been together for 15 years, married for 10." As with most of our generation, we jumped into the deep water together and never looked back. We've stuck together through thick and thin—and believe me there've been plenty of thins. She's been willing to put her career and aspirations second and to help me realize mine. She worked most of the time and still found time to take an active part in supporting and promoting my endeavors. One of her supervisors once told her, "There's no telling how far you could have gone in civil service if you hadn't followed Luke around all these years." And I know that's the truth.

We've known each other since about age 10. She was the

"girl next door." Of course, we lived in the country and "next door" was about three miles away. We did not date in high school. It was only after we went to different colleges and seeing each other became difficult that we began to date. Sometimes youth waste a lot of opportunities.

All the females in her family were sent to a girls' school, which is now Mississippi University for Women, to become school teachers. As she was finishing, her parents asked her where she might apply for a teaching job. Her reply: "Nowhere. I'm getting a degree in business." She's always had a mind of her own.

This independent streak showed up in our wedding. In those days, the woman usually promised to "love, honor and obey." She refused to promise to "obey," but she did promised to "cherish." It didn't bother me since I knew I was coming out ahead anyway.

We went to the Army together and our daughter was born in one of those old rambling, wooden Army hospitals in what today would be primitive conditions. All the new mothers were in a large ward and on the second morning were expected to get up and make up their beds.

My first teaching job was at a boys' boarding school where I coached all sports and ran a dorm and dining hall. Can you imagine a new mother with no kitchen and having to take all meals with a 6-month-old in a dining hall full of boys? She did it because it was what we had to do.

Our son was born in a regular hospital, but there were complications. After the birth, Sara's blood pressure went sky high and she was drifting in and out consciousness and pulling the IV out of her arm. I was assigned the task of holding her arm flat to keep it in. Later, I had to explain the finger-like bruises. But we were luckier than some. The same thing happened with a friend of ours, who had a stroke and died.

We grew up in an era when girls were not encouraged to

develop themselves physically. Consequently, Sara never played any games or sports. In college, PE was required. She learned to float on her back but never to swim on her stomach without sinking. Her tennis teacher said that she'd never had a student who made a perfect score on the written exam and yet never returned a ball across the net into the opposite court the whole semester. With this background, she found herself in a family of sports activists. Of course, she appreciated and understood the games, even though she couldn't play them. There's no telling how many games she's watched during our 50 years. And she didn't just watch all the time. When I was managing and playing on a softball team, she became our scorer, which is not an easy job. She's one of the few women I know who can quote and explain the infield fly rule.

And then I got a wild hair about starting a Ph.D. program at the advanced academic age of 35. She quit her job and we packed up two kids, ages 11 and 8, and headed for Knoxville. She found another job and didn't complain while we spent five years in a small two-bedroom student apartment. During that time I played two softball games a week in the spring and summer and our son played a game or two of something most of the year. And she made them all.

And she's the main reason I finished my degree. Many Ph.D. candidates do the course work and pass the oral and written exams but never do the research and write the dissertation. They call themselves ABDs, All But Dissertation. She said to me, "We've sacrificed too much for you to be an 'All But.' You're gonna finish." And I did.

After that we settled back into a normal life. I had a good position; she was in a really good civil service job. Then BGA called. She really didn't want to move again, so I told her it was her call this time, that I wouldn't go for the interview without her OK. I'm sure she told me to go because she knew I wanted to, again putting herself second. However, after the move you would have thought she worked for the chamber of commerce, as she bragged on her new home. So far, we've had 26 great years here.

And in thinking back, it's hard to believe that that brief ceremony on that hot August day was a half-century ago. But the calendar says otherwise. And we are not the same people who walked out of that little country church. We've been faithful to each other and each has allowed and helped the other to grow. I believe Lord Lyttelton was correct when he said, "How much the wife is dearer than the bride."

So I'll just say "happy anniversary" to my bride, my wife, my giant.

Earning the Pink Ribbon

It all began, as many life-changing events do, rather innocuously. It was a Monday evening and I was settled in my easy chair reading the paper. Honey was taking a shower. I was engrossed in a Gail Kerr column when she suddenly appeared beside my chair with a towel wrapped around her waist. "Feel this," she directed as she pointed to her right breast.

"Don't you think you should dry off first?" I retorted. This seemed to annoy her.

"I'm not interested in any of your foolishness. See if you don't think there's something in there that doesn't feel right." She was correct. There was a mass in one side that felt like a blob of Jell-O salad without the fruit "What do you think?' she asked.

"I think you need to call your doctor first thing in the morning," I replied.

She did and when she told the receptionist what the problem was, she said, "For something like this the doctor will see you immediately. Come on to the office." She did so, was examined, and sent to get a mammogram and an ultra sound that afternoon. The next morning, Wednesday, Honey's doctor called with the results and said, "You need to see a surgeon." Since the two surgeons we'd used in the past were not available, she recommended one and made an appointment for the next day.

Thursday, we met Dr. Burgess for the first time. After I found out that he was from Cornersville and had gone to UT, I figured that he leaned toward the practical. He does and he tells it like it is—doesn't dance around the facts and doesn't sugar coat things.   We liked that.   He'd examined all the pictures. He did a physical exam and then told us, "What you want to see is a smooth border on the mass. It feels smooth but the pictures show it as irregular. Either way it needs to come out but I need to know what we're dealing with before I go in. I'm scheduling you for a biopsy tomorrow. I'll have the results by Monday."

After Friday's biopsy we had time to reflect a little on our whirlwind week. A lot had happened in just five days and we had not had to worry with making any appointments or setting up any tests. The various offices had done it for us and had done it quickly and efficiently.

Monday afternoon the call came from Dr. Burgess' nurse. She said, "You need to come in tomorrow and bring your husband."

Honey replied, "It sounds as if the news is bad."

"It is," the nurse responded.

Honey informed her that we had a day trip scheduled the next day with Synergy Bank's Travel Club and suggested that we just wait until Wednesday for the "official" bad news. The nurse agreed. We had a great time on the trip.

Wednesday Dr. Burgess confirmed that the mass was cancer. The better news was that it was in an early stage. He gave us three choices: (1) Remove the mass only; go through 6 weeks, 5 days a week of radiation; and _maybe_ some chemo in addition. (2) Do a total mastectomy and reconstructive plastic surgery, no radiation, and _maybe_ some chemo.   (3) Do #2 with no reconstruction and _maybe_ some chemo and be fitted with a prosthesis.

Honey and I looked at each other while trying to digest everything. "What do you think?" she asked.

"I know what my choice would be," I responded, "but it's your body."

After reflecting a minute or so, she said, "Forty years ago I'd probably have gone with number 2 but now I think number 3 would be best. What are you thinking?"

"The same thing." I replied.

Later when she told our son what she'd decided, he was sort of taken aback and asked if she was sure that was what she wanted to do. She replied, "Yes, I'm sure. I really don't need that breast." He laughed and decided that she was still capable of making her own decisions.

The surgery was scheduled for the next Tuesday. As she set it up, the nurse told Honey that she would have go to the hospital the day before for a shot containing radioactive material. "Will it make her glow in the dark?" I asked. The nurse said that it wouldn't but that it would trace any spreading of cancer cells.

At that point Honey's Sunday School class, Bible study group, church friends, and many other friends had begun an intensive prayer effort. That gave us both a lot of comfort.

The surgery went well—so well in fact that Dr. Burgess offered to let her go home that afternoon. But Honey thought that a mastectomy ought to allow her at least one night in the hospital and declined. She was home before noon the next day all bandaged up with two drain tubes. One of my jobs was to empty and record the amount of drainage.

Honey was up and about immediately but did not have a lot of stamina for several weeks. Our friends brought food---a lot of food—and we received many cards, letters, and phone calls. We are fortunate to have a lot of good friends.

The pathology report was good—no spread to lymph nodes. Dr. Burgess has a steady hand or either used a ruler. The incision was straight as an arrow. He admired his work as he removed the staples. His nurse told Honey, "Surgeons have to have a lot of praise." He said that he would write a prescription for the prosthesis. I asked if he could stipulate the size. "Sure," he replied, "I've got any size from pole dancer on down. What would you like?" After careful consideration Honey opted to stay with a matching set.

At this point we thought we were home free but we had to meet with the oncologist. He showed us several graphs and quoted several studies. Honey showed up mostly positive but he said, "There's one more test I want to run. If it shows up on the high end, I recommend a round of chemo." There would be certain side effects; the most noticeable would be the loss of her hair. This news hit her pretty hard. When we got home, I just put my arms around her and told her that I was gong to love her with only one breast and that I'd feel the same if she lost all her hair. After all, the hair would grow back. We began the two-week wait for the test results.

The time dragged by but finally we were again seated with the oncologist. He had more graphs. Honey fell on the low end—the possibility of a reoccurrence was about 7% with no chemo—which meant she wouldn't have to go through that. Words can hardly express our relief.

The last few months have seemed like a bad dream but we learned a few things. (1) Breast cancer is curable, especially if caught early. You women out there pay attention to that. (2) We have some very talented doctors and excellent medical facilities in the county. They're both efficient and caring. (3) You can't have too many friends. (4) Prayer works.

CONVERSATIONS WITH ABIGAIL

I'm going to start this column off with a confession. I've become enamoured with another woman. I never thought it could happen at my age but it did. She's younger, of course, so she can benefit from my considerable years of experience. I've always liked red hair and Abigail's a strawberry blond. Close enough. She has freckles on her nose, a sparkle in her eye, and boundless energy—all of which are hard to find in more mature women. She makes me feel younger and tires me out quickly all at the same time. You readers who know Honey, don't bother telling on me. She has known for quite some time and, more importantly, she approves. You two must have an open marriage, you say. No. Not at all. You see, Abigail (who goes by Abby), is seven years old and is my favorite (and only) granddaughter. She is in the second grade at Walnut Grove School and just the right age for me to further her education with stories—some fact but mostly fiction.

During one of our conversations one day, she mentioned Alaska. The following exchange ensued.

Papa (her name for me): Abby, do you know anything about Alaska?

Abby: No. But I know it's cold.

P: Do you know how cold it is?

A: No.

P: Well, it gets so cold in Alaska in the winter that if you go outside and say anything, you don't make any sound. The letters just freeze as they come out and fall on the ground. So in order to know what's been said, you have to pick them up, take them inside, put them in a pot on the stove, and thaw them out. Then the sound comes out.

Abby screwed up her face in deep thought for several seconds as she analyzed my story. She does this a lot now when I tell her things. It didn't take her long to find a flaw in it.

A: That's not right Papa. When you say something, it comes out of your head and you know what you're saying before it comes out.

P: That's right, but if you're saying something to someone else, they don't know what you're saying until they hear the words.

She thought some more before replying.

A: I guess that's right.

P: And another thing, you should pick up all those frozen words, because you know what will happen if you don't.

A: No. What?

P: Well in the spring when the weather warms up, those words begin to thaw out. The short words like "a," "an," "it," and so on thaw first and you hear them. Then the longer words thaw and soon there are so many words in the air that it sounds like a football stadium during a game.

But I'd gone too far. The last part was more than she was willing to swallow.

A: Nana, (her name for Honey) Papa's telling tales again.

* * * * *

On another occasion we saw several birds, sitting on a power line over the road.

P: Abby, do you know what kind of birds those are?

A: No.

P: They're white-crested car poopers.

A: What do they do?

P: They sit on wires over roads and poop on cars.

A: Ooo. That's bad.

P: But they're not nearly as bad as their cousins, the black-crested people poopers.

A: What do they do?

P: They sit over sidewalks and poop on people.

A: Ooo. That's real bad.

Now when we're out and she sees birds on a wire she wants to know whether they're people or car poopers. If we're driving, they're always people poopers. If we're walking, they're car poopers. So we've been safe thus far. And Abby's been working on her identification skills so she'll be able to tell which is which when I am not with her.

* * * * *

On one recent Tuesday, her school had an in-service day, so she spent the day with us. Honey had a meeting until early afternoon putting me in charge. Since we didn't have any good lunch food in the house, Honey told me to take her out to lunch. So, after a morning spent reading, doing homework, and watching TV, I asked her where she wanted to eat lunch. I figured she'd want to go to one of those fast food places with ten miles of tubes all twisted together. But, no. Abby had other plans.

A: Papa, do you know about Friday's?

P: You mean T.G.I. Friday's?

A: That's it. Can we go there? I just love their flat iron steak.

P: Are you sure you can eat a whole steak?

A: Well, Papa, it's not very big.

With that, I agreed on Friday's. As I was running a couple of errands on the way and not heading toward our agreed on destination, Abby's voice came from the back seat. "Papa, you haven't forgotten where we're going to eat, have you?' She's good at reminding me of things when I get forgetful.

As we entered the restaurant, the hostess asked if she'd like a child's menu. "No, thank you," Abby replied in a very grown-up voice. "I'll use the regular menu today." She's gotten a lot more dangerous in restaurants since she's learned to read the menus. When the server asked for her order, "I'd like the flat iron steak, medium rare. And could you put some mushroom gravy on it, please."

She ate all the steak and most of the mashed potatoes before the dessert card attracted her attention.

A: Papa, this little Rocky Road ice cream cup is really good.

P: But you don't like nuts.

A: Oh, I pick the nuts out.

P: Are you sure you have room for ice cream after all that steak.

A: Papa, you can always make room for ice cream. You just take your hands and push things around a little like this and you have room. (She demonstrated.)

P: Okay. We'll get it if you'll promise me you won't suck the fudge off the nuts and I can eat them.

We collaborated on the dessert. She ate all of her part. So, what I thought would be a cheap date turned out just the opposite. I can tell this young lady is going to be high maintenance.

PART III

HUMOROUS STUFF
[WITH SOME SARCASM THROWN IN]

THE BUZZARDS OF
JORDAN HALL

Dick and Marie Jordan live in this big, old house in Franklin. It has tall columns and sits on a heavily wooded lot. Its back gate opens into Pinkerton Park. The Jordans have lived there for many years so they know the place has never before attracted the bizarre or unusual. Therein lies the mystery.

They came four years ago—two large, ugly buzzards. They built a nest in one of the tall trees back of the house and raised two young, ugly buzzards. When Dick told us about them, we kidded that he and Marie were getting old and slow and the buzzards were just waiting for them to stop moving so that they could have a good meal. We cautioned them about falling asleep in the hammock and advised them to keep moving at all times. We all had some good laughs about their unusual guests and thought the whole thing was over when the buzzards disappeared sometime that Fall. However, such was not the case.

The next Spring they returned to raise another family and the cycle has been repeated each year since to the degree that they can now be classified as family pets. Scottie, the dog, has quit barking at them and they walk around the yard with the Jordans like pet chickens. Dick has named them Lonzo and Gertrude and when he judges that they have not found enough road kill to eat, he buys a package of assorted, bony chicken parts for them. One day he gave them a Crystal burger. They ate the meat, threw the pickle away, and didn't seem to know what to do with the bun. Marie fussed about his feeding them.

She has feeders all over the yard to attract "good birds." Dick's response was, "You feed your birds; I'll feed mine."

As they became more like members of the family, they began roosting in the rafters of his mower shed. In doing so they began to arrange their new quarters to their liking. Dick has a red, one-gallon gas can that he keeps under the shed. Each night the buzzards put it out in the driveway. Their favorite rafter is directly over Dick's riding mower upon which they deposited large amounts of buzzard guano. Now, just plan bird poop is bad enough. That which is the end result of assorted dead and decaying animals is terrible. Dick thought he would solve this problem by spreading an old beach towel over the mower. The next morning it was out in the driveway with the gas can and the mower sported a coat of fresh buzzard dung.

Their determination to rearrange his mower shed Dick took as a challenge. He thought, "Surely, I'm as smart as a buzzard." So, he reasoned that the solution was to put something over the mower they couldn't move. A piece of plywood seemed to be a good answer. This seemed to tick the buzzards off to a great degree. Marie had a picnic table out back on which she had arranged a large number of seashells collected from a number of beaches around the country. The night the plywood went on the mower, the buzzards went out to the picnic table and threw all the shells out in the woods. You might guess that Marie was somewhat upset. Apparently, there is nothing so mean as a ticked off buzzard. They now have Dick wondering if he, indeed, is as smart as a buzzard—or two buzzards in this case.

Where will it all end? No one seems to know. Will Jordan Hall and Franklin become another Hinkley, Ohio? Will Lonzo and Gertrude bring other "smart" buzzards with them next year and take over Jordan Hall as a first step in taking over the whole town? Hollywood could make a movie, City of the Buzzards, along the same line as Planet of the Apes. Could Lonzo and Gertrude be space aliens in disguise? It's too bad Twilight Zone is off the air. It would make a good episode. In the meantime we're still advising Dick and Marie to keep moving.

FULL MOON RISING

Randy Moss' simulated mooning of Green Bay fans at the NFL playoff game back in January created a firestorm of indignant reaction from all quarters.   I suspect that his suggestive gyrations around the goal post after the simulation was what galled most folks. After all, he didn't drop his pants; he only indicated that he would have liked to do so.   And he was only simulating what Green Bay fans have been doing in fact for quite some time.   Apparently, a group of fans gather after each home game and moon the visiting team's bus as it leaves the stadium. Security officers have simply turned a blind eye to their act. I suppose they figure anyone who exposes such a tender, vulnerable body part to the rigors of Green Bay weather has already been punished. If course, its never been on national TV either. Moss was saying, in part, "Here's one back at you."

Now, I'm not defending Randy Moss in particular.   From what I read about him, he seems to be a jerk with a capital "J." But what about Jack Nicholson? Sports fans will remember his act a few years ago at Boston Gardens.   A rabid Lakers fan, Nicholson had been taunting the Celtics' fans while their team was behind. But when the lead changed and the Celtics' fans returned the favor, Jack dropped his pants and mooned the crowd. Of course, this was another incident which didn't make national TV.

Seems like a lot of folks are getting awfully upset about mooning—the act of displaying one's bare buttocks by dropping the clothing and bending forward. I suspect this has been going on since people have had behinds. We find it in literature at least as far back as Chaucer's _Canterbury Tales_ ("The Miller's Tale" to be specific) in the 14th Century. As general rule, the pointing of the body part by the mooner toward the moonee is considered a rude and insulting act. However, it can also be done playfully and for fun. Much of what goes on today seems to fall in the latter category.

For example, in 1995 a large group of Stanford University students assembled to protest something or other and decided to try to set a world record. It is unclear who counted the butts or whether they made it or not. And what UT fan does not remember when Peyton Manning playfully mooned a teammate only to have a female trainer get caught in the line of fire. She sued the University claiming it caused her severe mental anguish. Come on, give me a break. She got a view of what many women would have paid to see. And a trainer for a football team is shocked at a bare butt? Anyway, she got an out-of-court settlement and went off to be shocked at another university.

A good friend of mine who was a teenager back in the '60s relates that mooning was a favorite evening activity. Four or five boys would load up in a car and drive around town. They would pull up beside another vehicle at a traffic light just to observe the reaction of its occupants when they looked over and saw the boys in the front seat staring nonchalantly straight ahead but a set of buttocks pressed against the window of the back seat. This is called "pressed ham." The more adventurous ones would lower the window and hang outside. With the amount of road rage and weapons carried today, this would probably be a dangerous evening sport.

On a trip to Alaska a few years ago, we were traveling by train when our car steward related a story about a remote village we were passing through. It seems that the village lay on both sides of a small river. To get from one part of the village to the other by road required a trip of about thirty miles up to the nearest bridge. However, walking across the long railroad trestle was a quicker option and the one used most often. Because the tracks were private property and because the rail company was fearful of running over someone caught out on the trestle, they tried several ways to stopping this practice. Nothing worked and the only result was a long-running feud with the villagers. One day as our excursion train passed through, the whole population of the village—men, women, and children—were lined up on the road that ran parallel to the tracks. They turned as one and mooned the train. Each buttock was painted to look like a face. Our steward said they looked bad enough from the train. He couldn't imagine the view enjoyed by those who painted the faces.

The longest running mooning escapade I've ever heard of began back in 1979 in Laguna Niguel, California, when a patron of the local Mugs Away Saloon offered to buy drinks for anyone who would go outside and moon the passing Amtrak train. Many did and a mooning tradition was born. Today on the second Saturday in July, thousands throng to this small town and moon all the trains from early morning to midnight. Tee shirts are sold. The trains are crowded with passengers taking pictures of the mooners. Since this area is unlighted, night mooners must bring lights to illuminate their buttocks. Free drinks are no longer a part of the package.

Yes, mooning seems to be just about anywhere you care to look. In the film _Braveheart_, over a thousand Scottish warriors mooned the English army. It was recently featured in a strip on the comic page of _The Tennessean_. It has been defended in court both as a form of expression and as a form of political protest. A friend of mine says that the Constitution that gives us the right to bare-arms ought to allow us the right to bare buttocks as well. Maybe some folks ought to lighten up a little—sort of live and let live or moon and let moon, so to speak.

THE SAGA OF MR. LOVE

After the impoundment of Center Hill Lake, a family purchased a piece of property on which to build a lake house. On this land was the house site of the late Mr. Love, who had once owned a number of acres there. The old house was still standing and in cleaning it out, they discovered an old trunk. It contained nothing of any real value but among its contents were several packets of letters and post cards tied up with string. These missives were all from women and all were in the same vein. "Dear Mr. Love, I am a young widow with three children ages 5, 7, and 9. I am a good cook, can sew, and can weave cotton cloth. I have a pleasant disposition, am frugal and hard working. We are used to farm work and my oldest two can help about the place. I would be a faithful wife and good companion to you. If you have any interest in pursuing this, I may be contacted at . . ." The epistles intrigued them so they set out to learn more about Mr. Love and why so many women were offering to marry him. Their investigation revealed a man who was well-known and well-remembered in White County and one about whom they learned more than they ever intended.

Times were hard and with social programs practically non-existent, unattached women with no family support were especially destitute. But why would so many seek out Mr. Love, a life-long bachelor?

Well, it seems that Mr. Love was sitting around the feed store one day along with a number of other farmers when the talk got around to wealth. Mr. Love volunteered, "Well, I'm a millionaire." This declaration brought much laughter and scoffing challenging his statement. His reply was, "You all know I own a lot of land. I farm the creek bottoms but most of it is ridges covered with trees. And you know a tree is worth at least a dollar, and I know I must own more than a million trees. So, you see, I'm a millionaire in trees." This story got told around and somewhere along the line, the "tree part" got dropped and the story come to be that Mr. Love was a millionaire. This accounted for the letters from desperate women seeking a haven in the midst of hard economic times.

There is no indication that Mr. Love ever contacted any of his suitors. He remained a bachelor—but he kept the letters.

Another thing discovered about Mr. Love was that he thought it unhealthy for a person to expose too much of his skin to the air at any given time. Consequently, he took only one bath a year. Also, he only shaved once a year as well. And because of his fear of too much skin exposure, these yearly grooming chores were performed on separate days.

Another story about Mr. Love concerned a farming crisis he faced in the mid-1930s. Some years earlier Mr. Love had "gone modern" with his farming. He sold his mules and bought an old tractor. For a number of years, this seemed to have been a good move but then the mechanical beast just up and died on him. The mechanic who had worked on it for years reported that parts were no longer available and that he had done all the "creative mechanicing" on it that could be done. The junkyard was the only answer. As a result, Mr. Love found himself in quite a pickle. It was the middle of the Depression. He couldn't afford to buy another tractor or even a team of mules. With Spring just weeks away, how was he to get his crop planted? The situation was desperate indeed.

In some way the local County Agent became aware of Mr. Love's plight. Fortunately, he knew of a New Deal program which would grant tractors to destitute farmers, so he took Mr. Love to Nashville to file an application.

With some difficulty they found the correct building which contained many offices, many desks, and many people administering a large number of agricultural programs. This was all extremely confusing to Mr. Love who seldom left White County but he vowed to see it through.

After trying several lines, they finally found the right one and were given some forms to complete. Mr. Love did so but when he brought them back to the man at the desk, the man wasn't satisfied and had him do some parts over. He did so and finally got the man happy. He was then sent to another desk where he was told to change some parts of the first forms and was given some new ones to complete. After this man was satisfied, he sent Mr. Love to yet another desk where the process was repeated. This went on for quite some time—more desks, more forms, more changes.

After about five hours of this, Mr. Love was getting very exasperated but he needed that tractor. Finally, he arrived at the desk of a very pretty young lady. By this time he had accumulated quite a stack of forms which he presented to her. Now, it so happened that she had relatives in White County who had told her about Mr. Love. As she began to go over his forms, she realized who he was and said, "Why, you're Mr. Love from White County. I've heard about you."

About out of patience, Mr. Love put his hands on her desk top as he leaned over and demanded, "And just what have you heard about me?"

"Well," she responded, "one thing I've heard is that you only take one bath a year."

Mr. Love drew himself up to his full height and replied, "You've heard right, Miss. One bath a year is enough for anybody. How many do you take a year?"

"Why, I take a bath every day. Some days I even take two."

Mr. Love leaned down again. "Miss, I'd like to ask a favor of you. Will you stay right here at this desk and not go anywhere?"

"Of course, I will. But why?"

With his eyes flashing, Mr. Love responded, "Young lady, I think I've finally figured out how things work around here. And I figure before I get that tractor, I'm gonna have to kiss somebody's ass, and I want it to be yours."

There is a moral to this story: "If you ever have to perform this act, pick a clean one."

SKID TALK

We have some friends who have a place in Florida where they spend the winter. We spent a week with them during March enjoying the warm weather. Our host (Jim) has an uncle (John) who also winters there and this uncle has a long-time friend (Jack) who does the same. They play golf most every day and have set a goal to play all the courses which are within a reasonable driving distance. One day I was invited to accompany them.

Riding with them to a "never played before" course was a genuine experience. It was akin to a car trip scene from Clyde Edgerton's _Lunch_ _at_ _the_ _Piccadilly_ in which the old ladies expound on a variety of subjects. Only in this case it was the male version. Also, my host's uncle and his friend have a relationship reminiscent of Walter Matthau and Jack Lemon in _Grumpy_ _Old_ _Men_. The uncle's friend has been visiting the area for about fifty years and considers himself an expert on the locale and everything connected with it. Others consider him something else.

The verbal exchanges began as we were driving down the main street of Umatilla on our way out of town.

Jack: Better drive slow down through here. They'll get you.

John: Why do you say that every time we drive through here:

Jack: Because that's what Mama used to say every time we came through here in the car. She also said it to anybody who left the house to drive this way.

Jim: (the driver)   What would anybody want with me?

Jack: They don't want you. They just want your money.

John: I think it's a misuse of governmental authority. I think something ought to be done about it.

Jack: It's not misuse of authority. It's a revenue source.

They also had some comments on local construction.

John: They've been working on that building a month now. It wonder what it's gonna be.

Jack: Then, why don't you read that sign?

John: Well, they <u>have</u> put up a sign. Wasn't up a couple of days ago.

Jack: In case you can't read it, I'll read it to you. It says "Huddle House."

John: Why, I'll be. It's gonna be a Huddle House. When they get it done, I'm gonna hafta come over here at breakfast.

Jim: Do you like the breakfasts at Huddle House?

John: Aw, naw. I wouldn't eat there. I just like to hear the waitresses call out the orders.

* * * * *

Routes of travel was also a big item of conversation.

Jim: Jack, you made the tee time. Where is this course?

Jack: It's over on 27 down close to Clermont. I don't know exactly. I've never been to it.

Jim: Well, why didn't y'all come pick us up and we could have gone across on 44 and 19. That would have been the closest way.

Jack: Naw, it wouldn't. It would maybe be the closest from your place but it would have been fifteen miles out of our way to go down there and then come back up and go the closest way from here which is over on 32 down to 441 and then across on 68.

Jim: But if you were down at my place you wouldn't have to come back up to go your closest way.

Jack: Yes, we would because my way's closer. Just drive where I tell you. I know these roads.

Needless to say, we followed Jack's route. He had some observations on some of the other sights along the way.

John: What lake is that?

Jack: That's Lake Leven. It covers 17,492 acres.

John: Is that when it' full? During the dry season, it's way down. It is 17,492 acres then?

Jack: That's what it is when the water covers everything it can cover.

John: Well, I don't think that's right to count a half-dried up lake as big as it would be if it was full. I'm not sure that 17 whatever is right any way.

Jack: I know I'm right. You can look it up.

As we came near to our destination, locating the course became the paramount issue.

Jim: Which side of the highway is this course on?

Jack: The right, I think. But I'm not sure. We'll have to look.

Jim: I'm looking.

Jack: I'm looking, too. But I can't see for your hat, John. You're gonna have to take your hat off.

John: I can't take my hat off. It's holding my hair in place.

Jack: Well, I don't guess we'll find it then.

John: There's a big sign. Says it's a mile ahead but it don't say which way.

Jack: There'll probably be a sign at the turn that'll tell us.

John: We've come two miles at least. Why haven't you turned?

Jim: There's been no place to turn. It must be at this light up ahead. I'm gonna turn there.

John: Here's the road but I don't see a sign.

Jack: There's not one.

Jim: Well, I'm turning right.

John: Probably the wrong way. We always turn the wrong way and hafta turn around and go back. I wish we'd turn the right way sometime.

Jack: Well, smarty. There it is just up ahead on the right.

John: Well, you know what they say about a blind hog. He finds an acorn every now and then.

* * * * *

At the first tee, we presented the starter with our receipts.

Starter: Are y'all gonna hit from the back tees?

Jack: No. We're gonna hit from the gold up there. But now, you see this little short guy here with the white legs. Well, he's a pro and he's been trying to get us to hit from the long tees but we're not. He's a pro from up north. That's why his legs are so white.

Starter: Is that right?

Jack: Yeah. "Course he's a pro bowler. He's not worth a hoot at golf.

Starter: Really? A pro bowler. We've got a pro bowler who lives in this development right over there. His name's Dickerson. Do you know him?

Jim: No, I don't believe I do.

Starter: Are you sure? He bowled on the pro tour for several years.

Jim: No, I'm sure I don't know him.

Starter: Well, it's open. Y'all can hit now.

After playing golf the route home became a topic of debate.

John: (who's now driving)   I'm gonna turn here and go back another way. It'll be closer than the way we came.

Jack: That's fine.

Jim: How could this way be closer than the way we came? You said that way was the closest.

Jack: It was coming over here but going back this way is the closest.

Jim: That doesn't make good sense. How could there be two closest ways?

Jack: Because we're going in opposite directions. That makes the difference.

Jim: That still doesn't make any sense.

Jack: Well, I'll just have to draw you a picture sometime. Drive on, John.

The acreage of lakes came up again as we crossed a long, arching bridge over a narrow piece of water between two lakes.

Jack: On the left is Little Harris Lake. It's 12,746 acres. That's Big Harris Lake on the right. It's 15,179 acres. If you put them both together—and you can because they're joined—they are the largest body of water in Central Florida.

John: Did you take off any for the fill they did for this bridge? And I see over yonder that they've done some filling. Did you take that off?

Jack: I don't know about that. I just know what it is. You can look it up.

The selection of eating places also came up.

Jack: Where do y'all like to eat when you're down here?

John: We like to go to Cracker Barrel.

Jack: I can't believe that. Why don't you go to some "Florida" places and get a flavor for the area? Why would you go to franchise places?

John: Cracker Barrel's not a franchise place.

Jack: It's not?

John: Naw, they just serve good food.

Finally, our "closest" route home brought us back to the town of Umatilla. As we passed the "City Limits" sign, Jack said, "You'd better drive slow through here, John. They'll get you."

An Adventure in Moving

There are several companies around that rent trucks and trailers which are used mostly by do-it-yourself movers. About thirty years ago one of these had as its slogan "An Adventure in Moving." It was featured prominently on all sides of all its vehicles. Honey and I had several of these "adventures" through the years as we moved ourselves and both our children. Our experiences could best be described as "misadventures." The truck was too small. Although promised and reserved, the truck was not ready on time. We didn't get enough furniture pads. The turn-in office was closed. We could figure something was going to go wrong. We just couldn't predict what it would be. Even today when Honey and I see one of this company's trucks or trailers on the highway, one of us will comment, "There go some folks having an 'adventure.'" And we're so happy it's not us.

Recently, a friend of mine had "an adventure in moving" but he was not using one of this company's vehicles. If he had been, things would probably have turned out differently. Therein lies the tale.

Over the years my friend Wayne had become friends with one of his older neighbors, Mr. High. Mr. High had a large workshop filled with all sorts of tools and had the reputation of being able to make or fix most anything. However, by the time of this incident, Mr. High was well up in his eighties and his engineering skills had eroded over time.

Mr. High had owned a winter house near Sebring, Florida, for a number of years but was getting too old to make good use of it. He decided to sell it and offered it to Wayne at a good price. Part of the deal was that Wayne would help him move its contents back to Franklin. Wayne agreed which set the whole fiasco in motion.

First of all, neither had a big enough truck or trailer and Mr. High wouldn't hear of renting one. "I'll just build one," he declared. True to his word, he made the rounds of junk and salvage yards and hauled to his shop an axle, two wheels, and an assortment of metal bars and beams. Out of this he fabricated a flatbed trailer to which he attached wooden, slatted sides about four feet high. It had a taillight but no license plate. He didn't bother cleaning off any of the rust. When Wayne asked him about this he replied, "No need in painting it up. We're just gonna make one trip." Wayne didn't much like the looks of the contraption but he didn't have grounds to protest. He was just the driver.

Moving day came and they headed south, pulling the trailer with Mr. High's pickup. To Wayne's relief they made it all the way to Sebring without mishap. Plans were to load up one day, leave early the next morning, and make the 700 mile trip in one day.

Wayne couldn't figure out why Mr. High wanted to haul _that_ furniture back to Tennessee. It had been purchased from used furniture stores when Mr. High first bought the house thirty years earlier. Wayne thought it should just be taken to the dump but Mr. High wanted his stuff. They stacked it on the trailer and Mr. High put tarps over it and laced it down with several hundred feet of rope. The tarp only peeked through in places

They left before dawn the next morning. The trip was uneventful until they pulled into a rest stop near the Georgia line. The trailer with its load was listing precipitously to one side. When Wayne pointed this out, Mr. High replied, "It's just settling in good. It'll ride better now." Wayne had his doubts and could imagine all sorts of problems at high speed on the interstate but Mr. High was unconcerned.

They hit Atlanta after dark and, fortunately, after rush hour traffic. Suddenly, Wayne could feel an unseen force tugging at the rear of the pickup. Looking in his side mirror, he saw that they had a real problem. Sparks were flying everywhere. He let out an exclamation which roused a dozing Mr. High who saw all the sparks and shouted, "Good Lord, Wayne, the trailer's on fire!"

"No it's not!" Wayne came back. "It's lost its wheels!" The whole wheel and axle assembly had disintegrated leaving them pulling a sled full of furniture down the highway at sixty miles per hour. Somehow Wayne managed to get across five lanes of traffic and stop the truck and its strange-looking tow on the right shoulder. Luckily, there was no fire and both Wayne and Mr. High were unharmed. When they got out of the truck to check things out. Mr. High's first act was to walk a few yards away and relieve himself.

When he finished, he walked back to the truck and said, "Wayne, we need to go back up the road and get my wheels."

By this time Wayne could hear the screeching of tires as motorists tried to stop or avoid their debris and dull thumps when they didn't. "Mr. High," Wayne replied, "We can't go back for those wheels. Don't you hear that? There's no telling how many times they've been run over already." Mr. High cocked his head to listen but didn't say anything.

Cars disabled by blown tires and other problems began to stop all round them on both sides of the highway. One motorist who had managed to avoid the debris stopped to see if he could help them. As they were looking at the wheelless trailer, Mr. High sidled up to Wayne and said in a hushed voice, "Wayne you'd better watch this here big city fellow. I think he wants to steal my wheels." Wayne assured Mr. High that he didn't think that was a possibility.

Soon several police cars showed up. One stopped behind

the trailer with its blue lights flashing. As the officer got out and came toward them, Mr. High warned, "Better watch where you're walking officer, I just peed right there." The policemen just ignored him and began to assess the situation. Finally, he asked, "Do you want the stuff on this trailer?"

"Of course, I do," responded Mr. High. "It's my furniture." Wayne was hoping he was through with the load of house plunder but such was not to be the case.

"Okay," said the officer, "here's what I want you all to do. Unhook this thing and I'll have it towed. You can come back and get it. Here's my card. You all just head on to Tennessee before you cause any more problems." And so they did.

A few days later, Wayne brought Mr. High back in a bigger truck. He paid the towing fee and they rescued Mr. High's furniture. However, they left the trailer behind—a gift from a Tennessee craftsman to the city of Atlanta.

Mr. High has now gone to that great workshop in the sky. Wayne is enjoying Mr. High's house in Florida. No one knows what eventually happened to the furniture. But even today Wayne is a little gun shy when someone asks him for help in moving.

THINGS THAT EXPLODE

O ver the years I've had several friends who have had trouble with things that explode. Now, I'm not talking about things that are _supposed_ to explode like fireworks and dynamite although I've known some folks who have had some problems with these categories as well. No, I'm referring to common, everyday items that are not prone to blowing up. Some cases in point.

Sam's first wife had divorced him and he was living in a trailer. His job as a construction foreman left him little time for domestic pursuits, but ever so often he would make a trip to the store and pick up some food items he could prepare quickly. One day he noticed a display of canned biscuits. "Just like mother used to make" the sign said. They hadn't been on the market too long. He bought several cans and planned on trying them out that very evening.

As he started his meal preparation, he glanced at the directions on the can. He saw "preheat oven to 450°" and "place biscuits on a cookie sheet." So, he did. He turned the oven to the directed temperature, sat the can in the middle of the cookie sheet, slid it into the oven, and went about readying the rest of his meal.

He was peeling potatoes a few minutes later when the explosion came. It startled him so badly that he almost amputated one of his fingers. The stove door flew open and bounced several times before remaining down. A large ball of smoke and debris shot across the kitchen. After he regained his composure, he looked into the oven and saw the uncooked dough hanging from the walls and top like stalactites in a limestone cave. He just shut the oven door and let the dough cook. When it was done, he took a metal pan cake turner and scraped it off. The oven cleanup was easy compared to the stuff that had escaped into the kitchen.

Upon reading the _full_ directions on another can, he discovered his error. However, Sam says that he has really not developed a liking for canned biscuits.

Chuck was a _very_ good golfer. He was a traveling man who kept his clubs in the trunk of his car. After completing his calls for the day, he would head for the local course and get in at least nine holes.   He also played year around, weather permitting. It was a chilly morning in December when Chuck's episode occurred.

It was a Saturday and Chuck was rushing to make his mid-morning tee time. Marcie was still in bed. She didn't mind his playing but she wasn't about to get up and fix his breakfast. He was seeing to this when he remembered that he had neglected to warm his golf balls. All golfers know that you can hit a warm ball a lot farther than a cold one. In cold weather Chuck usually brought in several balls and placed them on the heat vent overnight but he'd forgotten this time. So he ran out to his car, grabbed several balls, and pitched them into the microwave. He set it for two minutes and began scrambling his eggs.

Chuck recalls that the explosion sounded about like a stick of dynamite. It was followed by a scream from the bedroom. Fortunately, the microwave's door lock held the door closed. A tentative inspection revealed that the inside was totally shred-ed with the glass tray reduced to fine particles much like sand.

Hurrying down to the bedroom, Chuck found Marcie sitting straight up in bed. Her mouth was open and her eyes looked about the size of saucers. "Honey," said Chuck enthusiastically, "I think we're going to be able to get that new microwave you've been wanting."   Chuck has always been one to find something positive in a bad situation.

ENGAGEMENTS, WEDDINGS, AND EVERAFTER [?]

June is here—the month of weddings. All my life I've heard of "June brides" and the fact that more couples are wed in June than in any other month. I understood that the month's popularity was rooted somewhere in early history but had no clue just why or how the custom originated. Then a few years ago I came across an article by a noted sociologist giving an explanation. This scholar did, indeed, trace this custom's origin to man's _very_ early history.

It seems that by June the waters of lakes and streams had warmed enough to bathe in, offering primitive folk the opportunity to get rid of the accumulated winter crud. And what better time to wed? Both the bride and groom would be freshly scrubbed making those first intimate moments much more palatable. Of course, this reason for June wedding has long since passed but the custom still lingers. It's sort of like having our school calendars reflect an agricultural society which no longer exists. But that's another story.

Anyway, all the engagement write-ups and pictures coupled with those from the ensuring weddings offer a fruitful field for critical observations. As everyone knows, there have been significant changes in male-female relationships in the last 50 years. No place are these more evident than in the engagements/marriage section of the newspaper.

At one time a male seldom appeared in an engagement photo. It was a "future brides" section. Only if they made it to the altar did we get to see the other half—usually in a stiff, formal pose. Occasionally, there was an action shot of the couple emerging from an archway of flowers or of sabers if it were a military ceremony.

But times have surely changed. At least seventy-five per cent of the engagement photos now include both parties. And these pictures can be very revealing. First of all, and contrary to the adage that "opposites attract," people tend to marry their own kind: young tends to marry young, old tends to marry old, fat tends to marry fat, homely tends to marry homely, and rednecks tend to marry rednecks just to name a few of the categories. The write-ups further confirm these observations. You never find a Vanderbilt graduate getting engaged to a person who is a high school dropout and just finishing Burger Boy's patty pressing and french fry course.

Other aspects of these photographs that speak volumes are the poses, the settings, and the clothing. The stiff, formal pose is out. More commonly both parties are draped around or on each other. I especially like the upper torso pose in which the couple faces each other but turns to the camera at about a forty-five degree angle. The woman usually has one hand lying somewhere on the man's upper chest. I always wonder about the location of her other hand and what activity it might be engaged in.

Where the pictures were taken and the garb of the happy couple also says a great deal. A while back a picture and article announcing the engagement of Smith and Jones appeared in the paper. The photo showed the couple reclining in the crevice formed by two large rolls of hay with tall trees in the background. Both were wearing jeans and Western boots; he sported a white, cowboy hat. Her tee shirt advertised a rock band, his an oil company. And you thought I could not recognize a redneck engagement? It's just like when you see the wedding picture of a couple in front of one of those miniature churches and read in the write-up that they were married in Gatlinburg's Chapel of Love and will spend their honeymoon in

Pigeon Forge bungee jumping and water sliding. I rest my case.

Previous to the "rolling in the hay" engagement photo, the paper had announced the betrothal of Jackson and Johnson. The picture of this couple featured a horse barn as the backdrop with both wearing identical white, Western hats. I remarked to Honey, "I'd be willing to bet they get married in those hats." Fortunately, nobody took me up on it. I didn't have any money riding on the outcome when the wedding picture proved me wrong. They didn't get married in _those_ hats; they chose more formal ones for the wedding. Hers was white with a flat crown and bridal veil. His was larger and black with a white band. He also sported a black jacket and a white shirt with a bolero tie. Obviously, their engagement photo had concealed the true depth of their taste.

When we look at these pictures—both the traditional and the unusual—it's sad to think that, statistically speaking, about half of these unions will end in divorce. Forever just isn't forever anymore. There are undoubtedly numerous reasons for this one of which has to be attitude. There is a minivan being driven around Franklin which verifies this point. It's driven by a woman in her thirties. I've seen it twice. On its rear bumper is a sticker that reads, "All men are idiots, and I married their King." What else is there to say?

LOOKING WHERE THE SUN DON'T SHINE

"Your doctor says you're in real good health." This statement came from the anesthesiologist whose job was to make sure I slept well during an impending surgery.

"Then I wonder how he explains the fact that this is my third time in the hospital this year," I shot back.

"Well…." She scanned my chart. "You are in good health. All they've been doing is fixing those parts that have gotten broken or bent pretty badly. All your vital organs are fine."

Her assessment was pretty well on target. I was sort of like an old car whose engine and transmission were in good shape but whose shocks, wheels, and exhaust needed attention. These repairs were the cause of my all too frequent visits to our local medical center.

And in addition to the obvious repairs, some in the medical field like to take preventive measures. That is to say, they like to look around for parts that need some work even though there's no outward sign of a malfunction. That explains what happened a while back when I just went for a _regular_ check-up.

"If you were my father, I'd make you go get it done. But since you're only my patient, I can only recommend _very_ strongly that you do so," so said my doctor—or as they are called today, my primary care physician. That's one of the consequences of getting old. Your doctor is young enough to be your son—or grandson in some cases.

Anyway, because I have had several friends who have had bad experiences with colon cancer, I decided to take the more prudent, although decidedly less pleasant, route. The next stop was the specialists who said, "There're only two reasons to do this at your age. (I just love the "at your age" qualification.) The first would be if you had symptoms which you don't. The second would be for prevention. And we'd only recommend it at your age if we figure you're going to live another ten years. Looks like you probably will make it, so I think we ought to go ahead with it and if everything's clear, we won't ever have to do another one. I was so overjoyed at being granted another "probably" ten years that I signed on for the procedure.

I had heard that the worst part of an endoscopy was the day before—absolutely a correct assessment. At certain times of the day, you drink a magic potion followed by a liter of water. Since a liter is about a quart, I just used that measure. During this procedure a person does not want to plan any long trips or activities which will take you more than thirty seconds distant from a facility. I have no idea what the formula is for this stuff but it would make a good remedy for clogged plumbing.

At about ten in the evening, the last thing consumed is ten ounces of a vile looking drink from a bottle. The nurse had written on the directions, "better chilled." Now, this is fake advertising at its worst. To say that something is "better chilled" implies that it is somewhere less than better or maybe even good at a warmer temperature. This could not be the case. It was so bad chilled that, had the concoction been warm, it would have gone completely off the scale of un-palatability. So much for the day of preparation.

* * * * *

The next morning I found all the hospital folks to be pleasant and efficient. I even knew one of the nurses. They got me "gowned" and into a small, curtained area where a nurse got an IV in me and gave me three pages of information on the procedure which she asked me to read. I noted that pictures would be taken. I asked if I could have an 8x10 glossy. "The doctor usually brings some for the patient," the nurse replied.

The information also said that they would probably pump air into my colon in order to get better pictures. It would feel like gas and when I awakened I should just get rid of it in the normal manner.

They wheeled me into the room where the procedure would be done and got me up on the table. I was told to roll over on my left side. As I was getting settled, I felt somebody bothering my gown from the rear. I looked back over my shoulder and caught one of the nurses who said, "I thought maybe I could get your gown up without you knowing it."

"Just go ahead," I replied. "I quit caring about things like that a long time ago."

The next thing I remember was a voice coming from a long way off saying, "Mr. Boyd, it's time to wake up now. Take some deep breaths for me." I managed to take one deep breath before going back to sleep. But the voice persisted, "Come on. You've gotta give me more than one." I don't know why they put you in that good sleeping mode and then wake you up.

After I was fully conscious, the nurse was working around getting everything unhooked and put up when I had a tremendous gas pain. She noticed me squirming around with a distressed look on my face and asked, "Is anything wrong?"

"The paper I read said that some air might be pumped in ...." I didn't have to finish.

"Oh, just go ahead," she encouraged. "I've got a husband and three sons at home. I'm used to it." The world needs more of these understanding people.

The doctor came in and he did bring pictures. They were not 8x10s but they were glossy. He let me keep them. He explained that there were no polyps, nothing abnormal, everything was clear. Wonderful news to say the least. I may die from something but it won't be colon cancer. It felt so good to be given another "probable" ten years. Heck, I may even shoot for fifteen or twenty.

How To "Fix" Zucchini

Zucchini, the kudzu of vegetables, is prolific. One hill can produce enough long green tubular fruit in a good season to feed a small southern town and have plenty left over for seed. It's the only vegetable that will cause Baptists to roll their car windows all the way up and to lock their cars at church on the hottest of summer days to guard against fellow members slipping a sack of zucchini inside.

It is as fast growing as kudzu and can, on occasion, be dangerous to pets and small children. A fellow once told me of an incident he had one summer. He was practicing chipping golf balls in his back yard when his two-year-old wandered too close to the zucchini section of the garden. Alerted by the child's screams, he found the youngster enmeshed in the plant's tentacles and being slowly drawn to its center. The rescue was affected with the help of his 60 degree loft pitching wedge which he used to flail the plant into submission.

With zucchini in such good supply, one would expect to find it featured prominently on restaurant menus. Such is not the case. To get diners to order it, chefs have to disguise it under the heading "vegetable medley." Order this and you get a few yellow squash, three or four carrot strips, a green pea or two, and a whole mess of zucchini. Most people won't eat it so restaurants end up throwing it away after selling it to unsuspecting customers.

However, in spite of its shortcomings, it does have _some_ food value and is eaten by _some_ people. Of course, the secret is in the recipe and the best one I know of was given to me by an old fellow from Dull, Tennessee.

The first step is to acquire the zucchini. Assuming that you don't have a garden or didn't plant any (which was wise), just wander about the neighborhood and look for backyard plots containing a large plant bearing long green fruit which is about to inundate the rest of the garden's citizens. This is zucchini and any home gardener will be more than happy to give you some. In fact, people have been known to form life-long friendships with those who will take zucchini off their hands. This step is known as GATHERING. It harkens back to that period in human history before the domestication of plants, dogs, or males when our forebearers simply wandered about and picked up what they could find to eat.

Next, measure the depth and width of your oven, go to your local lumber supply store, and have them cut you enough Western cedar slats 1/4 inch by 4 inches to fill this space. Southern pine can be used but there's nothing like the flavor that is imparted by the Western cedar.

Peel the zucchini and slice into 1/4 inch thick, round slices. Place the slices on the boards with just the sides touching. Do not overlap or stack. Lightly dust with salt and black pepper. Place on the middle rack of your oven pre-heated to 375 degrees and cook for 35 to 40 minutes or until the tops of the slices begin to bubble. This step is known as PREPARATION and harkens back to an early period in human history when our forebearers dressed virgins in the best of clothing and threw them into volcanoes to appease the gods of the mountain.

Remove the zucchini from the oven and while it is still hot garnish with sprigs of parsley and thin slices of red and green peppers. This step is known as DECORATION and harkens back to an earlier period of human history when our fore bearers painted their bodies all sorts of colors, donned ceremonial dress, and danced all night around a campfire drinking fermented beverages.

Allow the zucchini slices to cool 15 to 20 minutes. Remove

them carefully from the cedar boards with a spatula or other flat instrument, throw the zucchini into the garbage and eat the boards. This step is known as REVENGE and is the best way known to "fix" zucchini.

DEARLY BELOVED

Marriage proposals and weddings seem to be becoming more unusual with each passing day. Apparently, some folk are determined to out "special" everyone who has gone before. In fact, proposals are becoming so "special" that family and friends are being invited to them. Yes, you did read that correctly—the proposal. One lady's account of this new trend was especially chilling.

The proposal involved her sister's child who was getting proposed to in Washington State. Family and friends from across the country were invited. The lady telling the story lives in Maine and couldn't afford the trip so she didn't go. The couple has been living together for several years causing her to think a proposal should not have been such a big deal. Wrong. She was given this account of the event: All invitees assembled on a beach. The couple was not there. They were flying around in a seaplane which landed and taxied in to shore. The couple hopped out onto the beach where the boy got down on one knee and asked "the question" to the "surprised" girl. To everyone's amazement she said "yes." A cheer went up and another successful and "special" proposal went in the record book.

However, there was some fallout. Because the Maine lady did not go all the way across the country for the proposal, her sister is not speaking to her. And to top it off, the wedding will be in Hawaii and she's invited to it. She said if she couldn't afford to go across the country to the proposal, she surely can't afford to go halfway around the world to the wedding. She's in a "lose-lose" situation. Some folk have a hard time under-standing that the world does not revolve around them.

I heard another account along the same line. The girl was engaged and the wedding date set but they decided to elope. Groom was a military man and was later deployed. After he returned the girl decided that they needed to "renew" their vows. It had only been two years. This "renewal" will involve bridesmaids, groomsmen, bridal showers, a bachelor party, a full-dress military ceremony with exit through crossed sabers, and a big reception. In addition, the event will be held at his military post several hundred miles distant which will entail a lot of travel for a lot of people. The person telling me said that she thought the woman was trying to "have her cake and eat it, too," and cause a lot of people considerable inconvenience. Sure seems that way to me.

This last wedding story is not about self-centeredness but I thought it interesting. A friend of mine who is a retired minister reported that he will travel to one of our western states next spring to officiate at the wedding of one of his nieces. The ceremony will include a "ring dog." Yes, you did read that correctly. She's got an English bulldog she just loves and is making him a part of the ceremony. My first question was, "Is he housebroken?" My friends said that was not an issue since the ceremony would be outside. However, my friend does have some concerns. The dog does not like to be leashed and will have to come down the aisle without restraint. Now, what could possibly go wrong here? My friend has suggested that a trail of doggy treats be laid down the path to keep him on track and that he have some in his pocket when/if the dog gets to the front. Also, a good question might be, "Where does a 50+ pound unleashed bulldog go?" Answer: "Wherever he want to."

Additionally, you know the animal is going to be nervous. What if he raises his leg and marks his territory along the way? And what if he decided to stop and do #2 about halfway down? And since this breed is known for its flatulence, what if he wanders among the wedding party doing #1 ½ during the ceremony? And surely he won't be bringing the "real" ring. If a cat or a squirrel wanders into the area, the dog may not be seen until after the reception. I think all these and a few other scenarios are going through my friend's mind.

And what if the dog is overly possessive and attacks the groom as he kisses his bride? Can't you just see the news account? "Ring Dog Attacks Groom. The wedding of _____ and _____ this past weekend was thrown into chaos when the ring dog attacked the groom, biting him several times and ripping his tux beyond repair. The bride was also bitten when she tried to intervene. The couple spent their wedding night at the emergency room while the dog was placed in quarantine to check for rabies. Pictures at 11:00."

My friend is considering calling in sick.

FANS

We are nearing the end of the _regular_ college football season. Of course, with playoffs in some divisions and more bowl games than anyone would have imagined a few years ago, some schools will be playing into early January. This "extended season" gives the fans additional bragging time and excuses for holiday trips to such exotic places as Shreveport and Prairie View. And what would college football be without the fans—those devoted followers who plan their lives from August through December each year around their teams' schedules. So, let the sports writers write about the game; this column is about the fans.

At the outset it should be noted that the word is a shortened form of "fanatic." That fact in itself goes a long way in explaining the actions of some of these folk

The first thing most fans have in common is color. The true fan takes his team's basic color and incorporates it into every aspect of his life. That can, and often does, include his mailbox, barn, house, car, RV, boat, clothing, pets, and even his wife and children. And on game day he always wears "the color" especially if he attends the game. Retailers have caught on to this desire which allows the fan to wear "the color" from the skin on out including all accessories. A fan enjoys setting himself apart in this way even if his "color" doesn't go with or complement any other color. For example: (and I realize I'm on dangerous ground here even though one of my degrees is from UT and I enjoy watching Tennessee football) Tennessee orange—it doesn't go with any other color and doesn't even rhyme with anything but it does set the Tennessee fans apart and they're proud of it.

One morning last fall I was filling up with gas at one of our local stations when a very large RV with a car in tow pulled up to the pump across from me. The RV was orange and white and festooned with orange and white flags. The car was orange and white. The man and woman were both dressed in orange and white. The woman was driving; the man jumped out and began to wave his arms and direct her in maneuvering the RV into a position where the hose would reach the car's tank and both tanks on the RV. He caught me looking at his rig. Our eyes met. "I see you're an Alabama fan," I said. His muscles contracted uncontrollably causing him to squirt gasoline onto the side of the RV and a considerable portion of the pavement. Fortunately, nothing caused a spark which would have put us on the front page of area newspapers as well as TV at 6:00 and 10:00.

He soon realized that I was just kidding with him and we began to talk. His tags and other bumper information told me that he was from only a few miles south at Columbia. "Are you going up for the game on Saturday?' I asked.

"Sure are," he replied. "We're on our way now."

"But this is Wednesday," I observed.

"Yeah, we like to have plenty of time. We meet friends and do a lot of tailgating." His voice was enthusiastic. "For out-of-town games, we leave on Tuesday or on Monday if it's a long way off."

I knew I was in the presence of a true fan. For three to four months of the year, his world was nothing but highways, RV parks, parking lots, ball games, and a blur of orange. Could life be any better than this?

And a true fan's support for his team does not have to end with death. There was an article in one newspaper last month about a company that began six years ago marketing caskets in school colors with school logos. The article was illustrated by an orange casket lined in white with a Power T logo emblazoned inside the lid. What a way to go! They now have licenses with 47 colleges. Oklahoma is the number one seller followed by Alabama. And Tennessee ranks up near the top which should not be a surprise. They also have colorful urns for ashes if a fan goes the cremation route.

A couple of days later there was a letter to the editor applauding this creative appeal to the true sports fan. The writer even suggested that the idea be expanded to include tombstones. He was a NASCAR fan and suggested that stones could be carved into the shape of the car of a fan's favorite driver. He said that he could just envision a cemetery with all these race car tombstones lined up to look like the starting lines at Daytona or Talledaga. To each his own, I suppose.

Some fans are not content with just wearing their school's colors or having "the color" on most of their possessions. These put permanent adornments on their bodies. _Sports Illustrated_ did a piece on sports fans several years ago. One fellow featured was a Nebraska fan, a car dealer with an expansive smile. He had red inlays placed in his front teeth so that when he smiled, his teeth said, "Big Red."

Tattoos are another popular way of showing team support. Recently, I saw an article about an ardent Alabama fan who went this route. At the base of his neck in front was a red "A." On the back of his left arm was "Roll," on the back of his right arm was "TIDE." A red elephant was on his right upper arm with "Crimson" above it and "Tide" below. But his back said it all. Covering the whole area was a likeness of Bear Bryant wearing his famous hounds-tooth hat and leaning against a goalpost. The back tattoo alone cost $3500 and took over two years to complete. Apparently, where a fan's team is involved neither pain nor expense stands in the way.

The growing popularity of team related tattoos reminds me of a story I heard a while back. It seems that a fellow was a big fan not of just one team but of the SEC. So much so, in fact, that he had the faces of two legendary SEC coaches tattooed on his buttocks—Bear Bryant on one side and Johnny Vaught of Ole Miss on the other. As fate would have it, the man grew older and eventually developed a medical problem in his lower region. His primary care physician sent him to a young proctologist for treatment. Now this young doctor was not old enough to be familiar with these legendary coaches. So when he got him in position to be examined, the doctor was startled by these faces staring up at him. "What in the world is this?" he asked.

His patient explained that he was such a fan of SEC football that he had had the faces of SEC coaches tattooed on his behind. The doctor stepped back a little, squinted at the man's rear, and remarked, "Yeah, I can see Spurrier there in the middle, but who are those other guys?"

GEEZER GOLF

Honey once had a calendar: "365 Good Things About Getting Older." I could add one more for leap years—getting to play geezer golf. You see, when you get to be 65, golf courses let you hit from the front tees up near the women's tee box which gives you a nice distance advantage on your drives. The theory is that once you get old and dottery you cannot hit the ball very far.

I often play with a bunch of retired geezers. We tell people we are members of the USGGA, U. S. Geezer Golf Association. Some of us have been playing for many years. Others only took up the game after retirement. As you might guess, there's quite a variance in skill level but that's really not a problem. We're just happy to be still on the right side of the grass, to be able to enjoy each other's company, and to hit a good golf shot every now and then.

When we play, it is usual for the unusual to happen—and a good bit of it is not related to golf. For example: One day we invited Phil to go with us. He was recently retired and a pretty fair golfer. He came and rode down to the course with Pete. Phil and Pete also rode in a cart together. Pete was having some lower GI problems and during the front nine he had an accident. Since the damage was already done and because he didn't want to slow the foursome down by going to the clubhouse and cleaning up, he just played on. We all thought this very considerate on Pete's part. Phil, who had to ride in the cart with him, was the lone dissenter. He said riding in an open golf cart with him was almost unbearable. But the trip back to Franklin with him in a closed car was more than any man should have to take. Since that unforgettable day, Phil has declined to play golf with us which is probably a good thing. He obviously does not have a great deal of stamina.

There have been other unforgettable days as well. On one occasion I was driving one cart with Don in the passenger seat. Joe was driving the other with Jesse as his passenger. Joe is about my age but he's only been playing about a year. Both Jesse and Don are in their late 70s and late comers to the game. Also, neither could see very well.

The comedy of errors began on the first hole. We had teed off and were getting ready to hit our second shots when Joe turned his cart around and headed back toward the tee. "What's wrong?" I shouted as they passed us. "Jesse needs his sun glasses," replied Joe as they raced back up the cart path. I didn't know what we were going to do. There were several foursomes on the tee and we were holding them up. Just as we were about to wave the next group through, Jesse's cart turned around and started back toward us. I figured his glasses had fallen out of the cart and they'd found them. "Did you find them?" I yelled as they roared by. Joe leaned out and shouted back, "Naw. He had 'em on all the time." Things did not improve.

* * * * *

As already noted, Jesse and Don do not see well. So, early in the round Joe and I figured out that we needed to watch their shots and help them locate their balls. As I would stop beside Don's ball, there were many exchanges similar to the following during the day.

> Don: Why're we stopping?
> Me: That's your ball.
> Don: Are you sure? I thought I hit it over yonder a
>   piece.
> Me: No, I think that one's yours.

> Don: Well, let me see (as he gets out of the cart and examines the ball). Well, you know that is mine. I just declare.

In golf there are several cardinal rules on the green one of which is: don't walk in anyone's putting line. Many beginning golfers do not understand this. On one hole as Jesse was putting, Don walked across Jesse's line while going to his ball. Jesse's putt went between Don's feet in mid stride. The moving ball attracted Don's attention.

> Don: Whoa! There goes a ball.
> Jesse: Yeah. That's my putt.
> Don: Did I mess you up?
> Jesse: Naw, you didn't hit it and it wasn't going in anyway.

A hole or two later we hit up to an elevated green. When we got up there, Joe couldn't find his ball. We looked all over for it even in the traps. Finally, we got to looking at the balls that were on and by the green and asking what each was hitting. When Joe said, "I'm hitting a range ball," Don replied, "Oh, I've got that one in my pocket. I just picked it up. I thought somebody had just hit one up here off the range." We'd been wandering around like a flock of lost sheep and Don had what we were looking for in his pocket.

Usually these balls are not the best quality, are pretty dead, and don't go very far when hit. When this was pointed out to him, he said philosophically, "A ball won't go no farther than I hit it anyway." It's hard to argue with logic like that.

On the seventeenth hole, Jesse was putting when his floppy hat blew off for the umpteenth time. He started chasing it and encountered a wet spot in the grass just off the green where the sprinkler connection was leaking. He fell hard with one leg doubled back under him. I thought for sure he'd broken it. I was trying to decide whether it would be best to call the ambulance to the seventeenth green or take him to the clubhouse. But we helped him up and all his parts seemed to bend in the right direction. We chased his hat down but he missed the putt.

Thankfully, we only had one more hole to play and it was uneventful.

Postscript:

About two weeks later, the Women's Tournament, the LPGA, was held at the Legends Club in Franklin. Don was a volunteer. At church that Sunday, someone asked him just what he was doing. He told them that he was a spotter—that he found and marked the players' balls. The questioner's response was, "How in the world do you find those women's balls? You can't even find yours when you play."

"Yeah, I know," Don replied, "but those women mostly hit 'em in the fairway." There's a lesson there for all of us.

PUBLIC DISPLAYS
OF AFFECTION

When I am out and about, which I am a good bit since my retirement, I like to watch people. I'm telling you, there are some unusual sights out there just waiting to be looked at. Any mall is a good place or downtown during the Main Street Festival. But the best locations by far are vacation areas. Most of these folk are a good way from home and where no one knows them. As a result some don't give a rip what they wear, look like or do. This is especially true with public displays of affection (PDA). Now, by PDA, I don't mean tame stuff like holding hands. It's the mutual groping of each other's body parts I'm talking about. Seeing some of the things done in public makes me wonder what might go on in private. It's something to think about and it doesn't require much imagination.

A few years ago, Honey and I were at a resort area sitting on a bench eating ice cream. A couple came along, each wearing tight-fitting jeans. They were walking very close to each other with their inside arms across the other's back and their hands thrust into the other's back pocket. I suppose it is somewhat erotic to feel the pulsating muscle movement of your partner's buttocks.

A couple of nights later, we were doing the same thing— butter pecan on this occasion, as I recall. Another couple came by except their pants were loose fitting, so their hands were down the back of each other's pants. From the rear, it looked as if each pair of trousers was occupied by a hyperactive cat seeking an exit. That probably illustrates that most anything can be improved upon.

On another occasion, Honey and I were having a late dinner in Pigeon Forge at one of those places that serves family-style food and always more than you can eat. The restaurant was not crowded; in fact, we were the only diners in that particular section.

As we were looking over our menus, the hostess brought in a young couple and seated them by the wall directly across from us. They looked to be in their early 20s and for some reason this outing didn't look like a typical date. I suspected they had just come from the Chapel of Love or a similar establishment of the area which specializes in walk-in weddings. The boy wore a ball cap with "MF" for Massey-Ferguson Tractors on the front. He had it turned backward and kept it on for the entire meal. On the back of his gold tank top was a black outline of a couple, their limbs intertwined in a suggested position, with the statement: "Born to Love." A pair of baggy khaki shorts, which were sagged precariously low, and leather sandals completed his outfit. He sported several tattoos on his arms, shoulders and calves. They were mostly serpents, dragons and other creatures of fantasy. There was one ring in his nostril and several in each ear. As he seated himself, his shorts and top went in opposite directions exposing his Scotch-plaid boxers.

As far as body piercing was concerned, the girl seemed to prefer ears, eyebrows and the navel. She wore flip-flops and a tight short denim skirt low on her hips. Her red blouse did not come close to meeting her skirt and was cut in a way that exposed a considerable portion of her red bra. When she sat down her skirt went south, revealing the top of her red thong underwear and a tattoo of, what else, a monarch butterfly

They seated themselves on the same side of the table—boy on the left and girl on the right—and scooted their chairs as close together as the laws of molecular physics would allow.

They were facing the wall with their backs to the rest of the dining area. After ordering, their bodies seemed to merge into one as foreplay began. Occasionally, he would unlock his lips long enough to glance around to see if they were being observed. The girl didn't seem to care. I managed to avoid making eye contact. Just as things seemed to be rising to a crescendo the food arrived.

As Gilda Radner used to say, "It's always something."

As they began to eat, it was apparent that they were made for each other. He was left-handed; she was right-handed. They ate with their outside hands while both inside ones explored various parts of each other's bodies. It was multitasking at its finest. He seemed to enjoy making her giggle by sliding his hand up her back and under her top and snapping the elastic on her bra and then down and doing the same thing with the top of her underwear. Sometime both elusive hands would disappear to the front, at which point it was impossible to determine just what erotic activity was in process. However, they both appeared to be enjoying their partner's probing until the boy apparently stepped over the line—which to me seemed highly improbable. Anyway, the girl jerked him up short by grabbing the top of his boxers and giving him a serious wedgie. This slowed both "feeling" hands some, but the "feeding" hands made up the difference by offering food to the opposite mouths. The whole process reminded me or some of the grooming rituals of the Great Apes

They finished before we did and asked for take-home boxes. The waitress brought several along with some plastic bags. They proceeded to dump everything left into the Styrofoam containers and departed arm in arm carrying two plastic bags filled with leftovers. I remarked to Honey, "If they have a kitchen where they are staying, they won't need to come out for two or three days."

Another category of folks who are sometimes seen showing

affections in public is older people. They don't generate as much heat as the 20-year-olds, but when you see a couple who have been married 40-plus years arm in arm or holding hands, you can tell they really mean it—that they're in it for the long haul. I once overheard a teenager exclaim, "I just can't stand to see these old people holding hands!" I remember thinking that that young lady had a lot to learn. I sort of like to see it myself. At least we've got judgment enough to be discreet.

PUTTING PEOPLE ON

Mark Twain once remarked, "Sometimes I wonder whether the world is being run by smart people who are putting us on or by imbeciles who really mean it."

There are good arguments for the validity of Twain's statement in our present world. Of course, Twain himself was one of those folk who loved to put people on. And I found out early in life just how entertaining it is to engage in this practice. I suppose I come by it naturally because my father was a great kidder and storyteller. But one should remember that "putting people on" should never be mean-spirited or hurtful and if you dish it out, you'd better be ready to take it when it's turned on you.

The best "put ons" are not planned. They just happen as the situation presents itself. For example: A friend of mine ran into this ditsy female at a social gathering. When she inquired about his line of work, he told her that he was an announcer for a deaf radio station. She was impressed that such a service was provided and wanted to know how to tune in. He told her the call letters were WHAT located at 00.0 on the radio dial. She never caught on.

My career in "put ons" began rather early. I remember in high school our basketball team was playing in a tournament and when the brackets came out, our first round opponent was "Bye." When someone remarked that they had never heard of that school, I told them that it was a rural school in the next county. And when we appeared in the next bracket as the winner without playing, I told him that "Bye" had to forfeit because they couldn't' afford to travel that far. There was considerable sympathy for "poor, little Bye."

When I was doing my doctoral work at UT, we lived in an apartment unit with several students who were doing advanced degrees in psychology. They loved to psychoanalyze everybody so I spent a good bit of time "putting on" the psychologists. One fellow kept trying to figure out my motive for growing a beard. The things I said and did kept him bouncing between "trying to hide," and "trying to stand out." Finally, one day I told him I was doing it as part of a study being conducted by his own department and that I had to sleep over in the Psychology Department two nights each week. Of course, this got him all excited. "Tell me about this study," he demanded.

"Well," I replied, "they're studying the correlation between beard length and room temperature as to whether a person sleeps with his beard inside or outside the covers."

He mulled this over for several seconds before replying, "That sounds like an interesting study. Let me know how it turns out." And since I'd given him a "scientific" explanation, he quit psychoanalyzing my beard.

I play golf each week with a bunch of mostly retired fellows. Each week a different person is responsible for planning the event, selecting the course, and securing tee times. He also may add a "special" rule of his choosing for that day. A couple of months ago, the "special" rule was that each team could have one member hit a drive from the ladies/red tee on one hole. Our team was in the process of exercising that rule with our best and longest hitting member up on the red tee box preparing to drive when a golf cart pulled up behind us. It was a course marshal. He could see that Pete was swinging the club pretty well and gave me a quizzical look that seemed to ask, "What's that guy doing driving from up there?" I thought he deserved an explanation so I said, "That fellow is going through a sex change and we're letting him hit from there so he can get a feel for it."

The marshal nodded knowingly and winked as if to say, "It's okay. I won't tell anyone his secret." The rest of the group found a good deal of humor in the exchange. Pete was not particularly amused.

Honey and I have a single lady friend named Mona. Mona has a group of friends who gather regularly on a rotating basis at each member's home. We are not members of this group but Mona invited us on one occasion as her guests. We did not know many of the other members so a large percentage of the group was trying to figure out just who we were and what we were doing there. Apparently, one lady learned that we were friends of Mona so when we encountered each other over a bowl of salted nuts, she asked in a demanding tone, "Just how do you know Mona?"

I'm not sure just what came over me at that moment but I replied rather seriously and with a straight face, "Mona used to be the Madam of a whorehouse that I went to quite often." A startled look came on her face and her jaw practically fell on the floor. Her mouth opened and closed like a fish too long out of the water. Some sounds came out but no words. I just stood there munching nuts and letting her flounder. Finally, she pulled herself together enough to say, "You're kidding, of course."

"Yes, I really am," I replied. A look of relief came over her face. But then I leaned in close as if to let her in on a big secret. "She wasn't the Madam," I confided. She was again doing her fish imitation as I moved away to mingle with the other guests.

Some days later when she found out that I had _really_ been putting her on, she sent Mona a hand-decorated wineglass with "Madam" Mona painted on it. A suitable reward.

As I noted at the outset, those who "put on" often get "put on" as well and I've been the brunt of some pretty good ones over the years. But that's fodder for another column.

THINGS THAT LOOK LIKE OTHER THINGS

I have a friend from Texas who likes to brag about "Texas Things." He says Texans make "real" chili because it has no beans and is so hot that it eats holes through normal containers. Of course, I tell him that there wouldn't even be a Texas if it weren't for Tennessee folks like Sam Houston and Davy Crockett and others who were fleeing creditors and law enforcement personnel. In those days Texas had broken away from Mexico and was an independent republic. Farmers would paint "Gone to Texas" on their barns and leave their debts behind. I used to hear the expression quite a bit growing up. It described someone who had left for parts unknown. It was an earlier version of those who "went to Canada" during the Vietnam conflict.

Anyway, we were over at his house a while back and he was showing us, proudly, a rock he'd found shaped like the state of Texas. He'd run across it while hiking around Franklin. It was not perfect but it did have a basic "Texas" shape. I pointed out that he'd found it in Tennessee but that didn't even take the edge off his pride of ownership. Thank goodness Texas has not exercised one of the options it reserved for itself when it came into the Union—the option of splitting into five states. Just think of all this Texas bragging multiplied by five.

Not to be outdone, I began looking for state-shaped rocks and found one in the shape of Colorado. My Texas friend was not impressed. He said that it was not really square and with one corner chipped off, it looked more like Kansas. It's hard to one-up a true Texan.

People tend to find meaningful shapes in all sorts of things. A couple of months ago a fellow found a cereal flake in the shape of the state of Illinois. It was quite a news story. But no reporter ever asked this question: "What sort of weird mental condition do you have that causes you to examine your food in this manner instead of just consuming it?" It would be interesting to see him with a bowl of oatmeal or a plate of pasta. Why, I'll bet he could do a whole essay with a bowl of alphabet soup. However, this flake paid off for him. I think it sold for over a thousand dollars on E-bay.

I don't know why the cereal companies haven't picked up on this and exploited it. They could put state-shaped pieces in their boxes and give prizes to those who complete a map of all fifty states. Of course, they would hold out a couple of states and only put them in a few boxes. Just think how many extra boxes they'd sell to those folk who only needed West Virginia or Delaware to complete their maps. And breakfast would become something special in more households. It would bring families together as all members searched through piles of flakes for those "special" shapes. It would be exciting, educational, and fun. It would also lure children away for those 95% sugar cereals. And why stop with the U.S?" There could be a series on Europe, South America, Central America, North America, The Far East, and then the ultimate contest: The World. The study of geography would be stimulated.

The cereal companies would not be the only ones to benefit. Farmers would grow more grain; they'd need more fertilizer and more farm machinery. There would be a need for more boxes and more trucks to haul the boxes to stores. This whole thing could just snowball and act as a stimulus to the entire economy and bring us out of our current recession. Now, don't any of you readers get any ideas. I've already filed copyright and patent papers.

While I'm on the topic of food shapes, let's not forget the

"nun bun." I expect most of you have heard of this one, maybe even seen it. This bakery was baking some cinnamon buns and one turned out to look like Mother Theresa. The resemblance was striking. Of course, they didn't eat or sell it but put it on display in a case in their shop. A lot of people came by to look at it and many bought a sack of donuts or sweet rolls in the process. But then disaster struck. A thief broke in and stole it. One has to wonder just what he was thinking. Putting it up for sale would be an admission of guilt as would putting it on display. A reward was offered but to no avail. It's been several months now and the bun has not surfaced. Maybe someday the crime will be solved.

The face of Jesus turns up on a lot of things. For the life of me, I can't figure out how these folk "know" it's Jesus' face since no one really knows what Jesus looked like. It could just as easily be the face of Noah or Job or Ugga the cave man. These images are usually vague likenesses of the human face with no real distinguishing features. The most recent one was a small rock some fellow picked up. The photo in the paper showed sort of a face on it. He had proclaimed it the "face of Jesus" and said that it gave him a great deal of comfort just to carry it around in his pocket. If it makes him feel good and doesn't hurt anybody else, more power to him. One just has to hope that the fellow who swiped the "nun bun" doesn't find out about it.

A few years ago a family discovered the face of Jesus on the side of their freezer. They had an upright freezer on their front porch and their next door neighbor's porch light shining through some tree branches produced the image. The story appeared in all the papers; TV crews came out; hundreds would come each night to view the shadowy face. There was even talk of it having curative powers. The nightly mass of pilgrims clogged the narrow street and police had to be called to control the crowds. Finally, tiring of all this hoopla, the neighbor refused to turn on his light causing a heated confrontation. It would seem to me that the real face of Jesus shouldn't cause so many problems.

I suppose one moral of this piece would be, "Look around you. There's no telling what you might find." As for me, I'm looking for two rocks in the shape of both parts of Michigan. That'll put my Texas friend in the shade.

POPOURRI

This month's column consists of a few odd things I've been thinking about lately.

* * * * *

I'm sorry, but there's just no way a string bikini or thong underwear could be comfortable. How in the living world can a person concentrate on _anything_ they're supposed to be doing while a rolled-up piece of fabric about the size of a #2 pencil continually irritates very sensitive parts of his/her anatomy? I think a significant portion of the irritability we see among our younger citizens is caused by this fashion trend. And why do I pick on the young? Because this age group are the ones who aspire to be on the "cutting edge" of fashion. We older folk have learned better. I'm at the age where I don't want my clothing (any layer, that is) to touch my body in too many places at the same time. But not so among the young. Case in point: A while back I was trying to make a purchase at one of our local retail establishments and was being waited on by a good-looking, twenty-something year-old sales person.   Her disposition was just the opposite of her appearance. She was crabby, sarcastic, and didn't seem at all interested in locating the item I wanted. And I was trying to be nice. Finally, when she squatted to look on a bottom shelf, I saw the problem. Her low-rider pants and high-rider top separated to reveal red thong underwear. I wanted to say, "Honey, a pair of flannel boxers would improve your disposition considerably." But fearing being labeled a lecherous old geezer, I remained silent.

* * * * *

I have noted that a certain bodily function is making its appearance with increasing frequency on prime time TV. Things have gone from the sound of a flushing commode in the early 1970s on _All In The Family_ to graphic details of the functions of the lower GI and urinary tracks.

At first these functions were just mentioned—no visual images. But then one evening on an episode of _NYPD Blue_, there stood Andy and his partner at adjoining urinals in that drab precinct restroom. Over the sound of the splatter, they were discussing the probable guilt of the suspect they'd just left in the interrogation room. After that the restroom became a regular place to conduct police business.

And even the commercials have succumbed. One in the spring of last year showed two young executives standing at adjoining urinals. The only difference between it and _NYPD Blue_ was that the restroom was nicer.

I've been surprised that these scenes have not generated some protests. I don't mean from those who are offended by the acts themselves but from the distaff side because they've not been included. So far I've only seen men doing the peeing. There must be some women who are hacked off because they haven't been allowed to be as offensive as the men, although a young female doctor on an episode of _Grey's Anatomy_ came close. Surely a public outcry and possibly a lawsuit can't be far off. Where in the world will it all end?

* * * * *

For some reason Honey does not like for me to go outside. In talking with several of my friends, I've discovered that their wives feel the same about their going outside. I don't know just what it is in a woman's make-up that makes her want to deny simple pleasures to the man in her life, but this trait seems to be fairly common. This is true even if the couple lives on a farm or in an isolated house in a rural area. Going outside gives one a feeling of freedom, of primitiveness, of being close to nature—a feeling that is rapidly being eliminated by the growing population and new housing developments.

Now, I'm not advocating _complete_ freedom in this respect because a man's outside area is shrinking at an alarming rate. For example, folks in Westhaven should not go outside. There's just not room. You choose to live there, you have to give up some freedom.

On the other hand, we have a fair-size lot. The backyard is secluded. There is an overgrown drainage ditch running across the back. It's a perfect setting for going outside. The last time Honey caught me, she asked, "Why do you do that?" I gave her the answer which I suspect every male who has not had the feral state completely domesticated out of him feels deep in the roots of his being. "Honey, I'm just marking my territory."

THINGS THAT DIDN'T MAKE IT

There's no telling how many ideas for new products and procedures occur each day in the U.S. alone. Some come to fruition and make life better for many and a profit for those who thought them up. Others are duds. And some are such colossal duds that we wonder how such dumb ideas ever got into production. Some cases in point:

The "new Coke." All the corporate heads must have had a case of stupid at the same time to abandon the formula for the most successful soft drink of all time and try to market something no one would drink. Fortunately, they did not destroy the old formula.

Cars. Some of you older readers will remember the Kaiser, the Frazier, and the Tucker. These all came out right after WWII. The Tucker, "the car of the future," was ahead of its time. Many of its innovations were adopted by other car companies. And who can forget the Edsel produced by the Ford Motor Company. Some said it failed because its grill was an overt sexual symbol. I will not attempt to explain that. Curious readers can look up the Edsel and see what they think.

The metric system. There was a great push back in the 1960s for US to "go metric" and get into step with the rest of the "civilized" world. Actually, we now have a dual system with metric being used in science, medicine, and the size of bolts and wrenches but the common, everyday folk continue to slog along with our old English system—hard-headed to the end.

Another unit of measurement that has not garnered widespread acceptance is the smoot. Most folks have never heard of the smoot but its creation is an interesting tale—and even more interesting because it's true.

The Charles River separates Boston from Cambridge where the schools Harvard and MIT are located. The very long Harvard Bridge connects the two sides at this point. In the 1950s many students walked across this bridge to class. In the fog, snow, and other nasty winter weather for which Boston is famous, the trek seemed an endless one. With this in mind in 1958 the pledge master of an MIT fraternity decided that it would be a service to mark the bridge so that the walkers could note the exact distance remaining. He assigned this task to a group of pledges and, with true MIT creativity, declared that the distance would not be in any known unit of linear measurement but in "pledge lengths." For this "new" standard, the shortest pledge, one Oliver (Ollie) Smoot, was selected.

They went to the bridge, Smoot stretched out to his full 5'7", and chalk marks were made. The process was then repeated. After a time Smoot tired of getting up and down so much and was either carried or dragged the remaining distance. The length of the bridge was declared to be "364.4 smoots plus one ear." This figures out to be 2035 feet, give or take a few inches. Smoot declared that they were all cold sober at the time but there seems to be some debate on that point.

The next step was to make the chalk marks permanent with paint and to number every tenth mark (e.g., 10 smoots, 20 smoots, etc.). At the midpoint (182.2 smoots) was placed a special mark accompanied by the words "Halfway to Hell" with an arrow pointing towards MIT.

Since that October day in 1958 it has been the task of every new pledge class to repaint the markings. They also add a special mark for their graduating year.

There was great concern in the 1980s that the markings

would be lost when the bridge had to be renovated. However, they had by this time become well accepted by the public. Even the Cambridge Police Department requested they be maintained since they were useful for identifying the location of accidents on the bridge. The markings were saved and the new sidewalk was scored at 5'7" intervals rather than the usual 6'.

Because of its unwieldiness, the smoot has never made it beyond the Harvard Bridge. However, Google Calculator lists it as an optional unit of measurement and notes that 10 feet is 1.79104478 smoots. There are also conversion tables comparing the smoot to International, U.S., and Imperial units.

And what of Ollie Smoot, the short pledge who set the standard? Ironically, he became Chairman of the American National Standard Institute and President of the International Organization for Standardization. Truth is, indeed, oftentimes stranger than fiction.

COLLOQUIAL MEASUREMENTS

My friend, Dick Jordan, and I have lunch together on a semi-regular basis. We don't just eat and go, we have important topics to discuss—topics like odd names and nick names, traffic lights, and other important subjects. Dick is a writer/storyteller himself and has a wealth of stories about Franklin and Williamson County. Quite often he gives me ideas on things to write about. On one of our luncheon occasions, we got off on country measurements.

Rural folk have always operated on a different standard from their city cousins. A lot of city folk measure distance in time like "I'm ten minutes from the grocery store" or " five minutes from the mall," etc. Of course, they're speaking of car driving time while country people might be speaking of walking, horseback, or wagon.

Dick thought it would be a service if someone would develop a set of numbers to give these colloquial amounts some kind of standard so he came up with the following:

A smidgen –
something that is too small or
not enough to worry about
A few/several – 3 to 7
Quite a few – 8 to 15
Right smart – 16 to 24
Whole bunch – 25 to 50

To these I would like to add a "passel" which is an indeterminate large number or too many to count. It would fall 180° away from the smidgen.

Food preparation brings up some interesting measurements. I once knew a lady who started her biscuits with so many "handfuls" of flour depending upon how many would be at the table. This always seemed to me to be very inexact but she made awfully good biscuits. Good biscuit makers seem to mix the dough more by feel than by the amounts of the separate ingredients. And then there's the "pinch," as in "just a 'pinch' between your thumb and forefinger" but a cook with large or damp fingers is going to "pinch" a larger amount. I suppose that small a variance in the recipe would not make lot of difference.

Then there's the "mess," as in "We just picked a 'mess' of turnip greens" or "That's not enough corn to make a 'mess.'" My mother was always making statements like this about the amounts of vegetables from the garden. I recall asking her on several occasions just how much was in a "mess." Her reply was usually, "just this much," when she'd come in from the garden with a "good mess" of butter beans or peas. She'd always say, "Everybody knows how much a mess is." But I didn't. By simple observations I concluded that a "mess" was large enough for everyone at the table to have an ample serving. I also concluded that a "mess" would vary in direct proportion to the size of the family. We only had four. I knew families of ten or more. Surely they would need a bigger "mess" than we did. So I have concluded that a "mess" to a Southerner is a varying, indeterminate amount that everybody knows the size of.

"Pert-near" (pretty-near) is another Southern measurement that tends to vary with the situation. For example: "How close is your house to the river?" or to a fellow building a shed, "Is that wall straight?" both get "pert-near" for the answer. So we'd have to say that "pert-near" is fairly close, depending on what you're talking about.

Country distances are not measured in miles or time but in

"pieces" such as a "short piece" or a "little piece" or a "pretty good piece." In the spirit of Dick's push for standards, I'd like to propose that a "short/little piece" which is sometimes stated as "not too far" be established as ¼ mile or less and that a "pretty good piece" be set between ¼ mile and 5 miles if the person is walking and over 5 miles if the person is driving. This would be helpful to those asking directions in the country.

"Yonder" is a country term that's hard to get a grip on. It's a direction without a compass point reference or distance given. It's completely indefinite. "Over yonder" could mean within sight or ten miles away. "Up yonder" and "down yonder" are slightly more definite since they depend on the slope of the land—but not always. As ole Ernest used to say "see whatta mean?"

Then there's the "skosh." It's sort of like the "smidgen" except that it's enough to make a difference. Country folk probably don't know exactly how large it is but they know a "skosh" when they see or feel it. A few years ago a national clothing company had a TV ad for their full-cut jeans which said they had a "skosh more room in the hips." We older country folk knew exactly what they meant.

In reflecting upon this topic, it is evident that there is a definite need in this area. We all know that the Bureau of Standards in Washington is the repository of our nation's standard weights and measures. However, there's no place a person can go to discover how many there are in "quite a few" or how far a "short piece" is. This needs to be rectified. So Dick and I are going to establish a partnership to define country measurements and to establish a National Bureau of Colloquial and Country Measurements (NBCCM for short). We figure we'll have to start regionally since there's a lot of difference between New England, the South, the West, etc. Then, we'll have to reconcile the various regions into a National whole. Of course, there will have to be a building to house these standards. We envision a multi-million dollar state-of-the-art structure in a small-unincorporated Southern village like College Grove. All this is going to take a "right smart" of time. We'll let you know when we're "pert-near" done.

BASEBALL STORIES

We're past the All-Star break and into the last half of the major league baseball season in which 30 teams play 162 games each plus play-offs in order to decide which two get to play in the cold in late October for the championship. In a lot of ways, baseball is an odd sport, one in which the defense has control of the ball. Innumerable stories have come out of our national pastime. There's only space for a few.

In one high school game, I was on second with third occupied by a teammate. There were two outs. The pitch was in the dirt and blocked by the catcher but the ball bounded off toward first base. When I saw the fellow on third break for home, I broke for third. Seeing the third baseman getting in position to take the throw from the catcher, I slid into the base in a cloud of dust. There was an equally large cloud kicked up by my teammate who had changed his mind and slid back in from the home side. The third baseman took the throw and stood looking down at two base runners on his base. Apparently, he had not run into this situation before. Knowing we both could not stay there, my teammate broke for home and I headed back to second. The third baseman made a bad decision and threw to second getting me in a run down. The lead runner scored before they got me out so we did get a run out of the deal but we both had a hard time living down the fiasco.

A friend of mine played a couple of seasons of Class D ball down in South Georgia many years ago. One day they dressed at home and were on the bus to a game when the bus broke down. It got fixed, but they rolled up to the park just at game time. When their manager told them to hit the field, one player said, "But coach we're not warmed up."

The manager replied, "You're young. Just slap your gloves a couple of times. You'll be warm." And they did.

There have been numerous exchanges between player and umpire. Some are classic. Steamboat Johnson umpired back in the mid-1900s in the old AA Southern League. He got his nickname from his voice which was likened to a steamboat's horn. Everybody in the park could hear his calls without a microphone. One day he was behind the plate and the pitch was a curve at the knees on the outside corner. When he called it a strike, the batter said, "Ump, if you'd learn to call that pitch, you could call in the majors."

Steamboat replied, "Son, if you'd learn to hit it, we could both go on the same train."

Ted Williams was one of the greatest hitters of all time and noted for having a very sharp eye for the strike zone. In one game he was on a hot hitting streak and had a home run, a double, and a triple in his first three at bats. In his fourth plate appearance, the count went to 3-2. The next pitch was close, Williams took it, and the ump called it a ball. The catcher said, "Ump, you gave him that one."

"I may have," the umpire responded, "but I held him to one base."

Dizzy Dean was noted for his blazing fastball. He pitched in an era when many parks did not have lights. One day he was pitching the second game of a double-header and the light was fading fast. He needed one more out to finish the game and had two strikes on the batter when his catcher called time, went out to the mound, and said to him, "It's too dark to see anything. Give me the ball. You wind up and pretend to throw it and I'll pop the ball in my mitt." Of course, it's against the rules for the pitcher to get on the mound without the ball but Dizzy agreed. When the catcher popped the ball in his mitt, the umpire called, "Strike three," to which the batter replied, "Ump, you're blind.

That ball was a foot outside."

Yogi Berra was an excellent hitter but was noted for swinging at a lot of bad pitches. Of course, he turned many of these into hits. It was not unusual for a pitcher, trying to waste a pitch high and outside, to see Yogi bounce it off the outfield fence. However, one year the Yankee management decided to work to improve this aspect of Yogi's game. At the start of spring training, the batting coach began to work with Yogi. His big emphasis was to "think, think, think." In the first intrasquad game, Yogi came to the plate, took three pitches for strikes, and threw his bat down. When the batting coach asked him what was wrong, Yogi replied, "Can't nobody hit and think at the same time." They gave up and let Yogi continue doing it his way.

The Yankees were known as a team of sluggers—long ball hitters. But for some reason one year they decided to emphasize bunting which was not Yogi's long suit. However, there was one modification: if the bunt was on and the third and/or first baseman suspected it and began to creep in, the batter could swing away. Well, as fate would have it, Yogi was at bat with no outs and runners on first and second when the third base coach flashed the bunt sign. Yogi missed it, swung away, hit the ball into the outfield gap for a double, and went sliding into third when the throw missed the cut-off man. As he got to his feet, the third base coach said, "You missed the bunt sign."

Thinking quickly Yogi responded, "They were creeping in on me."

"Who was creeping in?" the coach asked.

Yogi answered, "The left fielder. Didn't you see him?" Thus ended Yogi's career as a bunter.

Yes, all you need to do is to get a bunch of old baseball players and coaches together and the stories begin to flow.

Remember: According to Yogi Berra, "It's tough to make predictions, especially about the future."

ABSURDITIES ABOUND
ALL AROUND

Is the world growing more absurd—or is it just me? For a while I thought it was just my advancing years causing me to lose touch with new age thought and practices. Now, I'm not so sure. You be the judge.

Late last year I saw this big "spread" in the Nashville newspaper about a new line of jeans this person had come out with. You would have thought that by now all the ways of constructing a pair of denim pants would have been figured out but, apparently, this was not the case. This person had come up with a method of construction for women's jeans that accentuated the butt and made it look larger. I thought that most women wanted to go in the opposite direction which goes to show how little I know. It seems that there is a certain ethnic group of women who consider a large, shapely butt to be a prized physical attribute and a major plus for attracting males. The article stated that interest was so great and sales so brisk that these new jeans were just flying (or maybe waddling in some cases) off the shelves at such a rate that retailers were having a problem keeping them in stock. So, my advice to you men out there: if you're shopping with your wife or spousal equivalent or significant other and she comes out of the dressing room with a pair of jeans on and asks, "Do these make my butt look bigger?" The answer is "yes." I suppose all of this goes to prove the adage, "Build a better mousetrap and the world will beat a path to your door."

Along this same line, I saw where there was an annual "Best Butt" contest held, where else but, in Paris, France. There was no mention of jeans being involved. The ones pictured were mostly bare. Of course, the French didn't use "butt." However, "derriere" was mentioned several times. There is both a male and a female division. You might think they would do like the Westminster Dog Show and name one "Best in the Show" without regard to gender but they don't. The piece didn't give all the judging criteria but I think shape, firmness, and complexion are some. Size didn't seem to count. It's truly an international competition. Last year's female winner hailed from Argentina. I don't recall where the male champion came from. So, all you Franklinites who think you've done about everything, here's a new challenge for you.

Recently, I ran across a short blurb about a new development in cosmetic surgery. It reported that this surgeon had come up with some procedures for use on women's private parts which would make them "more visually pleasing." Excuse me, but is this a major, or even a minor, problem? This "medical breakthrough" raises more questions than can be printed in a family newspaper. I'll just leave it to you readers to come up with your own. But I do have a couple that should be considered. First of all, who's gonna see it? It's fairly obvious when someone has had a nose job or a face lift or breast implants, but this is not something you'd want to show off at the Heritage Ball. And, also, it's not something most normal folk would photograph and hang on the wall in the family room. Secondly, who sets the standards? Is there a set of universally accepted criteria someplace of which most of us have been totally unaware? I'll just say that I've always subscribed to the adage, "Beauty is in the eye of the beholder." But before I went under that knife, I'd want to see some "before and after" pictures. What I think has really happened here is that a doctor has invented and solved a problem that nobody knew existed.

While I'm at it, I'll just finish up this piece by staying in the same anatomical area. Last fall I saw a newspaper article which reported that bottled, fake urine was showing up on the shelves of some of our local stores. Chemists report that there is no way to differentiate it from the real stuff. Another adage says, "necessity is the mother of invention," and I suppose this goes to show just how many people there are around who need to pass drug tests. It's gotten to the point now that testers cannot let "filling the cup" be a private act. And one ingenious inventor even came up with a way to get around that. At one test facility, a fellow was discovered with a bag of "clean" urine strapped to his body. To this reservoir was attached tubing and a fake appendage which made it appear to a casual observer that he was producing the sample normally. What will they think of next?

Of course, people have been trying to circumvent these tests for a long time. I remember back in the early 1950s when a friend of mine was drafted during the Korean War. He and several boys he know went together for their physicals. When several were sent in together to produce a urine sample, a fellow he knew remarked, "I'll never pass. I'm a diabetic," to which my friend asked, "Then how about filling up my cup, too?" He did, so my friend was rejected for his "diabetic" condition, but, ironically, the fellow who produced his sample was drafted and sent to Korea. Perhaps the testing was not as accurate in those days.

PART IV

SOME SERIOUS THINGS

THE BEACH

As one walks along the thirty to forty-foot-wide strip of sand at high tide, the beach has a look similar to many of the other beaches of the world. Men and women lie on towels or recline in chairs as they bask in the sun's rays. Some play in the gentle surf. A naked boy about two years old digs in the sand. A woman of about thirty-five wades out of the water shaking the water and sand from her bare breasts. No one seems to pay much attention. After all this is France.

Yes, at first glance this is just another beach. But a closer inspection of the sloping 150 to 200 foot high cliffs rising just behind the sand reveals World War II gun emplacements and concrete fortifications. And out to sea there are still remnants of the Mulberry Harbors which were towed across the Channel from England to provide docking facilities for the invading forces. For, you see, this is Omaha Beach, the bloodiest of the five D-Day beaches of 6 June 1944.

The Normandy coastline is concave at Omaha. As it curves to the north, the cliffs become lower and the land almost flat where the English and Canadian forces landed on beaches named Juno, Sword, and Gold. As it curves seaward to the south, the cliffs become more rugged ending at a promontory called Point du Hoc. Beyond this point lies the second American beach which was named Utah.

The light brown sand is very fine giving rise to the concerns of General Eisenhower and his staff as to whether it was stable enough to support the weight of tanks and other heavy equipment. Of course, it was.

Many who came ashore at Omaha on that fateful June day

never talked about their experiences. Perhaps they could not bring themselves to relive the horrors which they survived. A friend of mine's father was there. He has asked him on more than one occasion to go with him to the beaches. His father's reply is always, "Been there once. Don't need to go again." He will probably die without ever letting his son glimpse this part of his life.

The father of another friend was there as well. He has never related his experiences to anyone. When the movie, _Saving Private Ryan_, came out, he said to his father, "Dad, I understand the opening scene of this movie is extremely realistic. I'd like to know what you went through. Please go see this picture and tell me if that's the way it was." His father reluctantly agreed to do so after which his son asked, "Was that the way it was?"

"Yes, that was about it. They have the sounds and the visual stuff down pretty well." He paused a few seconds before adding, "But there's one thing they'll never capture on film."

"What's that?" my friend asked.

Tears welled up in his father's eyes as he answered, "The smell—the smell of death."

There was a German gun emplacement atop Point du Hoc which could rake the entire beach with its fire. It was doing tremendous damage to our troops. Realizing that the beachhead could never be established unless that bunker's guns were silenced, a unit of Army Rangers was given this mission. The only way to get to it was to scale the 200-foot cliff. Now, the cliff is not vertical and with outcroppings of rock and scrubby bushes for handholds, the climb is not particularly difficult. But add equipment and weapons and withering enemy fire and the 200 feet became Mt. Everest. The Rangers succeeded but about half of the unit was killed in the process.

I know another man whose uncle landed on Omaha on 6 June. He described him as the "runt of the litter"—a short, wiry man much smaller than his brothers. He was an Army Ranger.

The only thing his family ever heard him say about his part in the invasion was, "Well, I climbed Point du Hoc." Those few words said it all.

The beach was peaceful on 23 August 2004—more than sixty years after D-Day. There was no evidence of disabled and burned out military equipment, of bodies and body parts washing up in the surf, of the sand and water stained red with blood. Thankfully, time has erased all of this. Laughter floats up from a group running through the surf. The little naked boy continues to dig in the sand. The bunkers on the cliffs and the Mulberry Harbors stand as silent sentinels—vacant reminders of the significance of this place.

I kneel and scoop up three handfuls of the fine, brown sand into a plastic bag to bring home. Lest we are tempted to forget.

LES FLEURS DE LA MEMORIE

Standing as straight and tall as his eighty-plus years allowed, he stepped forward and was handed the wreath of flowers. There was a serious look on his face as his thoughts undoubtedly turned back to the events of that day over sixty years past—7 June 1944, the day after D-Day—when he landed on Omaha Beach. His name is Dismukes and he is from Texas but in 1944 he was a combat engineer and among many thousand other young Americans who landed on the bloodiest of the Normandy beaches. He fought across Europe and survived the war unlike many of his comrades who lie beneath the lush, green grass and white crosses in the American Cemetery overlooking Omaha Beach.

Five other World War II veterans fell in line behind Dismukes. The veterans of later service fell in behind them. We were honored to be included with the six who stood at the front.

The procession moved into the grounds of the cemetery, turned right, and stopped before the bronze statue, "The Spirit of American Youth Rising from the Waves," which is the centerpiece of the main memorial. We stood at attention as the notes of the Star Spangled Banner came from the loud speakers.

With the fading of the music, Dismukes stepped forward, laid the wreath at the base of the statue, and stepped back. We all did an about face turning to face the two U. S. flags flying in front of the thousands of white crosses. Taps were played. The veteran in front of me was wiping the tears from his cheeks. I saw no eyes that were dry. Along with many others, I sought out Dismukes and shook his hand.

That ended the group ceremony. Next came _Les Fleurs de la Memorie,_ the flowers of memory. Each one of us had a cluster of three flowers—a red rose, a small white flower, and blue heather. We went to locate our "special" graves.

There is an unusual story behind the flowers of memory. Two French teenagers from different families were living right behind the beaches when the invasion occurred. Although warned of the impending battle, they both decided not to leave and thus, were the first French civilians to greet the U. S. soldiers as they came over the cliffs. Later they were married and settled near where they grew up which is close to the American Cemetery. Over the years they met many Americans who came to visit the graves of their loved ones. An especially strong tie was established with one particular couple who came every year. One year this couple could not come and requested that their French friends decorate the grave for them. In doing so the French couple realized that there were many graves which were never decorated. Thus was born the flowers of memory.

They formed an association with the goal of getting French people to adopt undecorated graves to ensure that every grave is decorated at least once a year. Membership fees assist with the financing of this effort which has made significant steps toward this goal. The tour company with which we were traveling sponsors a number of graves which accounted for the three flowers in my hand.

Sara and I went to Plot A (There are ten plots.) to search for Row 21, Grave 41. It is the grave of 2/Lt. Benjamin A. Gallegos from Alaska. He had served with the 551st Bomber Squadron, 385th Bomber Group. He was killed on 28 February 1944 which is, ironically, the date on which our daughter was born thirteen years later.

I placed the flowers. Pictures were taken. Sara turned away. I stepped back and saluted Lt. Gallegos' grave with the words running through my head that I had just heard from a younger veteran as he was shaking Dismukes' hand. "My generation can never repay the debt we owe to yours."

"TOUCHING THE PENCIL"

In 1946 I began working as "extra Saturday help" in a grocery store in town. A person would come in and stand around until there was a clerk available. Then he/she would come up to the counter with a list and begin.

"I want three cans of English peas."

"You want the No. 2 size or the large size?"

"Oh, I don't know. Just the regular size whatever that is."

"What brand?"

"It don't make no difference."

The peas would be brought and placed on the counter.

"Let me have four cans of cream-style corn. Same size. Del Monte if you've got it. It's real good."

And so it would go until all the items on the list were transferred from the shelves to a stack on the counter. Then the clerk would take a scratch pad and note the price of each item before going to the lone cash register and ringing up the columns of figures.

One thing we saw a lot of on Saturdays was paychecks. Workers could pay for their week's groceries and get their checks cashed at the same time. We also saw a lot of workers who could not read or write, which meant that the endorsing of the check was an interesting process.

If the worker were unable to write, he'd respond, "I'll just make my mark and touch the pencil." He'd then turn it over and make his mark, usually an "X." Some of these marks were very elaborate and distinctive with curvy lines and curlicues on the ends. Then he'd hand the pencil back to me and I'd put the point down on the check next to his mark. Before I'd start to write his name, he'd touch the top of the pencil with his index finger. This act transferred his authority through the pencil to me, allowing me to endorse the check for him. In their eyes this made everything legal.

The late Pek Gunn, who was Poet Laureate of Tennessee back in the 1970s, wrote a little poem entitled *Touching the Pencil* about this practice. Actually, the poem is about Gunn's father, who never learned to read or write his name. It ends:

"He was proud to be my Papa,
I was proud to be his son,
As he smiled and touched the pencil,
I wrote William Carroll Gunn."

Now, you're probably thinking, "That's a nice little trip down memory lane, but what relevance does it have for me?" The answer is "none" if you just want to continue living in your own world oblivious to the basic educational needs of some of your neighbors. In fact, some Tennessee residents still in the 21st century have to "touch the pencil."

On a brighter note, most counties have an agency charged with addressing this problem. In my county it's The Literacy Council of Williamson County and Rita Dozier is its executive director. Those who read below the fifth-grade level and/or do not have basic skills in math are eligible.

The staffs of these agencies do a tremendous job. However, they never have enough resources to take care of all the needs, especially basic school materials and supplies. And they never have enough volunteers.

This is an area in which we senior, retired people can still be useful to our communities. If you can afford it, send a check to your county agency earmarked for materials and supplies. You'd be surprised just how much a few dollars will buy. But perhaps more importantly, you could give something that some of us now have in excess--time. Volunteer some of your time to work one-on-one with some of these folks. The agency people will be appreciative and I'll guarantee you'll get a lot more back than you put in.

As we grow older, we should be more cognizant of the fact that we ought to leave our world just a little better than we found it. One good way is to help some of these less fortunate than us to master a basic skill we tend to take for granted. If we do, we will leave behind fewer of our neighbors who have to "touch the pencil."

THE AUCTION

I went to an estate auction a while back. It was out in the country at a place where the family had not thrown anything away since about 1947. Instead they had erected a series of storage buildings that marched to the back of the property like a squad of infantry on patrol. There were a few treasures, but there was much junk as well.

The old fellow who was selling out and moving was there and easily identifiable. It was obvious why he was having to leave. He looked to be in his eighties and moved unsteadily about using a metal cane with four tips for added stability. His arms shook unceasingly with either Parkinson's Disease or palsy.

I had bought several items and was in the process of looking through a pile of stuff when I struck up a conversation with a young couple who had bought an old trunk. We were discussing what needed to be done to the trunk and how they might go about it. I noted by his build that he was obviously a weight lifter. He had on a shirt bearing the name of a fitness center in Lewisburg. I asked him if he were from there. He replied, "No, this shirt belonged to a friend of mine who was from Lewisburg. I'm a fireman and we served together for five or six years. He was one heck of a lifter. Could bench-press close to 700 pounds. But he died young—38. Took too many steroids. I sure miss him." I hoped to myself that this young man wasn't walking down the same road.

Later, we were in the back under one of the sheds. The item up was a riding lawnmower. From the crowd someone shouted, "Does it run?" The auctioneer turned to the old fellow and asked, "Does it, Mr. Evans?"

"Well, it was runnin' good when I drove it up here and parked it. I just wasn't able to drive it no more." His voice seemed to tremble in rhythm with his shaking arms.

I looked at the mower. It was covered with dust and bird droppings and had vines growing up on it in places. Conservatively, I guess it had been sitting there three years or so.

The bidding went on.

We moved to the back fence row. I was standing near the auctioneer who was carrying a portable speaker and a mike. He asked the fellow who was putting items up, "What's next, Calvin?"

"Four thousand bricks," Calvin shouted back.

The auctioneer turned to me and remarked, "Shoot, you know Calvin ain't counted them bricks."

But, there they were all stacked up in the fence row with vines and weeds growing over them.

The bidding was not particularly spirited and I bought them for thirty dollars on the theory that every homeowner can use a good brick every now and then. A friend of mine noted later that they come in handy when you've locked your keys up in your car. In that case I'm set for life.

After I bought the bricks, my weight lifting friend came up and gave me his name and phone number and volunteered to help me load them. I've found that people who go to auctions generally help each other out.

Mr. Evans also tottered over and showed me some more concrete items that were _really_ covered up with vines which went with the bricks.

We got to talking and he wanted to know all about me for some reason. When he found out that I had been Principal of BGA, he really began to talk.

"Yep, I wanted to go to BGA but we just didn't have the

money. My mama died and my daddy had to raise all us kids. I had to work a lot and got behind in school. Why, I was seventeen when I started eighth grade. I went out for football and made the team but I didn't get to play until I got into high school. I was on the first team from tenth grade on."

Of course, I knew that back in that era (c. 1940) age limits and years of playing were pretty flexible.

"Say, do you know Jackie Gordon?" he inquired.

When I replied that I did, his eyes lit up and he became more animated.

"Well, I played with Jackie. He was a good ball player. We had one play, number 43, and I was the main blocker on that play. Jackie's number was also 43."

As he got into the story, his voice went to a higher pitch and the arm that rested on the cane began to shake faster.

"We'd need some yardage and we'd get in the huddle and Jackie'd look at me and say, 'What about 43?' And I'd say, 'Just come on through, 43.' Yes sir, we made a lot of yardage on that play."

"And I run into Jackie here a while back and I said, 'Hey there, Jackie Gordon,' and he said 'What about 43?' And I said, 'Well, just come on through, 43.' Yes sir, we really had some good times back then."

I wandered on to look at more things leaving him standing there leaning on his cane, looking up into the hackberry trees, and recalling the days when his body was young and his arms didn't shake and when he cleared the way for number 43. I thought to myself, "This old gentlemen has some wonderful memories."

Yes, you can meet some interesting folks at auctions.

GIVING BACK

Here a while back on a visit to my dentist for a regular check-up, I got disconcerting news. He was in the process of selling his practice and retiring. Even though I'd been his patient for 25 years, he was only in his 50s. Surely he could stick around for a few more years until the rest of my teeth fell out. But he seemed determined to leave my teeth in the hands of an unknown practitioner.

I asked him what he was going to do, knowing that he was not about just to sit and rock on the porch. His reply caught me totally by surprise. "I'm joining the National Guard." Noting the incredulous look on my face, he elaborated. "My kids are grown, I've had a good practice all these years, so I think it's time I gave something back." I was ashamed that I'd been thinking only of my teeth while he has been thinking on something more important.

He went on to relate his experience of taking a military physical with a bunch of 18-year olds. They seemed to be wondering just how desperate the Guard was for recruits. Anyway, he passed with flying colors after being granted a few waivers. Of course, he's not going into combat; he'll be on active duty as a dentist. But he will be _serving_ and serving in a vital role.

Not long after my dental check-up, I fell into conversation with a fellow at one of our local restaurants. Somehow the conversation got around to the military. Noting his special interest, I asked, "Do you have someone in service?"

"Yes," he responded. "My son is in the Marines. He's in Iraq. Did you serve?"

"Yes," I replied, "I was in the 11th Armored Cavalry back in the 50s." He shook my hand. "Thank you for serving," he said sincerely.

Yes. I served. My dentist has gone to serve. We have come through in the last weeks several days which recognize those who served our country in years past—Memorial Day, D-Day, Flag Day, Independence Day. And coming up in November will be Veterans' Day to recognize all who served in the military.

In recent years when I attend a service or ceremony marking service to our country, I notice something that's very disturbing. When veterans are asked to stand, most of the ones up are older folk. I think this is a national tragedy and our country is the worse off because of it. We are raising an "entitled" generation. For the most part, they seem to think that everything is due them without anything being required of them—mostly takers, few givers.

Now, I know there are some bright spots especially in volunteer agencies at the local level. The Peace Corps is still in operation. There's National Make a Difference Day. The recent destruction along our Gulf Coast awakened the volunteer spirit in a number of people. It was gratifying to see the cooperation and effort that went into setting up the shelter here in Franklin. But only a small minority of our population actually gets involved at any level.

The obvious question is, "Is there a way to reverse this?" I think so but it will take time to change practices and attitudes. I think every able bodied and able minded citizen, male and female, between ages 18 and 30, should be _required_ to serve in some capacity. And the military would only be one option. Health services to rural or improvised people, teaching in inter-city schools, maintaining National and State Parks, fighting forest fires, cleaning up after hurricanes and other disasters are only a few examples that come to mind. When John Kennedy said at his inaugural, "Ask not what your country can do for you, ask what you can do for your country," he energized thousands of American.   We need re-energizing in this direction.

Of course, those serving should be paid. Many would be able to serve in their career fields. They should receive educational credit for service. One of the greatest investments this country ever made was the WWII G.I. Bill which made post-secondary education available to millions. The positive results have been incalculable. Investments in education always pay dividends. And what could be better than a situation in which both parties give and both parties receive?

These are only my thoughts. There may be better ways to effect a change in our national attitude. But I do know one thing: our country needs to have more of its citizens serving—giving something back.

SAM'S STORY

It is less than a week until 11 November. Old timers will remember it as Armistice Day when at the 11th hour of the 11th day of the 11th month in 1918 the armistice which ended the fighting in the Great War (WW I) was signed. It is now observed as Veteran's Day, a day to honor all those service people who have served our country.

When historians write the history of wars they, out of necessity, write the big picture—of causes, strategies, and outcomes. However, we should never forget that this "big picture" is composed of millions of tiny dots, each representing the actions of a single individual. It takes all of these "dots" to give the picture meaning and focus. But it is only by looking at the dots themselves that we see the real face of war.

As this Veteran's Day approaches, I'd like to examine one of these dots. He served in WWII. All these veterans are at least in their eighties now and are dying at the rate of about 1,500 a day. We don't have many years left to recognize the ones remaining. This is Sam Chused's story.

Sam, whose father immigrated from Russia in the early 1890s, grew up near Boston, Massachusetts, and was attending Clark University when the war broke out. He enlisted in late 1942 and went into aviation cadet training in the Army Air Corps. His training took him to states he'd never seen before—Louisiana, Florida, Texas, New Mexico, South Carolina, and Georgia. He was trained as a navigator/bombardier and received a commission as a 2nd Lieutenant.

After serving as an aerial instructor for several months, Sam received orders for the South Pacific Theater with the 500th

Bomber Squadron of the 345th Bomber Group. This unit flew B-25 Mitchell bombers. These were twin-engine, medium range, medium altitude, bombers which carried a 5-man crew. However, by the time Sam arrived in early 1945, his unit was flying low-level strafer-bombing missions as U. S. forces moved up the island chain toward Japan. "Low level" meant "very" low—just above the water or at treetop level over land. They were thus exposed to a considerable amount of ground fire with little margin for error when hit. Casualties were heavy.

Sam flew his first mission in early March. A month later he lost his best friend, Jukey Cohen, whose plane was shot down on a raid on the China coast. Two days later on a similar raid, Sam's plane was badly crippled and had to make a wheels up belly landing in a rice paddy by their home base. For this mission the crew was recommended for the Distinguished Flying Cross.

Sam and his flying buddies continued to flirt with death on these dangerous missions through the summer of '45. During this time he was awarded the Air Medal and received a Letter of Commendation. Then on 6 August, the first atomic bomb was dropped on Hiroshima. Two days later Sam flew his 25th and last mission which was to attack Japanese ships off the southeast coast of Korea. They found one and sank it but sustained a lot of damage from the ship's guns. Unable to make it home, they had to ditch in the South China Sea. Although injured himself, Sam helped to get the more seriously injured into a life raft before the plane sank. Fortunately, they didn't spend very long in the raft. A search plane spotted them and radioed their position to a U. S. submarine who picked them up and took them to Guam where Sam said he had the "best steak of my life."

On 9 August the second atomic bomb on Nagasaki brought the war to a close. Sam was recommended for the Purple Heart and promoted to 1st Lieutenant before being discharged. He had flown 25 missions and survived two crash landings. It was time to go home.

So Sam came home, finished his schooling in optometry, and became Dr. Sam Chused. He also married Lenore Cohen, his friend Jukey's widow. Together they raised five children, all college graduates, two of which are attorneys. They have been married over 60 years. Long-time Red Sox fans, they've lived long enough to see Boston win a World Series.

When Sam and Lenore moved to a smaller place a few years ago, their youngest son, David, who is an attorney at MIT and my son-in-law, was going through Sam's papers and noted that he had never received his Purple Heart. After several years and much paper work, everything was verified and Sam was invited to Hanscom Air Force Base, Massachusetts, to receive his medal. It was presented on 10 October 2006, over 61 years after the crash in the South China Sea.

About 25 of Sam's family and friends attended. Most expected a rather perfunctory ceremony but such was not the case. There were 25 or so military personnel in attendance. A three-star general made the presentation. There was a printed program outlining Sam's exploits as well as the history of his unit. David spoke for the family. And then the unexpected happened. Sam, who on the way to the ceremony had said things like "I hope they don't ask me to speak. I don't want to say anything," rose and walked to the podium. With no notes and no evident preparation, he gave an eloquent and detailed account of that last mission. It was a story none of his family had ever heard—one that he'd kept to himself for over 60 years. There were many wet eyes in the audience.

After a nice reception, Sam continued his modest, unassuming ways. He walked off and left his medal in its nice presentation case on the table. One of his family members rescued it for him.

Whenever I'm at a function where we older veterans are

asked to stand and be recognized, it never fails that a current soldier doesn't come by, shake my hand and say, "Thanks for serving." So Sam, even though its come very late, I'd like to say to you, "Thanks for serving."

Waiting For The Ass To Speak

The following is a talk which I gave at the start of one school year to our student body. Perhaps it would be appropriate as we begin a new school year.

Students, this is the first week of school. We've all got a long year ahead of us and many of you right now are wondering if you will ever see the end of it. You will. And there are some things you can do which can make the journey more pleasant and productive. This morning I'm going to tell you about one of those things by telling you a couple of stories.

The first story can be found in the 22nd Chapter of the book of Numbers. It is commonly known as the account of Balaam's ass. Although biblical authorities do not agree on its meaning, it contains an element which helps to illustrate the point I want to make.

The story occurred somewhere around 2500 B.C. after the children of Israel had escaped from bondage in Egypt and were headed toward the Promised Land. They had encamped on the plain of Moab, east of the Jordan River opposite the city of Jericho. They numbered in the thousands and Balak, the King of Moab was fearful that such a large number of people would consume the resources of his land. So, in order to rid his land of this threat, he sent messengers to Balaam, whom he knew to be a prophet of God, to ask him to put a curse on the children of Israel. Balaam apparently lived some distance away. These messengers carried money to pay for this service and they also wanted him to return with them to Moab to enact the curse.

They made their way to Balaam's house and made their

request. Balaam asked them to stay the night so that God would have the opportunity to show him what he was to do. During the night God spoke to him telling him not to go to Balak's land nor to curse the children of Israel since He had blessed them. In the morning Balaam gave God's word to the messengers and sent them on their way.

When Balak received this word, he refused to take "no" for an answer. He sent another set of emissaries to Balaam with promise of greater reward for the curse. Again, Balaam asked them to stay the night so that he might receive God's word. God spoke to him and told him to go with the men and to speak the words that God would give him to speak. The next morning Balaam saddled his ass and started on the journey to Moab with Balak's messengers.

However, for some reason not disclosed in the scriptures, God became angry with Balaam and sent an angel to stop him. The angel came and stood with a drawn sword in the path in front of Balaam. Balaam's ass saw the angel but Balaam did not. The ass turned aside and went out into a field to avoid the angel. Balaam's response was to beat her to get her back on the path.

Next, the angel stood blocking the road in a narrow place between two walls. Again, the ass tried to turn aside and crushed Balaam's foot against the wall. Balaam beat her a second time to get her back on track.

The angel's third appearance was at such a narrow place in the path that there was no place to turn. So the ass lay down which resulted in a third beating.

At this point the Lord enabled the ass to speak. She asked Balaam why he had beaten her three times. Balaam replied that it was because she had mocked him and that if he had had a sword, he would have killed her.

The ass then asked, "Am I not the ass you have ridden for many years? Have I ever done anything wrong to you?"

Balaam answered that she had not.

At that instant the Lord opened Balaam's eyes and he saw the angel of the Lord standing in front of him with drawn sword. His response was to fall down on his face before the angel who spoke to Balaam saying, "Why have you beaten your ass three times? I was sent to stop you but only your ass saw me and turned aside. If she had not done so, I would have killed you but let her live."

Numbers Chapters 23 and 24 tell the remainder of the story—of Balaam's journey to Moab and the events that transpired. However, since the illustration I want to use in a minute is contained in the Chapter 22 section, I will not relate the rest of the story.

Now, let us move forward in time a few thousand years and to another place—France in the 17th century during the time of King Louis XIV. Louis' reign lasted from 1643 to 1715. During this time France was the envy of the Western world and French manners, customs, styles, and culture were widely imitated. Louis' court was located at the ostentatious palace at Versailles which he had built. No other court in Europe displayed such opulence.

In addition to the open display of wealth, Louis liked to have unusual things surrounding him--especially animals. One of his favorite animals was a donkey, but not just any ordinary donkey. Louis had the royal tailor make various suits of clothes which the animal would wear while standing near the throne on days when Louis gave audience to his subjects. Around the court the donkey was known simply as "The King's ass."

It is said that one day two nobles, who were accused to some crime—probably treason, were brought before the King. Louis sentenced them to prison which, considering the nature of prisons in that day, amounted to a death penalty. After passing judgment on them, Louis gave them the opportunity to speak.

One of them being very quick-witted spoke thusly: "Sire, for some time we have been privileged to be engaged in the study of animals and specifically in methods of making certain animals utter human speech. If it please the King and should he be so kind to grant us a year, we could make your ass speak."

This offer intrigued Louis. He already had the best-dressed ass in any kingdom. One that could speak would be an even greater treasure. So, he granted the request and dismissed the two men.

When they got outside, the silent nobleman said to his colleague, "Have you taken leave of your senses? You know you cannot make that ass say anything. When the year is up, the King will surely cut off our heads."

"You are correct, of course," replied the first nobleman. "But you must look at the situation in a different way. I have bought us a year of freedom and that is a very precious thing. And much can happen in a year: The ass may die. We may die. The King may die."

Still not losing sight of the precariousness of their situation, the second nobleman persisted, "But what if _none_ of these things happen?"

With a shrug of his shoulders and a look of unconcern on his face, the first nobleman responded, "Then, perhaps the ass will speak."

Now, boys and girls, I am sorry to have to tell you that during my many years in education, I have known too many students who have adopted the tactics of that French nobleman in dealing with their academic work. That is to say, they were willing to rock along throughout the year while doing nothing—and worse, not even intending to do anything—to alter their situation or to ensure a desirable outcome at the end of the school year. They simply enjoyed their "year of freedom" with the vague hope that some miracle (_i.e._, the ass speaking) would change the inevitable and make things okay for them at the end.

Students, I stand here to advise you not to adopt this approach to your academic work for this school year. The only account I have ever been able to find of an ass speaking is recounted in the 22nd Chapter of the book of Numbers. That was several thousand years ago. I do not think the ass will speak for any of you this coming May. So, I advise and urge you to get started on your academic tasks immediately. Do not wait for "the ass to speak."

During the years I was Principal of Battle Ground Academy, I tried to say something "special" to the seniors as the end of the year approached. Since the time of graduations is at hand, a re-presentation of one of these talks seems appropriate.

THREE LESSONS FROM A LITTLE BIRD

As this school year draws to a close, we will do a number of things for the last time—for the last time this year, that is. Since this is my last time to talk to you this year, I'd like to address the seniors who will be leaving us in a very few days. Of course, the rest of you are expected to listen in.

Good rules for life and for living can be found in many places. One good source is the Book of Proverbs in the Old Testament. Here you will find such passages as:

> "The fear of the Lord is the beginning of wisdom.
>
> "The way of a fool seems right to him but a wise man listens to advice.
>
> "He who ignores discipline comes to poverty and shame."

If you would like a more modern source, H. Jackson Brown, Jr. has come out with _Life's Little Instruction Book_. It contains a number of "new proverbs" which in many cases are old proverbs in modern dress. A few are:

> "Never compromise your integrity.
>
> "Do more than is expected.
>
> "Don't expect life to be fair.
>
> "Stop blaming others.
>
> Take responsibility for every area of your life."

As I have stated, good rules for living can be gleaned from various sources. Many can be found in stories that teach good morals. These are as old as Aesop and as modern as Thurber. Since this is the last time I'll get to speak to you as a captive audience, I'm going to tell you one last story. It has not one, but three morals which are good guides in life.

Once upon a time, there lived a little bird in central Illinois. He was a migratory bird and was accustomed to spending his winters in Florida. He had a time-share condo somewhere in the Panama City area.

Well, one year winter was slow in coming (something to do with the jet stream no doubt) and he was late in leaving. One morning he awoke and felt a certain chill in the air. He started flying south immediately, but, alas, a fast-moving storm soon overtook him. Fear gave added strength to his wings but his frantic flying only postponed the inevitable. The storm caught him just as he crossed the Cumberland River near Nashville.

Ice began to form on his wings and even though he put forth more effort, he flew slower and slower and lower and lower. Finally, exhausted, he fell to earth in a barn lot near College Grove. (You see, that's how I found out about this. Mrs. Pettus, one of your English teachers, lives in College Grove and is a personal friend of this particular farmer.)

The little bird lay there in the barn lot, his life slowly ebbing away. He knew he was about to die and he thought about how foolish he had been for not leaving earlier with the rest of the flock. (There's a good lesson here on procrastination but since that's not my main point, I'll just throw it in for free.)

Just at that moment a large creature of the bovine persuasion walked out of the barn and deposited a large volume of fertilizer right on top of the little bird. With what seemed to him to be his last ounce of strength, he managed to free his head. He thought, "Dying was bad enough, I'm now going to die in this humiliating position."

But, he did not die. The fertilizer was warm. It began to melt the ice and the little bird could feel his blood as it began to flow through his wings and bring new life to his frozen body. When he realized that he was not going to die after all, he became so thankful and overjoyed that he began to chirp and sing and the entire barnyard was filed with his song.

As the little bird's song grew louder and louder, high up in the barn one yellow eye opened, then another. The barnyard cat had been sleeping in because of the storm and had not had breakfast. He began to search for the source of the song and found the little bird trapped in the cow pile. The cat very unceremoniously took the little bird by the head, plucked him out, shook him vigorously to remove most of the clinging residue, wiped him around on the ground a few times, and ate him.

Now, as I said, this story has three morals or lessons you would do well to remember as you go through life.

Number one: Those who put you in it are not always your enemies.

Number two: Those who take you out of it are not always your friends.

Number three: When you find yourself in it up to your necks, (as you will more than once in your life), it's best not to chirp and make such a big racket about it.

I wish for you successful exams, a happy graduation, and a fruitful and rewarding life.

COUNTRY COME TO TOWN

Honey and I have been to Paris (TN), London (KY), and Rome (GA) but our globetrotting had never taken us to New York (NY). That gap was closed this past December when we took a trip to the Big Apple with Cumberland Bank's travel club. We toured Manhattan by day and saw Broadway shows at night.

Our coach pulled out of Franklin at 4:30 a.m. and right off the bat an incident at the airport portended an eventful few days. One of our group sat down in a chair at the security check point and found $4000 on the floor by her feet. She turned it in and we learned later that it had been claimed. I hope they left her a reward.

To quote David Letterman, "New York is a happening place." It is truly a "city that never sleeps." The noise produced by the movement of people and vehicles only abates a few decibels after dark. There are thousands of cabs in the city and they're all yellow. Viewed from 20 floors up the streets resemble a beehive in full production.

Everybody seems to be in a hurry but only those walking and riding bicycles or the subway are getting anywhere quickly. Traffic just crawls even though many of the streets are one-way and 4-lanes wide. Since stores don't have back doors or delivery entrances, the outside lanes are filled with delivery vehicles most of the time. UPS drivers must think they've died and gone to heaven. That leaves the two center lanes with there being some blockage on one of them in almost every block, which leaves the goers all fighting over one lane on an alternate basis.

I'm telling you drivers in New York deserve combat pay.

Just why 8.2 million people (according to our guide) would want to wad themselves up in one place like that is beyond me. One day as we sat in our coach in heavy traffic going nowhere, one of our party said, "I'm not going to complain about Franklin traffic when I get home."

The buildings are tall and everything in between them is paved over. It's almost impossible to find a clod of real dirt any place. However, there is Central Park. To their credit New Yorkers have left something like 825 acres of natural land in the center of Manhattan Island for public use. It's a pleasant contrast to the concrete and asphalt surrounding it. We were told that apartments with a view of the park have very high rent.

We went to Macy's which touts itself as "the world's largest department store." A few years ago we visited Harrods's in London which made the same claim. I don't know who is right. I just know that Harrods's has a big meat department with fresh carcasses of various animals hanging around. Macy's doesn't— but does have the annual Thanksgiving Day Parade as well as the first escalators in the world. They have wooden treads. They have also been declared "historical" so Macy's cannot get rid of them. (We Franklin folks could understand that.) There's only one company that can work on them and they charge many hundreds of dollars an hour to do so. History is expensive anywhere you go.

Actually, we were at Macy's for breakfast and a fashion show. The breakfast was excellent. I'm not an authority on fashion shows. I did notice that the outfits were black. The commentator lady said that it was true that most New Yorkers did wear black but that New York fashion people were making a bold move and introducing color—brown. BROWN! That's a color? She was serious. Most of us found it humorous. We should have brought sunglasses. Just imagine how bright, flashy and even gaudy wardrobes will be with all that _brown_ streaking through the fashion world. What will they go to next? Maybe gray.

Some of us noted that Victoria's Secret was also advertising a fashion show. We asked our tour person if we could get signed up for that one as well. She said "no" — because Victoria did not serve breakfast.

At one Broadway show our seats were in the midst of a bunch of folks from Alabama. It was an old theater with the seats covered with that old fuzzy material. One of our group had on pants made of similar (but newer) material. During the first act, her pants and the seat effected a permanent union and when she stood up at intermission, the pants stayed with the seat. This caused quite a stir. Taking it in stride, she said that she could not imagine anyone being either shocked or stimulated by her 68-year old behind. The Alabama folks were real nice to her which proves, I suppose, that people from that state can be civil to Tennesseans if football and/or Philip Fulmer are not involved.

One evening we had a great dinner at Sardi's. Its walls are covered with caricatures of famous people who have dined there. I did not notice anybody making drawings of any of our group.

One afternoon we walked along the waterfront and looked out at the harbor and the New Jersey shore. We could see Ellis Island, the port of entry for millions of immigrants, and the distinctive Jersey railway station where they began their journeys to various parts of the Country. We could also see the Statue of Liberty. One of our group told of the emotional experience of seeing it for the first time in 1938 at age 15 as she came on a ship with her family as they fled Hitler's Germany. Her last night in Germany was _Krystal_ _Nacht_, the night of the broken glass, when the Nazis attacked the homes and shops of Jews throughout the country.

We also learned of the island in the harbor that is up for sale for one dollar. The catch is that there is an abandoned Coast Guard station on it and whoever buys it has to restore the facility and convert it to some viable economic use. It's only accessible by ferry. I gave them Calvin Lehew's name.

Ground Zero and St. Paul's Chapel. If you go to New York, don't miss this. The space is clear and clean now, almost sanitary in appearance. Just looking at it, it's hard to imagine the events of 9/11 and after. But the Chapel that sits across the street from the site is a different story. This small church was used as the relief center for the rescue and clean-up crews. Its pews are scarred and scratched from the equipment of the workers. George Washington's pew was cleared of its historic items and used for foot massages—an appropriate use considering the condition of the feet of many of his soldiers at Valley Forge. There is a large pile of uniform patches from the many units from around the nation and world who came to help. The church's iron fence became a depository of posters, letters, flowers, and other items from all over the world. Some of these are on display inside the Chapel: the U. S. Flag made from the hand prints of all the children in one school, the poster from a school in Tennessee, thousands of letters. This place has become not only a shrine to the _people_ of the disaster but also a tribute to the indomitable _spirit_ of America. As one of our group remarked, "Pearl Harbor, Omaha Beach, and this place. A real American can't help but get emotional at all of them."

Back In Time

This month's column relates to the struggle for equality commemorated by Dr. Martin Luther King's birthday on January 16. Since my early years during the 1930s and 40s were spent on large cotton plantations in Mississippi which my father managed, I have some understanding of just how far our Black friends have come. And those who worked to change the system are deserving of recognition.

In October of 2001, Sara and I attended the Southern Festival of Books in Nashville. One session featured Vernon Jordan who made a name for himself during the 1960s as a Civil Rights attorney for the NAACP. More recently he served in the Clinton White House and headed the Democratic team which was responsible for the transfer of power to the Republicans as Bush took over. He was from Atlanta originally and had a new book out.

He was introduced and came to the microphone—a tall, imposing black man with a deep, resonating voice and much gray in his beard and hair. He said that since people were always asking him about the book's title, he would deal with that first.

I'm going to tell the story _just_ _like_ Mr. Jordan told it.

After growing up in Atlanta, he went north to college. One year he applied for a summer intern program with a major insurance company, was accepted, and sent to their Atlanta office. When he walked in, there was great consternation among everyone. It was the 1950s and he was black. After a quick huddle, he was assigned to a small branch office in a black section to Atlanta where there was nothing for him to do.

So he quit.

But he needed a job for the summer. His parents knew somebody who knew somebody who got him a job as chauffeur and butler for a rich family in Buckhead. Mr. Smith was up in years but still very much the head of the family. Vernon's task was to drive him each morning after breakfast down to his private club where the morning was spent playing cards and visiting with his cronies. After lunch at the club Vernon would drive him home where he would have his afternoon rest before puttering around the house for the remainder of the day. This schedule meant that Vernon had nothing to do most afternoons.

Mr. Smith had a nice library containing most of the classics of literature bound in beautiful leather. Vernon began spending his afternoons in this library reading. One day as he was sitting in one of the large, leather wingback chairs immersed in a book, Mr. Smith happened to walk in. He was dressed in his usual afternoon attire—boxer underwear and no shirt with a cigar in one hand and a glass of Southern Comfort in the other. He seemed startled to see Jordan.

"Vernon, what the hell are you doing in here?"

"I'm reading, sir."

"Hurmph, I never had a nigger that could read."

"I can, sir."

"Well, why don't you read down in the basement? I've set up a room down there for you all."

"There're no books down there, sir."

"Well, take some of these."

"Mr. Smith, I don't think you'd want your nice books down there in that basement."

"I guess you're right. Well, read then." He threw up his hands and walked out.

At dinner that evening, Vernon was dressed in his butler/waiter outfit and standing near the table with a white table napkin folded over his left forearm when Mr. Smith said, "

I have an announcement."   All the family stopped eating, put down their utensils, and sat expectantly awaiting the message from the family patriarch.   Mr. Smith turned, gestured toward Jordan, and announced, "Vernon can read."   Hence the title of Jordan's book, _Vernon Can Read_.   After a collective gasp at such unusual news, the family took up their knives and forks and resumed eating.

A few days later there was another exchange between Jordan and his employer.

"Vernon, they tell me you're going to college."

"That's right, sir."

"Are you going to be a preacher or a teacher?"

"Neither one, sir.   I'm going to be a lawyer."

"Hell, can't no nigger be a lawyer."

"Well, I'm going to be, sir."

Mr. Smith just shook his head and walked away.

A number of years later the University of Alabama was being integrated.   One of the black students was a strikingly beautiful young woman.   For this reason the TV cameras seemed to focus on her and the NAACP attorney who was escorting her—Vernon Jordan.

Many miles away in Atlanta Mr. Smith was now in an exclusive health care facility where some of his long-time employees stayed with him around the clock.   He was dozing in his chair with the TV on when his companion roused him excitedly.   "Mr. Smith, look who's on TV!"

Mr. Smith squinted at the set.   "Who is it?"

"It's Vernon, sir."

"What's he doing?"

"He's integrating the University of Alabama."

"Hurmph," grunted Mr. Smith, "I knew that nigger'd never come to any good."

Jordan spoke matter-of-factly and without bitterness about the prejudice he and his people had faced not many years ago.

He also spoke in glowing terms of a young black woman who is "quite a writer" according to Jordan and who is involved in several noteworthy literary projects. "I know she's good," said Jordan, "she helped me write my book." It was refreshing to see someone of such prominence give credit to the one who really did the work. Many ghostwriters don't get recognized.

We need more people around like Vernon Jordan.

TRAINS

In the 1930s the main line of the Illinois Central RR ran across the back of our place. My brother and I loved to go down to the crossing and watch the big, black locomotives come through pulling either freight or passenger cars. We loved to hear the steam whistle as it blew for the crossing. We loved to wave to the engineer who always waved back. We counted it an extra bonus especially in winter if the fireman had the boiler door open as he shoveled in coal from the tender just behind the cab. If the train was a freight, one of us would count the cars and the other would count the hobos. A hundred-car freight was a long train. Sometimes we could count almost a hundred hobos sitting in boxcar doors, riding on the tops, or clinging to ladders in between. We also waved to the hobos. Sometimes they waved back. Apparently, the railroad bulls weren't too strict on hobos in our area.

On the passenger trains, we liked to see the people, especially in the dining cars with the white tablecloths and shiny silverware, the height of luxury. Sometimes they'd wave to us, two little barefoot tow-headed urchins in overalls. I wonder what they might have thought about us. I suppose to us those trains represented places and sights we never thought we'd ever go to or see.

On the outskirts of town was a railroad water tank and coal tipple. We loved to watch the locomotives leave the train cars on the main tracks and chug over to be replenished. The fireman would climb atop the tender and throw back the round cap to the water tank. The engineer would ease the engine forward slowly stopping when the fireman could reach the

chain that hung from the end of a large down spout. He'd pull
the pipe down, swing it around, and drop the curved end into
the tank's open hole. He'd then pull another chain down and
hold it until water filled the tank to overflowing. When both
chains were released, the counterbalance would raise the big
dripping pipe to its original position.

Coal was taken on in a similar fashion except that no pipe
was involved. The tender's coal bin did not have a top. There
was a long slide or chute coming from the bottom of the tipple
and aimed toward the tracks. The engineer would position the
coal bin directly below this slide. The fireman would pull a
chain which would unleash an avalanche of coal and a big black
cloud of coal dust. Some of the lumps would bounce out of the
bin. After the train left, some of the poor living close by would
bring crocker sacks and gather up the scattered coal to use for
fuel.

If we were in town when a fast train came through, Daddy
would take us down to the depot so we could watch the mail
car hook the mail sack. There was a device that sat by the track
that looked like a giant c-clamp. A man from the post office
would bring the mail sack, clip each end of it to two chains, and
position it in a vertical position. As the train came roaring
through, a man in the mail car would swing a metal arm out,
hook the mail sack, and swing it inside.

Our family seldom rode on trains. Greyhound buses were
cheaper. On the rare occasions when we did, Mama always
packed a lunch. "Dining cars cost too much," she'd say. I never
slept on a train or ate in the dining car until I was in college and
traveling with the football team. It was just as luxurious as I'd
imagined.

I had an uncle who was involved with trains. He was a
switchman in the Illinois Central rail yards at McComb, MS.
Today all switching is done electronically. One night he got
careless and stepped from between two boxcars and into the

path of a switch engine. It ran over him cutting off his left leg at the knee and causing other assorted injuries. He got a new leg and a lifetime pension from the railroad but folks said he was never right in the head after that which helps to explain why he ended his life with a .45 automatic a few years later.

Trains have played major roles in songs, stories, plays, and movies. Who can ever forget that heart rending scene in Fiddler On The Roof in which Tevye sits with his daughter at that God-forsaken whistle-stop as he prepares to send her away to be with her lover knowing he will probably never see her again?

One of the first big western movies was The Great Train Robbery. And it was followed down through the years by others like The Orient Express, Strangers on A Train, Throw Mama From The Train, and Polar Express.

From its very beginning, country music has celebrated trains and those involved with running them. In fact Jimmie Rodgers, one of country music's pioneers, billed himself as "The Singing Brakeman," and often was pictured in railroad overalls and cap. He wrote and sang many songs about trains, e. g., "Brakeman's Blues," "Hobo's Meditation," and "Train Whistle Blues." Some of the better known country music train songs are: "City of New Orleans," Fire Ball Mail," "Freight Train Blues," "I'm Movin' On," "King of the Road," "Night Train to Memphis," "Orange Blossom Special," and "Wabash Cannon Ball."

A more recent country music performer who focused on railroads was Boxcar Willie who dressed as a hobo and appeared on the Grand Ole Opry where he sang train songs.

Kate Campbell, a local artist, wrote and sings a haunting song entitled, "Trains Don't Run from Nashville." It begins, "I'm sittin' in a restaurant drinking coffee black; they call it Union Station but it ain't got no tracks." She goes on about standing on the platform and seeing loved ones off to war as well as welcoming them home. She laments the fact that her lover has gone off somewhere up north and she longs to be in his arms once more-—and she would go to him but "trains don't run from Nashville anymore."

No. Passenger trains don't run from Nashville or most other places anymore. The great railroad era is past. The great steam locomotives are gone. Everything is diesel now. The red cabooses are gone from the freights. The little electronic device on the coupling of the last boxcar does a better job—so they say. Today's youth cannot lie in their beds and hear the sound of a steam engine's lonesome, mournful whistle drifting through the night and wonder and dream and fantasize about it. They'll never know what they've missed.

MEMORABLE LINES

There are some lines in plays and movies that just stay with us. They strike a chord and become, in a word, memorable, and a part of our literary baggage. For Honey and me, one such line comes from an old Western movie of the 1940s, _Colorado Territory_, starring Virginia Mayo and Joel McRae, both well known in the acting field. We came across this movie in the mid-1950s when we were first married. Television was still in its infancy with only a station or two in most cities. They all signed off after the 10:00 P.M. news except for Saturday night when a late movie was shown. A free movie was quite a treat. We had invested $45 in a second-hand, black and white TV, so we'd pop some corn and watch the movie almost every week. You got no choice. You just had to watch whatever was on which was why we saw _Colorado Territory_ three or four times in the span of six months.

The movie was actually a tragedy not one of those romantic oaters in which the boy and girl ride off into the sunset. The movie opens with Joel getting out of prison. He'd been a participant in a robbery in which the loot had never been recovered. Sure enough he picks up the loot and Virginia and they head off to live happily ever after. But the authorities have been watching and chase after them to recover the loot. The movie is a series of hairbreadth escapes from various posses and bounty hunters. Finally, with a large posse on their heels, they pass through a small mission where the padre is lamenting the fact that his chapel is incomplete without its bell. They are chased up into the hills where they both are killed in the ensuing gun battle, each falling upon the other as their blood intermingles. The last scene is at the mission and the chapel bell is ringing. When asked where he got the money for the bell, the padre replies: "From two happy people who passed this way." Honey and I have used this line facetiously ever since.

Who can ever forget the gasp that went through the audience when Clark Gable uttered that famous line at the end of *Gone With The Wind*: "Frankly, my dear, I don't give a damn." It was the first cuss word most people had ever heard in a movie. You see, in the early 1940s those words were reserved for boys on the playground or for when our fathers hit their thumbs with a hammer. Nowadays nobody much seems to give a damn about how many cuss words there are in the movies or on TV.

At the end of the movie *Casablanca* another perfunctory criminal investigation is launched with the words: "Round up the usual suspects." I still hear that line today when someone figures an investigation is going no place. Oddly enough, the *most* repeated line from that movie wasn't even in the movie. Impressionists of the day always had Humphrey Bogart saying: "Play it again, Sam." Sam was the piano player in Rick's bar and Bogart did ask him to repeat a song, but not with those words. I wonder if the ones who came up with the business name, "Play it Again, Sports," were aware of this.

In Arthur Miller's play, *Death of A Salesman*, down-and-out salesman, Willie Loman, brags that he used to be tops in his field using only "a shoe shine and a smile." And when confronted with hardships, he says, "It goes with the territory." I hear that line quite often today by people who, I'm sure, have no inkling of its origin.

Shakespeare penned many memorable lines. I particularly like one that comes from the courtroom scene in *The Merchant of Venice* when the judge rules that Shylock The Jew's contract is, indeed, valid and that he may cut "a pound of flesh" from the breast of the Christian. But as Shylock prepares to collect his debt, the judge adds that the contract calls for _exactly_ a pound and should he cut even an ounce more or less, he will be in violation of the contract and be dealt with by the court. Of course, he casts his knife away as the Bard shows the vile Jew being thwarted by the Christian. When teaching this period of history, I use this scene as an example of anti-Semitic attitudes of the day as well as our source of the expression that signifies excessive punishment or retribution.

In the play, _Crimes of The Heart,_ one of the sisters keeps asking: "I wonder why Mama done it? Why did Mama kill herself?" Toward the end as she herself is beset by all sorts of problems, she attempts to end her life by hanging herself from the light fixture but only pulls it out of the ceiling. Then, dragging the rope and fixture behind her, she turns on the gas and sticks her head into the oven. This doesn't work either but it causes her to reach a conclusion: "Now I know why Mama did it. She was just having a bad day." Yes, "having a bad day" is still causing people to react in all sorts of ways.

When Honey and I run across an investigation (usually political) of something that's of questionable existence in the first place, we refer to it as a "strawberry investigation." It comes from the scene in _The Caine Mutiny Court-Martial_ in which Captain Quegg assembles all his officers around the mess table and with a gallon of sand tries to determine that someone made off with the leftover strawberries which did not exist. There are a lot of folk out there looking for leftover strawberries that don't exist.

For some reason I'm not a big fan of the play, _The Fantastiks,_ but I love one line near the play's end. The play begins with Boy and Girl in an idyllic setting. Eventually though, Boy has to go out into the world. When he returns, battered, soiled, bruised, and cut, wearing tattered clothes and a forlorn expression, someone asks, "What happened to him?" The answer, "Life happened to him."

Indeed, "life happens" to us all and we're going to have some "bad days" because they "go with the territory." However, we all get to decide if we will be "two happy people who pass this way."

SOME THINGS I'VE NOTICED

I've noticed that an increasing number of folks are opting for what used to be called "face-lifts." The proper term today, I suppose, is cosmetic surgery because it's performed on just about any part of the body. Many people will go to just about any length to counteract the force of gravity and the natural aging process. They seek to challenge the truth in the riddle: "What do you find between the breasts of an older woman that you don't find between the breasts of a young woman?" Answer: "Her navel." I loved the recent comment of fellow columnist, Cathy Clarkson, who described a woman who had undergone a severe face-lift as having a look of perpetual surprise on her face. I know one woman in town who's had one and every time I see her I can't decide whether she looks the same but different or different but the same. But, more power to these folks. They're doing their part to keep Franklin beautiful.

I've noticed that the excessively wealthy continue to be excessive. They continue to seek one-of-a-kind possessions or those that no one else can afford in order to set themselves apart—to put themselves in a "special" category. This past summer it was reported that $350 shoes were passe'. If your stilettos didn't carry a tag of at least $1000, you were not really "special." And $600 handbags were so bourgeois that "special" people wouldn't be seen with anything costing less than $5,000. Then, there was the handbag for "really special" people at $52,500. Recently, I saw where wannabes, who can't afford to own one of these bags, can rent one for a week. It seems as if these folk spend a goodly portion of their time seeking exclusivity. In a sense they are trapped by their wealth. It's also sad that they think that the only way they can define themselves is by their possessions. The idea of noblesse oblige is entirely foreign to them. Also foreign to them is the idea that possessing luxury goods does not give them a right to inconvenience others. I don't know how many times I've seen, usually at crowded restaurants, fancy cars parked across two spaces so that other cars cannot be parked next to them. If your car is too good to take a chance on door-dings like the rest of us, keep it at home and call out for pizza.

Probably the saddest group is too large a number of professional athletes. They have physical ability and multi-million dollar contracts but lack both class and taste. One recent episode proves this point. A free-agent running back, who admits to fathering nine children with seven different women from several states, signed a new contract and received a substantial signing bonus. In an interview he claimed to love his children and wanted to provide for them. What did he use the bonus for? A luxury sports car and some jewelry—all for him, nothing for the kids.

If he could come back, I wonder what Diogenes might say to some of these folk. He was the Greek philosopher who founded the philosophy of Cynicism, who walked through the market place in Athens at noon with a lighted lantern peering into people's faces as he unsuccessfully looked for an honest man. He also preached against excessive possessions. His home was a large, earthen water pot turned on its side. He owned only a cloak (for wear during the day and for cover at night), a staff (for assistance in walking), and a bowl (from which to eat). However, one day he observed a youth drinking from a public fountain using his cupped hands, so he threw his bowl away realizing that it was an "excessive" possession. Yes, I'd like to take ole Diogenes into a Louis Vuitton handbag shop and listen to his blistering comments.

I've noticed that newspapers still can't get everything right when they put words together. The caption under the picture of our newly enlarge hospital noted that the "Williamson Tower was _builted_ next to the old part." I'm not sure but that sounds like some sort of double past participle. We've all heard a lot recently about obesity in this country. On the same page with an article on this topic was one with the heading: "Church widens door for female ministers." I have too many women friends to make any comments on that one. And why is it so difficult just to check the source of the quote being used? One reporter began her article with the line: "All we have to fear is fear itself according to Winston Churchill." Of course that was our President Franklin D. Roosevelt. Just because he and Churchill were contemporaries, doesn't mean they're interchangeable.

Ever so often I feel like that caustic, crusty Baltimore newspaperman of the early 1900s, H. L. Mencken. One night as he was checking copy and noting the high incident of errors, he remarked: "The older I get, the more I admire and crave competence, just simple competence, in any field from adultery to zoology." But if that ever happened across the board, Jay Leno would have to do away with his Monday night "Headlines" segment.

I'm always on the lookout for false advertising, signs that aren't right, and other things similar. Not long ago I met a moving truck on a Franklin street with just the driver in the cab. The sign on its side read: "Two Men And A Truck." Where was the other guy? I just knew somebody waiting to be moved was going to be short-changed. But them, about 200 yards down the street, I met another truck from the same company. Its cab held three men. I figured they were going to the same job and on average they were okay.

Since I have a little antique business, I'm always noticing unusual items that are advertised for sale at estate auctions. An ad for one such sale listed a large bear trap and a hornet's nest. I assume the latter came without the hornets. The writer of another ad must have had an overdose of phonics in school. Among the items in his auction were a "shifferrobe" and a "Duncan Fife" table. So far, the most unusual listing I've seen was a "coffin (un-used)." Has anyone ever seen a used coffin for sale? They're usually one-owner items. They are not something a person uses for a few years and then trades in on a fancier model. Thank goodness for that or we might find some of these extra-fancy coffins parked across two burial plots.

TRAIN WRECKS

It seems that people of Western Culture have always been fascinated with vehicles which would take them to other places.   This helps to explain the great love for trains and railroads that has existed in this country for nearly 200 years. It also may help to explain the undue interest we have in the wrecks of these vehicles which have long been celebrated in story and song.

Jimmie Rodgers, one of country music's pioneers, had worked on the railroad and billed himself as "The Singing Brakeman." He wrote and sang a number of railroad songs, one was "Wreck of the Old 97," which has one verse:

"He was going down grade, making ninety miles a hour
When his whistle began to scream.
He was found in the wreck with his hand on the throttle.
He was scalded to death by the steam."

If you want to hear it played and sung by an authentic country band, go to the Farmers' Market at The Factory some Saturday morning and listen to the Franklin Square Pickers.

One spectacular crash occurred late one night when a freight rounded a curve and was confronted by a piece of heavy construction equipment blocking the track. Unable to stop, the locomotive demolished the obstruction which caused several cars to derail. Fortunately, no one was killed or injured. Law enforcement officials did an outstanding job of sleuthing and arrested two local construction workers. It seems that these two had gotten drunk and discovered that they'd never seen a train wreck—so they caused one.

Very early it became important that trains run on time. In

fact making sure that trains were on time became an obsession with some railroaders who gained reputations for always meeting their schedules.   Casey Jones was one of these and I suspect it was this obsession which drove him that night of 30 April 1900 to climb up into the cab of the train that was running late, determined to make up the time before he reached his destination.   He pulled the freight at breakneck speeds down into Mississippi and had made up most of the time before he came upon a stopped train on the main line near the town of Vaughn.   Unable to stop, he yelled for his fireman to jump before he rode the speeding locomotive into the crash.   Casey was killed but his fireman survived.   This so-called "heroic" ride has been celebrated in story and song ever since.   Today one can visit The Casey Jones Railroad Museum and Park in Jackson, TN.

Tennessee has had its share of rail disasters.   On 9 July 1918, two passenger trains, each going 50 miles per hour, collided head-on in the Belle Meade area of Nashville.   A curve in the track blocked each engineer's view until it was too late for either to stop.   The wooden passenger cars telescoped into each other causing 101 deaths.   Local butchers were called in to cut out the wedged bodies of the dead.   This wreck still ranks as Nashville's worst disaster.

Many of you will recall the Waverly disaster of 24 February 1978.   Two days earlier 24 cars of an L&N Railroad freight train had derailed in downtown Waverly.   During the clean-up operation, a tank car containing liquefied petroleum gas exploded causing 16 deaths and destroying a good portion of the downtown area.   One piece of the tank car was blown over 330 feet.   Since the area had been evacuated, most of the deaths were among the emergency clean-up personnel.

Our current rail line, which is the CSX, was the L&N, one of the oldest rail lines in the South.   Perhaps that was its main problem—the oldness.   Its equipment was aging as was its tracks and roadbeds. This was probably the principal cause of the rash of derailments which occurred with increasing frequency during the '60s and '70s. Fortunately, the line no longer was carrying passengers by the '70s. Even though there was a great deal of damage to rolling stock, roadbeds, and cargo, there were few deaths and injuries.

The news media and especially the TV stations loved to cover these rail catastrophes. There was always live coverage of the wreck scene with shots of the twisted rails and jumbled boxcars and interviews with local residents and members of the train's crew. One prominent person who was <u>always</u> on camera at <u>every</u> wreck was Colonel Phil Hooper.

Colonel Hooper was a retired military man whom the L&N had hired to be its chief trouble-shooter and spokesman on these occasions. He was a tall, wiry man with sharp features and a great deal of poise in front of the cameras. He exuded confidence and positivism as he explained what had caused the disaster and what the railroad was doing to get the line back to running again. His trademark was a white Stetson hat which he always wore.

It seemed that few of these derailments occurred around major cities. Most were out in rural areas or near small villages. Colonel Hooper was charged with getting to the scene quickly and getting it organized. This included preventing looting and maintaining the safety of the crowds which always showed up.

Rural people often have ways of dealing with situations which are different from those of their urban cousins. I once heard Colonel Hooper relate a story about a derailment which illustrates this point.

There is this very small town in Middle Tennessee which has a long, steep grade beginning right at the edge of town. One night an L&N freight train came through and derailed about halfway up this hill. A part of the train was several boxcars filled with the product of the Jack Daniels Distillery located in nearby Lynchburg.

Colonel Hooper got to the scene quickly and found a mob of people all around the wreck scene. He quickly located the local law enforcement folk and found the person in charge of this group. Colonel Hooper's first words to him were, "Officer, you and your men have got to help me get this wreck organized."

An incredulous expression came over the officer's face as he replied, "We <u>have</u> got it organized, Colonel. We've got 'em in one line and we're only letting 'em get two bottles each." A disaster for the railroad had been turned into an "early Christmas" for local residents.

TEACHING ABE

About thirty years ago and in another county, the Director of Continuing Education came to see me with a pitiful story. She had worked hard and gotten a grant to set up an Adult Basic Education (ABE) Class. She even had the class formed but, alas, she had no teacher for it. That's where I came in. The fact that I had never done that type of teaching nor had any training in that direction did not deter her in the least. Her position was: "With a Ph.D. you should be able to teach anything." It's hard to argue with that type of faulty logic. Reluctantly, I agreed to give it a shot.

The class was a hodgepodge. No two students were on the same page. Even those who were working for the same goals were at different stages which meant that instead of teaching a class of twelve, I was teaching twelve individuals in the same room. Another handicap was the fact that the grant had included no money for materials. I begged and borrowed some; the students bought some; beyond that I was dependent on my imagination. What in the world had I gotten myself into?

After we got started, the things we didn't have were eclipsed by what we did have—people who wanted to learn something, people who had some goals, people who wanted to learn to read or to write or to use numbers, people who wanted to earn a GED high school diploma. The class met for three hours one night a week. They came early, stayed late, and were reluctant even to take a break. Some brought burgers and drinks because they didn't have time to eat between their jobs and class time. It was refreshing.

Most reacted to the classroom situation as if they were

elementary students again—almost as if they were young children. They'd tell me anything. I found out more than I even wanted to know about their homes, jobs, and personal lives.

There was one couple in the class—an elderly black man and his wife who had spent their lives as tenant farmers. Now, too old to work in the fields, they lived with one of their children. Since they had always wanted to read and write, they were taking this opportunity to learn. It was touching to see them helping each other form their letters and listening to them struggle with "See Dick run" and "See Spot jump." But they were so proud to be reading and writing those things which had been a mystery to them all their lives.

One lady who was about forty and a line supervisor at one of the local plants was studying to pass the GED test for her high school diploma. She and her husband had worked hard and had a nice house but she wanted to be able to say that she'd finished high school. It was obvious she was intelligent but there were some common things she was just clueless about because of the gaps in her education. One night she came in and asked me, "Can you help me figure out if the carpet store is cheating me?" I told her I'd try if she could give me some details. To her credit she had everything written down.

"I'm gonna have carpet put down in my living room. The carpet man said it would take this many yards at this price per yard. I think he's got too many yards there but I don't know how to figure the yards."

She had the measurements of the room but had no concept of square feet or square yards. I quickly showed her how to determine the square footage and turn that figure into square yards. She worked a few minutes with her pencil, looked at her results, and smiled. As she folded her papers and put them back in her purse, she said, "I'm gonna be glad to talk to that man again." I suspected that her gut feelings about the estimate were correct.

Another student looked to be somewhere in her 20s. She was tall, raw-boned and rather plain looking—your typical country girl who was no stranger to hard work. You could tell that by her hands which were large and callused. She had quit school early, gotten married, and produced three children. She was working toward her high school diploma so that "I kin git a good job when my kids git older."

This girl was not dumb but she had been exposed to little in the way of basic academic skills. She worked hard and did pretty well with math but anything related to English was a complete mystery to her.

One week she was absent. The next week I was at my desk sorting out some materials. She walked in and up to where I was working. I glanced up and said, "I missed you last week." Her reply caught me totally off guard.

"Yes sir, I'm sorry about that. But I just couldn't git here. My husband beat me."

I jerked my head up and looked at her more closely. She had on a high-neck, long sleeve shirt and dark glasses but I could see the bruises on her cheeks and the healing cuts around her mouth. I didn't know what to say but managed to stammer out, "I'm sorry."

She continued, "He don't want me to git no learning. He don't want me to be better 'un him. But I'm gonna keep on."

All sorts of emotions welled up in me—anger at her husband, sympathy for her, and a feeling of frustration at knowing of such an injustice and not being able to do anything to stop it. But the thing that so amazed me was the matter-of-fact way she talked about it. It was as if it had happened in the past and was going to happen in the future. She just accepted beatings from her husband as part of her lot in life. The course ended a few weeks later and I never saw her again.

Every so often I reflect on my short stint as an ABE teacher and the students I had. I'm sure the black-couple are dead by now. The carpet lady is probably retired. But the one that really troubles me is the girl who got beaten. I just hope that somehow, in some way, she was able to find a better life.

THE VETERAN

I did not know P. G. before the War. He and his family became good friends of ours in the 1960s. He walked with a limp.

He fought in World War II. He was one of those veterans of which the country is currently losing about one thousand per day. His part in the War will never make the history books— but it should. For you see, war is more than major generals, important battles, new weapons, and innovative tactics. War is the individual soldier, the common "dogface," as he was called in World War II—the one who was face to face with the enemy on a daily basis, who suffered through all the privations and hardships, and who was always thankful when the sun went down that he had survived another day.

P. G. was one of those. He was an infantryman—Company B, 119th Infantry, 30th Division. He carried an M-1 rifle weighing 9.5 pounds and firing nine, 30-caliber rounds before being reloaded—a primitive combat weapon by today's standards. He landed on the Normandy beaches in June of 1944 and fought through the hedgerows of France.

After almost fifty years, P. G. decided it was time for him to revisit the area where he had fought. He and his wife, Ruth, signed up for a tour of Europe but went a few days early, rented a car, and returned to Normandy. The beaches were serene compared to 1944. But their serenity belied that titanic struggle that had taken place there. Many men had died including P. G.'s best friend. Ruth said that in their long years together, she only saw him cry twice—once when his mother died, the other was when he stood at the military cemetery at Normandy.

At first P. G. was not at all certain he could locate and retrace the route of his old unit. But familiar sights began to trigger the long-forgotten memories that had been burned into his brain by the heat of battle. Fortunately, the hedgerows, houses, and villages of rural France had change very little over the years. As they drove inland, 1944 came back. He was able to point out fields and hedgerows they'd fought across and through, where a German machine gun emplacement had been, and where other incidents had occurred.

He stopped the car near a farmhouse and remembered that they had searched it to make sure there were no Germans hiding inside. It was occupied by a woman and her two small children. She became hysterical thinking they would be harmed. No one spoke French so they couldn't tell her they were not going to hurt her or her children. She was quite relieved when they left without bothering them or any of their meager possessions.

They drove into a small village. P. G. said, "We liberated this village. In fact, I helped clear out that store right there. The people who ran it lived above it." They got out of the car and went into the store and managed to communicate to the clerk in charge what they were doing there. He got extremely excited and begged them to stay until the owner returned. The store's current owner was a descendent of the 1944 owner and had been in the store when it was liberated. The clerk knew he would want to meet P. G. but his return was several hours away and P. G. and Ruth could not wait and be sure of meeting their tour group on schedule.

As they drove on, P. G. continued to recognize places and recall events. Finally, they came to the place that he would never forget. It was where on the night of 29 June the German land mine took his left foot and part of his leg ending his participation in the War and making "disabled" a permanent part of his veteran status. P. G.'s battlefield journey ended here on the same ground where his real journey ended in 1944.

P. G. never talked much about that fateful night—not even to those closest to him. After his death Ruth made contact with Bill Picketts, the soldier who was with P. G. when he was wounded. Although it had been over fifty years, he said that the events of that night were engraved in his memory so deeply that he would never forget them. He wrote down the story for her.

Bill Picketts was not a member of P. G.'s outfit. He just happened to be in that sector and was recruited to go on a recon patrol that night. He had never met Cpl. Coop before but was impressed with his athletic appearance and serious demeanor. To Picketts, he seemed to be a person determined to do any assignment the best he could whether he liked it or not. Pickets thought they would get along well since "he seemed to be my sort of soldier."

They were briefed in the afternoon, memorized aerial photos of the patrol area, and searched the area with field glasses to determine possible routes. Their mission was to locate the German main line of resistance (MLR). They were to cross the Vire River near the village of Le Moeuf. The territory on both sides of the river was a "no man's land" since our forces had lost contact with the German Army. Our Intelligence Section (G-2) needed to know the location of mine fields, outposts, and the main German line.

Shortly after 11:00 p.m., when it was fully dark, they blackened their faces with soot from a blackened mess kit and were guided through their lines to the river. An engineer paddled them across in a rubber raft and would await their return. P. G. took the point, the most dangerous position. Picketts followed about fifteen feet behind. They moved to the left parallel to the river until they came to the place where they were to turn away from the river. After the turn their pace became slower and they crouched closer to the ground as they moved into the unknown.

P. G. stopped frequently to check the ground for trip wires and other evidence of mines or the passage of military vehicles. When P. G. stopped, Pickets would kneel and wait until he moved forward again. There was brush and a hedgerow on their left. As they approached a gap in the hedgerow, they moved more deliberately and Picketts dropped back a little. Such a place would be a good location for mines or an outpost. P. G. got near the gap and stopped to check the ground. Picketts relates, "I kneeled and just as I arose and started forward, there was a loud explosion that sent me to the ground. I thought someone had thrown a grenade. The air was filled with dust, smoke, and small debris. My night vision was gone and there was a ringing in my ears."

Picketts stayed down fearing the area would be raked with machine gun fire—but none came. Shortly, he heard P. G. call quietly, "Picketts." He crawled up to him and found that they were in a minefield. P. G. said, "I've blowed my foot plumb off."

In Picketts own words: "He was certainly brave and determined. We used a belt and he helped me put the tourniquet above his knee. We used a trench knife to tighten the strap. Coop remained cool and self-possessed. The leg below the knee was mangled. We tried to do something to stabilize the situation. He did not indicate that he was in pain and I hoped that was the case. He was still losing some blood. With my help he was able to stand."

By putting his left arm on Picketts' shoulder and using his rifle as a crutch in his right hand, P. G. was able to walk. They headed back toward the river. Progress was slow and they stopped to rest once or twice. After each stop it was more difficult to continue, but after what seemed an eternity, they made the river.

After making P. G. as comfortable as he could and resting a

few minutes, Picketts went for help. He started walking fast at first but then began to run. This movement attracted the attention of some of our troops across the river who began shooting at him. Seeing the tracer rounds going just in front of him convinced Picketts to slow down and blend into the terrain. Finally, he got back to the engineer and the raft and told him the situation. The engineer went for a boat while Picketts headed back to where he'd left P. G.

The boat came in a short while. They were having a hard time getting P. G. to his feet and into the boat because he was getting weaker and could help very little. As they were struggling to get this done, Picketts noticed a soldier standing motionless to his right. He gestured to him and hissed, "Don't just stand there, help out." The soldier did not move or reply. After they got P. G. into the boat and started to shove off the silent soldier tried to get into the boat and go with them. That's when Picketts realized he was a German soldier. They rowed away leaving him.

Picketts ends his account with: "We could have been captured that night. But, I am certain of one thing, had I been on the point and called to him, he would have done the same thing for me."

But the land mine was not the end of P. G.'s story. He came home, got a new foot, married his sweetheart, and had a productive career and life. He fathered three fine sons, two of whom I was privileged to teach. He was active in the Disabled American Veterans (DAV) association and served as Commander at the local, State, and 6th District levels. He was a contributor to the betterment of his community. He never lost his zest for life.

P. G. has been gone sixteen years now but he should not be forgotten—neither he nor those others of his generation and his war. I know I'll never forget him. He didn't make Tom Brokow's book—but he should have.

PHILOSOPHY—
FROM GREEK TO COUNTRY

Philosophy in Western Civilization was begun by the Ancient Greeks. Not only did they originate it, they also carried it to a breadth and depth unequaled by any subsequent people. All the basic philosophical questions were posed by the Greeks. Since then, we've just been discussing, re-hashing, and arguing about these questions. In my limited experience, they are seldom answered in the quantified sense. However, the free exchange of ideas on a question often produces a different perspective and a deeper understanding. And that's what these Greeks were after. They called themselves "philosophers" or "lovers of knowledge" and they sought knowledge in all fields. They originated the symposium which literally means "drinking together." After a meal they would have a cup of wine and exchange ideas. Today, if you go to a symposium, you hear an exchange of ideas on a topic—usually minus the wine.

It's truly amazing some of the conclusions reached by these "lovers of knowledge." Without using the modem scientific method, they concluded that blood circulated through the body, that the earth was round, and that the earth revolved around the sun. They even calculated the earth's circumference, missing it by about 20% because of very primitive means of measuring, but their principles were sound.

Greek philosophy passed to the Romans who were a much more practical people. The Roman symposium was more drinking than idea exchange. Then, during Medieval times philosophy, science, and everything else was captured by the

Church which rejected any ideas posed by non-Christian thinkers. The Scholastic philosophers of that age would debate such questions as, "How many angels can dance on the head of a pin?" — which, of course, was a great benefit to mankind.

But the Renaissance came and the Greeks were re-discovered and in the 17th century Rene Descartes came up with a real answer to one of those basic questions from the ancient Greeks: "How does man know that he exists?" Descartes said, "*Cogito, ergo sum*," "I think, therefore I am." I don't think anyone has done better since.

Along this line my friend, Otey Walker, has a story about Descartes and his demise. Otey, whose mind tends to run off in alternate direction at times, relates that Descartes was having coffee one day in a coffee shop in the Netherlands. A server came by his table and asked if he wanted a refill to which Descartes replied, "I think not." Of course, he immediately disappeared. That's an intellectual story you can tell to folks to see if they're really intellectual.

When I was at UT working on my doctorate, we lived in an apartment building with this very young couple. He was studying philosophy. One afternoon he was telling me about the test he'd had that day. The prof had come in and written "Why?" on the board. That was the test. He said that he's written several pages but was not sure how he'd done. I told him my answer would have been much shorter: "Why not?' He assured me that my answer would not have been acceptable and that I would have failed the test. However, he never could explain "why" my short answer was not just as good as the short question. He changed majors at the end of that quarter.

Incidents such as these have led me to conclude that today's world is filled with what I call pseudo-philosophers — modern sophists who ask "deep" questions in order to show off their own brilliance. This is a favorite tactic to question a person's belief in God. Two exchanges:

"Do you agree that everything that exists must exist in some amount?"

"Yes."

"Then, if something exists in some amount, it can be measured."

"Yes."

"Do you believe there is a God?"

"Yes."

"Then tell me what is the measure of God—if He does indeed exist.

Of course the asker is making an absurd comparison between a concrete unit and an abstraction like an idea, a thought, or a concept. It used to be that a thought could not be measured but in recent studies researchers have been able to chart a thought through the brain. Who knows what else might be measurable?

And yet another:

"Do you believe in an all-powerful God—one who can do anything?"

"Yes."

"Then, can God make an object so heavy that He could not lift it?"

Of course, the question that's really being asked is "Could God put a limit on Himself?" I think most would say that he could—if He were disposed to do so.

Some of the purest thinkers I've ever run across have been country people with little formal education. They care little for philosophical sparing or extended verbal exchange. They tend to cut to the chase and look for a practical answer. A smart aleck used to like to ask the question, "What would happen if a force that couldn't be stopped ran into an object that couldn't be moved?" Then he would sit smugly back and let the person wrestle with it. One day he posed his question to an old, grizzled farmer who gave it a minute or two of thought before replying, "I think you'd have something that couldn't be described." Could there be a better answer?"

A perennial question is the "half full/half empty glass. I think the common analysis is that those who see the glass as half-full are optimists and those who see it as half-empty are pessimists. However, the best response I ever heard came from an old country fellow who maybe had an eighth grade education. He'd sent his son off to college and the boy had come home on a visit armed with all sorts of new and unusual ideas. They were out at the barn and the boy asked, "Dad, can you tell me if that bucket is half full or half empty?"

After giving it a little thought, his father replied, "Well, Son, I'd say it just all depends."

"On what?"

"On whether you're pouring water into it or out of it."

It's hard to get the best of a "real" philosopher.

DUSTY DELTA TOWNS

To a country boy growing up in the '30s and '40s in Mississippi, they were the most exciting and mesmerizing places he could imagine—those dusty Delta towns sprouting as if by magic out of the surrounding cotton fields. In this flat landscape, the water tank announced the town's presence long before it could be seen because a building taller than two stories was a rarity. The boy had never been anywhere and to one accustomed to dirt roads, coal oil lights, and no plumbing, places with paved streets, electric lights, colorful neon signs, running water, and indoor bathrooms were sights to behold. The boy lived for Saturday afternoons when farm work was set aside, the model A was taken from the car house, and the family went to town to buy a few staples. He got to go to the picture show and see a Western and, if his daddy was feeling generous that week, get an Orange Crush from the ice-water filled drink box at the grocery store.

These towns were all different, yet they were all the same. The common elements made them more alike than different. Just change the directions where certain parts were in relation to other parts and peoples' names, and it would be hard to distinguish one from another.

This town sat astride Highway 61, the Delta Highway that runs from Memphis to Vicksburg. There were two traffic lights although they were unnecessary except for Saturdays. But a traffic light on 61 was a symbol of importance so the town resisted all efforts to eliminate either of theirs. Lesser towns only had blinking caution lights. Insignificant places had nothing at all.

East of the highway between it and Deer Creek was the white residential section and the school, grades 1-12. Since it paid higher salaries than other schools in the area, it had no trouble getting teachers. However, with the higher pay came certain restrictions: no smoking in public, required church attendance, no dating on a school night, and numerous other infringements on teachers' personal liberties.

The business district, a block long and two blocks wide, lay on the west side of the highway. Its western boundary was the main line of the Illinois Central RR. There was nothing fancy, no boutiques, just the basic stores. Most were run by native Southerners except for the Jewish and the Chinese establishments, one each. The Jewish family owned a clothing store. The large, extended Chinese family lived above and ran a grocery store. There were several children of various ages, none of which went to school. Nobody seemed to care. Mr. Booth ran the corner drug store. His brother, Elmo, worked there. Elmo had never been to college but Mr. Booth taught him how to fill prescriptions so he could help out in the pharmacy. This lasted until the State inspector dropped by one day and caught Elmo mixing potions. Mr. Booth then sent him to Ole Miss where he got a pharmacy degree and became legal.

Of course, the town had no public facilities or drinking fountains but you could go into the drug store and ask for a glass of water—no charge. Mr. Booth got tired of so many colored (I'll use the term that was used then.) folk asking for water so he started asking them if they wanted city water or country water. Since they were in the city, they'd say "city water" and be given a shot of carbonated water. It didn't take long for word to get around that the city water at the drug store wasn't fit to drink. Of course, a white person could still get a drink there.

The picture show was bare bones—just a long box with seats and a screen. The small lobby had a ticket window and a popcorn machine. The ticket booth had a back window where colored folk could buy tickets and go to the balcony by an outside stairway. They didn't have access to the popcorn.

Along the tracks and a little to the north was a cotton gin, a Federal Compress and Warehouse Company, and a mill which processed cotton seed into meal and hulls for cattle feed.

West of the tracks was the colored section of town. The streets were not paved. The men worked in the gin, compress, or seed mill or hired out to do odd jobs. The women worked as domestics for white families across the highway. When a nearby plantation needed day workers to chop or pick cotton, a truck would be sent to drive slowly through this section with its horn blowing. Those wanting to work came out and hopped aboard, bringing hoes or sacks but rarely any lunch. There'd be water provided in the fields.

There were no businesses in the colored section of town unless you counted the fellow who cut hair under a shade tree in his front yard or the bootlegger or the juke joint that was only open on Saturday.

There was a school but the terms were sporadic. Colored children were expected to work as soon as they could use a hoe or pull a cotton sack. Books were mostly hand-me-downs from the white school. The State touted itself as "separate but equal" in education. It was always separate but never equal.

The business district was a bustling place on Saturdays. The boy loved to see all the people especially the crippled colored man who walked in a sitting position and the colored man with no legs who sat on a wheeled platform and propelled himself about with his hands and the little shoe shine boy with the homemade box who could really make that cloth pop at ten cents a shine and the police chief with the big gun on his hip walking around maintaining order.

Now days the town's still dusty but it doesn't bustle like it did 70 years ago. A by-pass routes traffic around town. Since the civil rights movement of the '60s coloreds began to vote and now hold a number of elective offices. They have proved to be just as honest or corrupt as the whites were before them. When one fellow commented that it was hard for a white person to live there with the blacks running things, he got this response: "It serves you right. You kept them in ignorance and peonage for a hundred years after the Civil War."

Sometimes it takes a long time for the pendulum to swing.

A Chance Encounter

In January 2003 Honey and I went to Sea World in Orlando, FL. It was not crowded.

We were going down a long, wide ramp to one of the exhibits when we came to the entrance gate. No other tourists were in sight either to our front or rear. The gatekeeper was an older fellow as many of the workers there are in the winter. He hailed us as we entered. "Where you folks from?" When we replied that we were from Tennessee, he said that he'd gotten married in Tennessee. It appeared that he wanted to talk and since we were not in a hurry, we walked over to where he was sitting atop the barrier fence. His permanent name badge said his name was Bob.

He said that he was from Ohio but had come to Tennessee to get married because there was no waiting period. He also said that he was stationed for a time at the Millington Naval air station in Memphis during World War II. "So you were in the Navy?" I asked.

"Yep. Navy pilot."

"What did you fly?"

"Torpedo bombers off the carrier Hornet. Say, if you've got a minute, I wanna show you something." He reached in his billfold. "Now, don't think I try to show this to everybody. But I just got it recently and I'm so proud to have it."

He handed me a small black and white photo. There were three people in the picture. Two of them were young airmen in World War II flight uniforms. The one on the left had what appeared to be bandages around his neck and forehead and a pained expression on his face. The other had his flight cap on and appeared uninjured. The third person was on the left and standing a little in the background. He was a Japanese soldier holding a rifle.

"That's me and my gunner the day we were shot down and captured. We were both 22 years old. Guess which one's me." I guessed the wrong one.

"How long were you a prisoner?" I asked.

"Six months—and then the war was over."

"I don't suppose you were treated very well."

"No, and they didn't feed us very well either. I lost ninety pounds in that six months."

He continued, "There's an unusual story behind that picture. It was taken by an official photographer of the Japanese Navy. He was under strict orders not to take pictures of any prisoners. But for some reason he took this one. Then, he had to hide it for fear it would be discovered. Over the years he forgot about it. Recently, he was preparing to remodel his house and was going through some stuff to throw away and found it. He wondered if we were still alive. He had recorded our last names so he got one of the Japanese newspapers to run the picture and the story behind it. Now, it just so happened that there was an American businessman in Japan for just that one day—the day the picture ran. It interested him so he brought it home and got all the veterans' journals to run it. Of course, I'm a member of several veterans' organizations and I saw it.

"The photographer had given a phone number to call. He wanted verification that the callers were really the ones in the picture. I called him and he was a little dubious. He had already gotten five or six calls from people who claimed to be the prisoners but they could not give him adequate verification. I said to him, 'Well, I don't know what you need but I can tell you that one of your soldiers attempted to kill my gunner. He tried to cut his throat and then beat him in the head. He was given no medical attention so he wrapped his long underwear around his neck and head to stop the bleeding.' The photographer replied, 'You're the one.'"

"He came over here recently and brought me this picture. I'm really proud to have it. He's 86 years old."

"Is your gunner still alive?" I asked.

"He sure is—and we're still in contact with each other."

I told him that I thought his story about the picture was most unusual. He said that he was thinking of writing about his war experiences. "I'm eighty years old but I guess I could do it." I encouraged him to do so.

At that point I thought his story was finished but such was not the case he delved into another aspect of it.

"Another thing that's going to come out of this is I'm going to get the Purple Heart. I'd always thought that medal was just for those wounded in combat. Of course I wasn't shot or anything. And when the war was over, I wasn't interested in any medals-only going home.

"But my children discovered that there were other categories and encouraged me to make application. I was injured a little when my plane went down—some cuts on my head and one leg. I was able to verify this through the treatment records at the Japanese hospital we went through before being sent to the POW camp.

"And then there was the time the Japanese officer came in our barracks and shouted, 'Roosevelt is dead! War will soon be over! America has lost!' I jumped up and shouted back at him, 'Like hell we have you SOB!' For that he beat me across the back with the flat of his sword for about ten minutes. I've still got the scars from that one. Of course, I had plenty of witnesses to verify those injuries. Everything's been approved. I guess they'll send it to me in due time."

"If anybody deserves a Purple Heart, you POWs surely do," I said.

We took our leave and went on our way to see the manatees.

I was glad we'd stopped. You never know when you might run into an old veteran with a story to tell--a hero waiting to be discovered.

Now And Then:
A World of Change

She is always impeccably dressed with no hair out of place and no flaw in her makeup. She has an engaging personality. Her daughter was the salutatorian at one of the area's college prep schools and has now earned her Ph.D. at Vanderbilt. She is a vice president at one of the local banks and is well thought of throughout the community. It would appear that she is living the so-called "American Dream," but it was not always this way for this black woman.

In a recent conversation, she recalled how it was when she was growing up near Franklin. She remembered that Saturday was always a special day because they got to go to town. Her mother would have her and her sister dressed well and looking nice. People who didn't know them often asked her mother if she were a schoolteacher.

One thing they got to do was go to the drug store and get an ice cream cone. They loved this weekly treat. They would go in and stand over to the side of the soda fountain where they would be served. White people would be sitting on the stools at the counter enjoying their sodas and ice cream. She says, "We would stand there eating our cones and thinking just how wonderful it would be if we could sit on the stools. I know it really wasn't much but it seemed a big thing to us back then." Surprisingly, she is not bitter about such treatment. "That's just the way it was in those days," she recalls.

Thank goodness things have changed in the last fifty years. Now this lady can eat in any restaurant in town and she can go to the drug store and get an ice cream cone and sit on one of the stools.

One can probably find thousands of stories similar to hers throughout our region.   And, appropriately, this month we observe Martin Luther King Day to recognize Dr. King's and others' efforts to ensure that black people be allowed to "sit on the stools" and to be afforded the same rights and privileges as other citizens. This year Dr. King's Day is the 19th; the next day is Inauguration Day—a juxtaposition that should not go unnoticed.

I never thought I'd live long enough to see a black person elected President, but I have.   You see I grew up in the segregated South and saw many of the practices which my black banker friend had to endure. These practices were seldom in writing but everyone knew what they were. They were necessary to "keep them in their place" which was always a position of inferiority. When I relate some of these practices to my younger friends, many can't believe I'm not making them up. Some examples.

All water fountains, restrooms, and waiting rooms were designated with signs as "white only" or "colored only." They could go to a movie but they entered by a separate entrance and sat in the balcony which was reminiscent of the old slave balconies of white churches and usually they did not have access to the concession stand located in the white lobby. They could not go to the front door of a white person's house but had to go to the rear. They could not enter a white café where all the customers and servers were white. Of course, most of the cooks in the back were black but that incongruity was ignored probably because many white families had black cooks. There were no dressing/fitting rooms for backs in clothing stores, because a white person would not buy a garment that had been tried on by a black person. And, of course, they could not return or exchange items after purchase for the same reason. In stores whites were always waited on first.   Even if a black person had been waiting a while to buy some hinges at the hardware store, he had to step aside for the more recent white customer.

On the large (2000+ acres) cotton plantations of the Mississippi Delta which my father managed, the black tenants were kept in a state of peonage. If a tenant had a debit balance on the books, he could not leave for another plantation unless the debt was paid. If he did so, the sheriff went after him and brought him back.

The South took great pride in being a society that was "separate but equal," a doctrine that was even upheld by the courts. However, a blind person could see that the things that were always "separate" were never "equal." This was especially true in education where the black schools got the out-dated, worn out throw-aways of books and equipment from the white schools. Education for the children of rural farm workers was almost nonexistent. A teacher might come to the local black church for a short session when the demands for field work was slack—winter or in the late summer after the crops had been laid by and before the fall harvest season. The prevailing philosophy was that you needed no "book" education to work in the fields.

The town schools met more regularly but they never had enough books or equipment. I remember talking to one of my teachers at Ole Miss in 1950 about his visit to one of these schools. The children were doing copy work and one little boy proudly brought his up to show him. Seeing the puzzled look on his face when my teacher couldn't figure out what he was seeing, one of the other students said, "It's upside down," to which another added, "Yeah, and it's backards, too." The table had only one copybook for about eight children and this little boy had been on the wrong side. My teacher turned the paper upside down and there was the perfect mirror image of the copy work. There's no telling what this smart little fellow could have learned if he'd gotten on the right side of the copybook.

The justification for inferior education for blacks was that they couldn't learn. I wouldn't try to guess how many times I heard that argument as I was growing up. It's been proven wrong countless times. The Tuskeegee airmen of WWII is one good example. In the 1970s I kept hearing that blacks were not smart enough to play quarterback. By that time I'd gone to graduate school with enough different folk to know that intelligence was not the exclusive possession of any race.

Not long ago my eight-year-old granddaughter overheard some of us discussing the era of segregated schools. She was shocked that such a time ever existed since she has friends of all colors and races. That's as it should be.

So, we should all stop this month and reflect on Dr. King and the many others who helped to bring these changes about— who helped my banker friend to be able to sit on a stool at the drug store and eat her ice cream cone with everybody else.

A LEVEL PLAYING FIELD?

We're at the beginning of a new sports season during which we will hear participants described as "scholar athletes" or " real professionals." Those terms connote players who play by the rules and are real credits to the game. On the other hand, there will be plenty of stories about players who get their transcripts altered to make them eligible for college scholarships, who finish their college eligibility with a melange of courses which only leads them to a career in the NFL or NBA, who take all manner of banned substances to gain a physical advantage over the competition, and accounts of coaches, boosters, and fans who aid and abet such behavior. And then, we've had the advent of the "thug athlete" with an arrest record as long as your arm but still able to play. What was once unheard of is now commonplace. And these negative aspects of sports has filtered down to the lowest level with youngsters as young as 8 or 10 being sought out and recruited "for the future" by some programs.

A year or so ago a sports writer capitalized on some of this negativity to make his NFL pre-season predictions. He predicted the two super bowl teams and the winner without using any football statistics. He ranked each team on the basis of their players' arrest records, seriousness of the charges, and the number of convictions. His theory was that these type players made a team tougher and more aggressive which were traits needed to win a football championship. Thank goodness he was wrong but the teams he picked did have good seasons.

At times these negatives seem to dominate the picture of sports. It often appears that Haywood Hale Broom, that old-line sports announcer with the loud sport jackets, was correct when he stated that "sports do not build character, they reveal character." He was probably right for the most part but I think sports, if used in the right manner, can be a valuable tool in the development of positive character traits.

A friend of mine was an outstanding athlete and played several sports in high school and both football and basketball at the college level. His mother was happy for him to play as long as he followed her rules of conduct. One of her stipulations was that he keep his grades up. He relates an incident when a bad grade report came in the mail. His mama proceeded to march herself down to the practice field and drag him off in the middle of a scrimmage. And he didn't put on another pair of shoulder pads until he got his grades up. He said he learned a valuable lesson that day and for the rest of his career, he never had a grade problem. One has to wonder if that could happen in today's world. One coach who used his sport as a positive teaching tool was Bobby Dodd. Dodd was a coaching legend at Georgia Tech back in the mid-1900s when Tech was a member of the SEC. There was probably not a coach in the country more widely respected than Dodd. A couple of stories illustrated this.

On January 1, 1953, Tech played Ole Miss in the Sugar Bowl. I was the equipment manager for the Ole Miss team. Nobody could remember when we had last been to a major bowl. Tech was a perennial bowl contender. Nevertheless, the game was hard fought ending in a 21-14 Tech victory. One reason for Tech's win was a skinny halfback named Billy Teas. He was about six feet tall and may have weighed 160 pounds but when he got into the open field, it was like trying to hem up a water bug. The next year was Teas' senior year. About halfway through the season, Teas had an excellent game and ended up lacking three yards to break Tech's career rushing record. That weekend he and two or three friends went out and got into trouble. Dodd dismissed them all from the team. There was much speculation among sports writers the next week about Teas, Dodd, and the rushing record. Many predicted that Dodd would allow him to play one series, get the record, and then send him on his way. That did not happen. Billy Teas never put on another uniform for Georgia Tech. On Coach Dodd's teams everybody, whether stars or fourth-stringers, was subject to the same standards.

I once heard a referee tell a story about officiating one of Tech's games. That was back in the day when a coach could blackball an official if he didn't like the way he officiated. That meant that the official could no longer work games for that coach's team. A few blackballs would put an official out of work. This particular game was a close one with Tech a few points down late in the fourth quarter. Tech was driving for the winning score and threw a little flare pass out into the flat right in front of the Tech bench. The receiver made the catch, spun off the defender, and headed down the sideline to score. However, as he whirled, the heel of one shoe caught the sideline and kicked up a puff of chalk dust. Seeing this, the official ran over and put his foot at that point to mark the play out of bounds. As he did, he looked up and there was Coach Dodd standing just across the sidelines with his arms folded looking at him. He said, "Coach, I'm sorry I've got to call this one on you."

Dodd replied, "Don't worry about it. If you didn't call it, you'd never call another game for me."

All Coach Dodd wanted or expected was a level playing field. He would see to the rest. It's sad that there are those in sports today who do not embrace this philosophy.

THE MINSTREL SHOW

February is Black History month, a time set aside for special emphasis on the contributions Black people have made to our society. One could wonder why the shortest month of the year was chosen but I won't go down that road. Anyway, 2012 is a little better than most years since the month has 29 days.

One contribution Blacks have made is that musical genre we call "The Blues." It is, of course, not happy music. It's mournful chords and lyrics speak of and to the downtrodden and relate stories of pain, suffering, and heartbreak in every aspect of life. Who can ever forget that mournful line, "I hate to see that evening sun go down." The blues began among Black folk and, for the most part, in my home State of Mississippi.

An article in a recent edition of my alumni magazine revealed that Ole Miss has been the leader in establishing a center for "documenting and preserving African American blues culture." One of the center's projects has been to establish the "Mississippi Blues Trail" which recognizes and marks locations all over the State where blues related events occurred or where blues people lived or performed. It is an on-going project with 129 sites marked so far.

There are some white folk on the list but the vast majority are black, as they should be. They're the ones who created the music. Some names are easily recognizable: Muddy Waters, Bo Diddley, B. B. King, and W. C. Handy. Others: Pinetop Perkins, Gatemouth Moore, or Papa Lightfoot are more obscure. And there are places like that dusty Delta crossroads where legendary bluesman, Robert Johnson, met the devil that midnight and sold his soul in exchange for supernatural musical ability.

A special one to me is number 21, Port Gibson, home base of The Rabbit Foot Minstrel Show. As a youngster the only culture I was exposed to was agriculture. The only entertainment venue I know anything about was the local picture show where we saw cowboy movies on Saturday afternoons. The first stage production I ever saw was The Rabbit Foot Minstrel Show with an all-black cast.

This was a tent show which traveled around the State in the 1930s and '40s giving Saturday night performances in small towns. About a month before the show posters would appear around town announcing the event. Early in the week of the show, large trucks would roll in to a field on the outskirts of town where a large tent would be erected. A smaller tent housed the performers and roustabouts who didn't have home trailers.

Because the plantation Daddy was managing owned the land, we always got free tickets. I don't know what the admission price was but I suspect it was less than a dollar. A day's labor in that era was a dollar. However, this show had very early mastered the tactics of present-day communication companies of selling you a basic package and then charging for extras. The ticket got you into the tent. There was a roped off center section of folding chairs for white only with another ticket booth. If you wanted to sit there, you paid more. Otherwise, you sat in bleachers at the back or on each side. About half of these were reserved for "colored" who came in large numbers. It was the only chance they ever got to see a black person in a staring role in anything.

The show was really vaudeville with black performers. There were singers, musicians, dancers, acrobats, and comedy skits, some of which were rather risqué for the time. I remember one. Two men meet on the street:

#1.   Where's you gwine?

#2.   I's gwine home. I got off work early.

#1. Well, let me give you some advice 'cause I know you ain't been married long. When you go in 'de front do', you needs to make a lot of racket.

#2.   Why is dat?

#1.   "Cause you don't want to embarrass nobody. 'Cause sometime you might hear 'de back do' slam. I knows 'cause I's a man what's been at both do's.

Before intermission the emcee would introduce new performers that would be doing an encore show after the main show — for an additional charge. Tickets to the encore were sold during intermission. When the main show ended, those not staying would leave and the crew would break down the bleachers. Whites from the bleachers who were staying could find seats in the center section (at no charge). Coloreds had to stand. There was always a young, good looking blues singer in long tight dress in the encore.

The Rabbit Foot Minstrels taught me at a very early age that Black people have a lot of talent in many areas. I'm glad they're finally getting some recognition.

PART V

Semi-Serious
and/or
Semi-Amusing Stuff

THINGS TO DO WHILE DRIVING

Some things are okay to do more than one of at the same time, *i. e.*, things that don't impinge negatively upon other things, such as going to the bathroom and reading the sports page. But there are not many activities that should be attempted while you're piloting a two-ton machine down the road. However, people continue to engage in this risky behavior even as more laws are passed to try to curb it. Some cases in point.

Cell phone use has become so common until it is hardly worthwhile even to discuss it. It just seems that a growing number of drivers apparently think a car engine and a cell phone cannot operate independently.

Texting is several times more dangerous than using a cell but it's all too prevalent, especially among younger drivers. One sweet young thing, who had rear-ended another vehicle on the interstate, admitted she had been texting. When asked why she didn't stop or exit, she stated that she'd just gotten a text and since she didn't plan on stopping for a while, she didn't want to be rude by not replying immediately. Wonder what Miss Manners would say?

Two activities are quite common during morning rush hour: eating breakfast (both sexes) and applying make-up (women), although I did see a man once shaving with an electric razor. One woman did all her make-up on her commute to work each day. She had a tray built over the center console which was stocked like the cosmetic counter at Macy's and a little pull-down magnifying mirror attached to the sun visor. She did most of her work at stoplights but would continue her application on the move if the light changed too quickly. Breakfast seems to be a little easier to manage than lunch because drivers tend to order fewer courses. During one lunchtime I saw a woman come through a stop light on Highway 96E with a burger in one hand and a large drink in the other. I suppose she was steering with her knees but I did not want to chance getting close enough to find out.

Upon retiring a fellow I know lamented all the reading time he was losing. His job had required him to make two round trips to Knoxville each week. He said he had no idea how many books he'd read by just propping them up on the steering wheel. And he never had an accident which I thought amazing. Thank goodness he retired before he killed himself or somebody. Any reader who might be thinking of trying it, I have three words for you—Books on Tape.

It was a small article buried in the back pages of the newspaper but the heading caught my eye. It said, "Sex at 70." Although I'm a few years past that, I read it just to see if anything new had been discovered. It turned out the "70" was not years but "MPH." This couple had posted on their face book page the claim that they had indeed performed this act while traveling down the interstate with the cruise control set at 70. Since the article did not give particulars, readers were left to speculate on the mechanics of the matter. They said they chose 70 rather than a faster speed because they didn't want to break any laws. Wonder how the trooper's accident report would have read if they'd run under the rear of a stalled semi?

This last one could be put under the heading, "Good Grooming Counts," and I'm indebted for it to Ms. Celia Rivenbark, a columnist in Wilmington, N.C. She reported on an accident in Florida in which a woman rear-ended another vehicle while attempting to drive AND shave her bikini area at the same time. She explained to the officer that she was on her way to a date and wanted to look her best. Ms. R. thought she was working on the wrong area since she'd seen her mug shots and reported the woman had "a face that would stop a clock and raise hell with small watches." The article did not say whether a straight, safety, or electric razor was being used. To her credit, however, the woman did take some precautions. Her ex-husband (Yes, you did read that correctly.) was in the passenger seat handling the steering wheel, leaving her only the foot pedals and shaving to deal with.

Please do not try any of these at home (or on the road).

THE "WALK-OFF" FOLKS— THEY'RE STILL AMONG US

In an old Negro tale about the Creation, there is a scene about the Lord making people. It seems He found some clay that was to His liking down close to a riverbank and set about constructing all sorts of folk. As each was finished (except for the brain) He would set him/her down leaning up against the riverbank. Well, He had not had time to get the brains in when darkness caught Him. Since He was tired, He decided to return the next morning and do the brains. But when He came back, He found that all His new people had just gotten up and walked off—without their brains. And these "walk-off" folks have been reproducing and messing up the world ever since.

There are some of their descendents around Franklin. I suspect that they are not natives but have migrated here from other regions. I've encountered a number at 4-way stops. They don't seem to be able to count to 4 or to understand that if two cars arrive at the same time, the vehicle on the right goes first. Even worse are the ones who can't handle a 3-way stop and have no idea what a "yield" sign means. These are probably the ones that are so vocal against round-abouts because they are unable to yield to the left and merge at the same time. I hope they never try to drive across England where this process is reversed.

Around Franklin we have an abundance of well-designed and constructed entranceways and business signs. Most are of stone or brick and are works of art in and of themselves. Usually there is a name incorporated in the design. What's hard to understand is why they go to all this expense and then plant shrubs in front of the name. In two or three years, the shrubs grow up and obscure the name. The only place I've ever seen this process corrected was at Centennial High school. Students laid out a nice school name sign in colored rock on the side of the hill in front of the school. Then they planted shrubs all around it. I remarked to Honey that those in the front would soon hide their handiwork. However, within a few months, the plantings in front of the sign had been removed. There are several subdivisions that could learn from these teenagers.

For some reason I quite often run into store clerks who cannot make change. I suspect that some of the "walk-offs" have gravitated to this profession. Recently, my bill at one of our local sandwich places was $11.12. I handed the young lady a twenty and twelve cents. As she stood looking at the bill in one hand and the change in the other, this exchange occurred:

"What's this for?" she asked holding up the twelve cents.
"So you won't have to give me back any change."
"How do I punch it in?"
"I don't care how you punch it in as long as you give me back nine dollars."
"Are you sure that's right?"
"Of course, it's right. What else could it be?"

Another clerk walked up and showed her what to do. As the numbers came up on her screen, her face lit up. "He's right," she said, amazed that a person my age had such facility with figures.

Usually, tour guides for major companies are very knowledgeable and add considerably to any trip. However, Honey and I encountered a "walk-off" not long ago in New England.

Boston streets seem to run in a lot of odd directions due to the fact (so the natives say) that they were laid out on the colony's cow paths. Using that as a basis, life-size fiberglass cows had been placed all over the city and local artists had been invited to decorate them any way they chose. We saw "John Han'cow" with excerpts from the Declaration of Independence all over her as well as "Pic'cow'so" done in the abstract. They were eventually to be auctioned for charity. These critters were anatomically correct in that they all had udders. In telling us about them, our tour guide said, "These cows aren't really correct physically. They're female at the back but they all have horns which make them male at the front." I let out a gasp.

"Don't correct her," commanded Honey.

"I cannot let such ignorance run loose among the general population," I replied. So at the next stop, I drew her aside and pointed out that horns on a cow had nothing to do with its sex. She replied that she was aware that some Western cows had horns which led me to inform her that a cow's geographical location also had nothing to do with its sex either. She did not seem convinced. Proof of this came a couple of day later as we traveled through Vermont. As we passed a pasture full of dairy cows, she remarked over the PA system, "You can see all these cows on the right. Some of them are Western cows because they have horns."

"She's hopeless," I said to Honey. And we found out how hopeless when we encountered a battle site from the war of 1812. She informed us that most people thought we fought England in that war but we had actually fought Canada.

"Are you going to tell her?" Honey asked.

"No," I answered. "If she won't listen to an old farm boy about cows, she surely won't listen to a historian about history."

I'm sure some of you heard about this "walk-off" out in Oklahoma a couple of years ago. It made the national news. He bought a new Winnebago RV and drove it to a football game. On the way back home on the interstate, he set the cruise control at 70 MPH and went into the back to make himself a cup of coffee. Of course, it ran off the road, crashed, and scattered debris all over the place. Fortunately, (or maybe unfortunately for him) he was not serious hurt and the roaming RV didn't hurt anyone else. "Walk-offs" like this fellow need to be taken out of the gene pool. Anyway, not content with just this exposure of his gross stupidity, he sued Winnebago for not telling him in the owner's manual that he couldn't operate the vehicle in that manner. The whole thing would be laughable except that he apparently got a jury made up of other "walk-offs" who awarded him $1,750,000 and a new RV. In the likely event that there were others out there like him, the company changed its manual.

It's dumb actions like this which cause all the excessive, dumb directions on products. My prescriptions all have directions like "take one pill per day by mouth." It makes you wonder just where folks have tried to stick them.

So, watch out for these "walk-off' folk. You never know when you might come across one. They're all around us.

"Walk-Off" Criminals

Regular readers will recall that my last column was about the "walk-off" folks—the ones who, at the Creation, walked off before the Lord could give them brains. These people have been reproducing and messing up the world ever since. That column was about general "walk offs." Today's is about a specific group—the "walk-off" criminals. These are the ones who can't even do the wrong things right.

It's fairly common for the body of a homicide victim to be discovered after erosion from a heavy rain has partially exposed the corpse or when wild animals have dug up part of it. The account always says that the victim was found in a "shallow grave." And this early discovery of foul play many times leads to the apprehension of the one who put the body there. Now, if I were to be asked to teach a course to a group who had plans to do away with someone, my first and most important point would be "dig deeper." In other words, emulate the ones who disposed of Jimmy Hoffa several years ago. They had to be accomplished professionals. There's just no telling where or how deep he is.

Some of the dumbest "walk-offs" are those who try to steal, especially from banks. I particularly like the account of a would-be robber who wrote a hold-up note on the back of one of his deposit slips on which was printed his address and then left it with the teller. The police were waiting for him when he got home. Then there was the brilliant thief who wrote a hold-up note on the back of a general deposit slip in the lobby of one bank and then went across the street to another bank and presented it to a teller. The teller informed him that she could not honor it because it was written on a slip from the bank across the street. He was surprised when he went back over to that bank to use it to find the police awaiting him.

Some thieves don't have much finesse. They're of the "smash and grab" school. They smash a window or door, grab what they can, and run off before the police can arrive. One such operator targeted a jewelry store. He didn't plan very far ahead so he just grabbed something at the scene to use as a smashing tool. It was a manhole cover. You know the fellow had to be strong just to pick one of those things up much less to throw it through a window. But he did, grabbed what he could, and ran. When he saw the police coming toward him, he turned and ran back the other way. He was caught when he fell into the open manhole in front of the just-robbed store.

Some burglars figure out ingenious ways to enter stores and homes. Reports of burglars who get stuck in tight spaces trying to enter are fairly common. One family came home from a night at the theater and heard shouts coming from their chimney. Since it wasn't close to Christmas, they called the police who, with much effort, extricated a rather sooty burglar.

Another fellow tried the same thing at a restaurant. He spent several hours stuck in the chimney before opening time the next day. However, he had a novel defense. He said he was hungry and was just trying to get in to get a sandwich. This plea fell on deaf ears.

There was one gang committing home burglaries who figured out a way which by-passed alarms on doors and windows. They would climb up on the roof, chop a hole in it, drop down into the attic, and then knock a hole in the ceiling of a room. After sacking up all the valuables they could find, they left the same way. However, on one job they misfigured and broke through on the front porch. All this commotion attracted the attention of a neighbor who was taking his dog for a late night stroll, which led to the end of their careers in crime.

Some burglars are able to get in but have a problem getting out. One fellow hid someplace in a large department store just before closing time and was locked inside. His plan was to gather up a bunch of stuff and just walk out. He assumed the doors could be opened from the inside. They couldn't. He was found the next morning by the store manager asleep on a couch in the furniture department with two pillowcases full of watches and jewelry.

Another "walk-off" broke into a house while the family was on vacation. He attempted to exit through the garage but was trapped as the house door locked when he pulled it shut behind him and the garage door opener malfunctioned. He survived for eight days on Pepsi and dry dog food before the family returned and he was carted off to jail.

One has to wonder why some criminals are so dumb that they keep things that tie them to crimes. Early last month there was a rash of store robberies around Nashville by folks wearing Halloween masks. Acting on a tip, the police searched one fellow's car in which they found his mask. He named his fellow pranksters ending this particular crime spree.

This past January we were treated to the saga of one Christopher Daniel Gay, a 33-year-old career criminal with 25 convictions all for some type of theft. Considering his age and the number of convictions, one wonders why he didn't consider going into another line of work. Anyway, Gay escaped from a prison transport down in Georgia and began a journey to Coopertown, TN, to see his dying mother. He stopped off in Atlanta and stole a tractor. As he passed through Manchester, he hooked it to a Wal-Mart trailer containing $300,000 in merchandise. He was spotted near Coopertown and led police on a back-road chase before he finally mired up in a field about 50 yards from his mother's mobile home and escaped into the woods. The authorities said that they'd let him see her if he were captured or if he'd give himself up. But no, he stole

Crystal Gayle's tour bus and made it to Daytona, FL, before he was captured. Since he was wanted in so many states, his mother died before the extradition process could be completed. Questions: If he just wanted to see his momma, why didn't he just sneak home through the woods rather than come roaring in with a tractor-trailer full of stolen goods? Why didn't he just surrender? Why did he head off to Florida?

During this escapade, he was pictured as a good Christian man, sort of a Robin Hood, who always tried to provide for his family—even is it was with stolen goods. His family said he aways made them laugh. How sweet. And before the dust had settled, he became sort of a folk hero when a country song, _The Ballad of Christopher Daniel Gay_, appeared on the Internet. I suppose that just goes to show that there's a lot of sympathy for "walk-offs" in our society.

THERE OUGHT TO BE A LAW?

The late humorist Will Rogers, who got much of his material straight from the newspapers sometimes would walk out on stage, unfold a paper, and say, "There's not much humor in the paper today. Congress is not in session." That's not true at present in our fair State since both our State and local bodies are in full swing.

Metro Davidson County just passed a "Chicken Bill," making it legal for people to keep up to six chickens on their residential property. Supporters of the bill were ecstatic with one saying that their eggs would make a huge difference in the flavor of chocolate chip cookies. Does anyone really believe that?

One Councilman said that they were not going to allow this new law to turn Nashville into another Key West where chickens are classified as "wild animals" and are protected. Honey and I spent some time there over the holidays. It's common to see chickens scratching around in flowerbeds in the affluent neighborhoods and wandering about at will. Roosters crow most of the time. We had breakfast one morning in the courtyard of a restaurant where hens roamed amongst the tables, herding their biddies and begging for scraps. This would probably be frowned upon along Belle Meade Blvd.

I suspect this law is going to be challenged because it's highly selective and discriminatory. It only pleases folks who want fresh eggs. What about those who would like to keep a cow for fresh milk or a sheep for wool or a donkey for transportation or a couple of goats to mow the grass? I predict the introduction of other "animal bills."

The "chicken bill" has yet to be reported on the national news but it probably will be. Why do Southern lawmakers get involved with issues that make Southern people out to be a bunch of redneck country bumpkins? There are plenty of examples.

Who can forget the "Roadkill Bill" a few years back which made it legal for residents of our State to eat animals that had not survived collisions with cars? It made the national news and conjured up images of hillbillies racing around on our roads in beat-up Fords looking for supper.

Another bill that made national news was introduced by a Metro Councilman some years ago to build a UFO landing pad in Nashville. His rationale: If there are UFOs and if they come around, they will need a place to land and Nashville should show its hospitality by providing such a site. Of course, there were no specifications for just what type pad a UFO might require but the fellow was determined to get one ready. Fortunately, his bill was rejected but not before the Country had a good laugh.

A couple of years ago our State Legislature passed a bill which affected only one barber shop in one small town which had an aquarium. The bill made it legal for barbershops to have fish for "decorative purposes only." Apparently, fish had been banned from barbershops in order to ban the practice of people sticking their feet into vats of small fish which eat off the dead skin.

Unfortunately, Tennessee is not the only Southern State afflicted with this type legislation. There was a report on TV that a Louisiana Parish's (County) legislative body was preparing an ordinance that would ban the wearing of pajamas in public. The obvious need for such a law was the observation of one man who did so and exposed his private parts to pubic scrutiny. They showed a picture of the man--from the rear-- walking into a shopping area. He was a large, dark-skinned fellow and the PJs were a light colored gauzy material. One could only imagine the front view. But, come on, a law? Surely they have statutes on the books about indecent exposure. Why not cite him for that and leave the rest of the folks who want to wear PJs of thicker material in public alone? No word yet on the outcome.

We can only hope that some of our State or local lawmakers do not get wind of this. One can only imagine the spirited debate on a law we don't need to solve another problem we don't have.

And back to the chickens. I grew up with yard chickens and know first-hand that they produce more than just eggs. So you need to be careful when you walk around the yard bare footed. That stuff is hard to get out from between your toes.

NAMES, NICKNAMES, AND ODD PLACES

It was Shakespeare who said, "What's in a name? A rose by any other name would smell as sweet." This would lead one to believe that it doesn't make much difference what we call things or people, that the name has no bearing on the object. I don't think that's true. Names have both a denotation which simply designates the thing and a connotation which is its emotional essence. Parents should think about this when they name their newborns but many don't. A name which is cute for a toddler might not be cute for an adult trying to make a mark as a professional. It can take quite an effort for a person to rise above his/her name. Some do and are stronger because of the struggle. That's the basis for Johnny Cash's hit, "A Boy Named Sue." Others are dragged down by their names and never rise above mediocrity.

Some parents with last names of famous people, e. g., Washington, Lincoln, Einstein, etc., like to name their kids for those historical folk. I once knew a "George Washington" — not the original; I'm not quite that old. He said he always had trouble making dinner reservations. He'd get comments like, " I suppose Martha and the kids are coming, too," before the restaurant person would hang up on him.

One summer I was in a special program with a fellow from East Tennessee named Martin Luther Dale. I figured he was from a long line of Protestant ministers and was named for the one who had nailed up those 95 theses on the church door in 1517. When I asked him if that was the case, he replied, "Naw, my folks never heard of Martin Luther. I just had one grandfather named Martin and the other named Luther." Sometimes accidents happen.

When I was young, the thing to do with twins was to give them names that rhymed. I had two cousins named Natalie and Katalie. The first "a" in each name was long and the last syllable was pronounced "lee." In high school I played baseball with a pair named Billy Wray and Billy Clay. They were both left-handed and odd in some other ways as well.

Sometimes parents give their kids names that are better suited for the opposite gender. I've noted that this is mostly true of parents who wanted a boy but got a girl. One of my high school English teachers was named John Henry Still. She was a good teacher and said simply, "My folks wanted a boy." She never married and I couldn't help but wonder if the name didn't have something to do with her spinsterhood. In this same vein, someone told me of a girl they knew named Werdna. They wanted a boy and had picked out Andrew for his name. When a girl came, they just turned the name backwards. And when I came to BGA, I kept looking for a boy named Lawrence only to discover he was a girl. She's an adult now and still complaining because she gets mail addressed to "Mr. Lawrence _____." Why is she surprised?

And you don't have to be a person to be a victim of letter reversal. There's a little town in Mississippi named "Trebloc." The place was originally named "Colbert" but when they applied to get a post office, they were informed that there was already a Colbert in the state with a post office so they just turned the name around. And while we're on place names, there's a little town in Pennsylvania named Intercourse. It means intercourse in the sense of trade and commerce because the founders hoped it would be such a center. It didn't happen. The next little town is named Paradise which gave rise to the local joke that you have to go through Intercourse to get to Paradise. I'll not pursue this any further.

I suppose the most melodious name I've ever run across was the name of a woman who a late friend of mine went to college with back in the early 1900s. Can you say, "Arabella Balla from Ashtabula, Alabama?" Doesn't it just flow off your tongue?

One good place to find unusual names, and especially nicknames, is the obituaries. One thing I've noticed is that many death notices for females do not include the age. What difference could it make at that point? They're dead. I suppose some are just vain to the end and even beyond. The age of one woman was given as "not too old but old enough." Several great-grandchildren were listed so you do the math.

One lady who died at 73 was named Shirley Temple _____(her real name). She was undoubtedly named for that child movie star of the 1940s. Another lady's nickname was listed as "Sheba Eagle Wolf" which led me to believe that she had some Native American connection. One lady's real name was "Sunshine" and she had lived for 85 years. With such a long life one would hope that she had lived up to her name.

The men are not to be left out when it comes to unusual given names. How about "Evangelist _____" who died at 86? The write-up didn't say whether he was one or not but I can imagine that when his parents selected his name in about 1920, they wanted him to be. And then there was "Andrew 'Andy' Jackson Jones," age 60. I suspect the Jones parents wanted a distinctive given name to go with a very common last name. They could have selected "John Paul Jones" but being good Tennesseans they went with a native son.

I suppose the moral to all of this could be that there are interesting things all around us. All we've got to do is look.

WAS IT REALLY ABOUT FOOTBALL?

The first NFL game I ever saw was "live and in person." In those days football had yet to take over TV. I was stationed at Fort Knox and Honey and I went to the 1956 Kentucky State Fair in Louisville. The morning was spent looking at various exhibits. Honey couldn't understand why I wanted to see the hogs but I thought 600-pound porkers were well worth looking at. The Baltimore Colts were playing an exhibition game (That's what pre-season games were called in those days.) in the afternoon and we had tickets. It was an unforgettable experience in many ways.

First of all, the former Commissioner of Baseball and current Governor of Kentucky, Happy Chandler, was introduced. He was resoundingly booed by the crowd. Obviously, he was not popular in the Louisville area.

Secondly, the fairgrounds field was a combination baseball/football facility. Our seats were in temporary bleachers on the east side facing into the sun on a very warm day. Honey was pregnant with our first child and the sun was so hot on her stomach that she worried it might cook the baby. There were several fellows on the row in front of us who spent the entire game mixing drinks, getting drunk, and sliding off their seats into our legs. Honey grew weary of all this and began kicking the guy in front of her in his lower back so hard that I thought she might bruise his kidneys. By this time he was so soused he didn't feel much pain but he did respond to her kicks. And to top it all off, about mid-way of the fourth quarter, our section of bleachers collapsed. They sort of swayed to one side and kept on going until they were flat on the ground. We just walked off and no one was injured.

Even though conditions were not the best, we were witnesses to an historical event that afternoon. The starting quarterback for the Colts was a rookie, a local boy who had played at the University of Louisville. Some fans around us were saying, "They're just starting him because he's local. He won't last in this league." But he did last. Johnny Unitas went on to great career with the Colts and Honey and I saw his first start in the NFL.

Soon the NFL came to TV on a regular basis and you could watch a game every Sunday afternoon. Certain teams were shown in certain regional markets. We had no teams in the South so we had to watch the Washington Redskins each week. It wasn't long before the networks decided that two games each Sunday would be good and another at night would be even better. This pretty much filled up the Sunday time slots but it wasn't long before some network executive began to think outside the hash marks and Monday Night Football was born.

My first reaction was: "It will never work. Nobody plays football on Monday night." But as we all know, it has worked. Whoever came up with the idea figured that America's desire for football was insatiable, and only one game nationwide in prime time would garner a very large audience. And I became one of the millions of regular viewers.

In the 1960s Andy Griffith came upon the entertainment scene with the comedy record, "What it was, was football." After a few years as a regular viewer of Monday Night Football, I came to realize that "what it was, was NOT football." There were some good games but most were just average and a few were real clunkers. What drew me and many others to the TV set each Monday evening were the three individuals in the broadcast booth: Frank Gifford, Don Meredith, and Howard Cosell. I don't think this team was put together by design. It was probably like the ten-year-old with a new chemistry set just mixing various potions together to see what might be produced. The result was a team with unusual chemical properties.

Both Gifford and Meredith were former NFL stars. Cosell had worked in various sports but I don't think he'd ever really done football. Gifford, a former running back, did the play-by-play. Meredith, a former quarterback, was the analyst. Cosell, a man of outstanding intellect and vast vocabulary, asked penetrating questions and made comments about most everything in a voice of an unusual tonal quality which irritated a lot of folks. On more than one occasion in the middle of one of Cosell's long discourses on some topic, Meredith would break in with, "Howie, why don't you use a word or two the rest of us can understand?"

Cosell had a propensity for giving people nicknames. Early on he began to refer to Meredith as "Dandy Don" which sometimes became "Danderoo" or "Dandy man." Meredith did not appreciate this moniker and on one early broadcast when he thought his mike was off, Meredith said, "Howie, if you don't quit calling me 'Dandy,' I'm gonna slap the hell outta you." Gradually a mutual respect developed and Meredith accepted being "Dandy Don."

At the start of each game, the players would be introduced by showing their photos and giving the colleges they had attended. One night Otis Sistrunk's photo came up. He had no neck, no hair, and heavy-lidded eyes. He looked like a thug that you'd not want to meet even in a lighted alley. He'd not gone to college.

The following exchange ensured:

M: Where'd he go to college?

C: The University of Mars.

M: Do they have good teams?

C: Of course they do. And mainly because they recruit good players from all the planets, especially Pluto. (Pluto was still a planet then.)

From then on Otis was always referred to on the program as a graduate of the U. of Mars.

This crew was very good with tight, exciting games but they were even better with the dull clunkers. They had to be creative to hold the viewers' attention. They'd talk about most anything. The camera crew would pan the stadium for interesting people—children sleeping, adults sleeping or doing unusual things. One night the camera caught a couple making out in the dark confines of the upper deck. On another, the camera focused on a fellow in an odd looking coat. When he realized the camera was on him, he gave it a middle finger salute. Meredith responded, "That probably doesn't mean we're number one." The best come-back I ever heard from Meredith came when the camera focused on a really good looking woman. She had her chin in her hand and was sort of rubbing her long-nailed fingers over her face. She ran one of the long nails up her nose and really reamed out one nostril. Meredith's response: "Well, she was almost perfect."

Recently, I watched some of the Monday night game. The announcers are good but they don't even compare to Dandy, Howie, and Frank.

LOST IN SPACE

I'm old enough to remember the genesis of the world's space programs and even after 50 years, "space things" continue to hold a fascination for me. A few years ago an article entitled "Sex in Space" caught my eye. Several scientists in different fields were weighing in on what they though might be possible or not possible in space. Knowing the ingenuity of humans, I figured sex in space was a no brainer. So did the scientists. They were also discussing whether a baby could be born in a weightless environment—another topic that I found intriguing. As it turned out, what they were really speculating on was whether or not a space colony could exist and function in a more or less normal fashion. I suppose it never hurts to plan ahead just in case.

And only a few days ago, I read of another break-through that will go a long way in fostering space colonization—the successful distillation of urine. Yes, you read correctly. Scientists have developed a process that will turn urine into a drinkable liquid. I hesitate to call it water but whatever the process is, the equipment for it is compact enough to be taken aboard spacecrafts. Now, I've never been lost in the desert and had to survive by drinking my own as some survivors have reported. _Maybe_ I could do that but there was something about the account that gave me pause. I'll just bet the urine from the whole crew will go into a common tank and everybody will have to share. That would bring the togetherness of a space voyage to a whole new level. And I cannot imagine that being a positive selling point in the recruitment of astronauts. My suggestion: mix it with a little Tang to make it more palatable.

After all, Tang went to the moon and is still available. But what should really be disturbing to future space travelers is "what's next?" If they can figure out how to recycle urine, what else might they find to recycle? I'll just let you readers use your imaginations on that one.

As this is being written, there is a rocket poised to blast off for the Space Station carrying supplies, tools, and equipment to be installed. At the last minute, they had to take some of the tools out in order to take something to unstop the toilet. Yes, that's right, the space toilet is stopped up. Of course, it's a Russian-made toilet which may help to explain its current condition. But just the fact that this has happened makes me wonder about the practical sense of some of these space scientists. Everybody and his dog knows that plumbing is going to mess up no matter where it is. So, why didn't they include a plunger and some drain opener with the original equipment on the space station? Of course, I'm being facetious here because this device does not use water for flushing but fans. Maybe they need a bunch of those Southern funeral home fans with a picture of the funeral home on one side and the Lord's Supper on the other.

In a report on this space toilet problem, one of our local TV reporters (a female) said, "Until help arrives they'll just have to make do." Loud laughter erupted from the whole news team.

I began to wonder because the reports didn't say if they were going to have to send a special "Space Plumber" to do the job—maybe one with "plumber pants." I can just visualize him squatting down to his work with half his butt hanging out. This is not a pretty sight on Earth and I can't imagine it being any better in space. And I wonder what's got the thing stopped up. I wonder if he'll find a John Glen bobble head doll or some hygiene product that should never been put into it to start with. There's just a lot to wonder about in space.

When I first heard about the problem, it seemed to me that

the solution was rather obvious. Space is pretty big so why not just dump the waste outside. It would freeze solid in an instant and it's not like a space-walking astronaut is gong to step in it. But then I thought further and realized my error. Space is, indeed, pretty big. I'd say it's about the biggest entity we know about. But only a few years ago, we felt the same way about the oceans. We thought them so vast that they wouldn't be hurt by us humans just dumping whatever we wanted to get rid of into them. Coastal cities like New York would put their garbage on barges, haul it a few miles out to sea and dump it. We finally came to realize that dumping stuff like this plus all the toxins flowing into the sea from polluted rivers was killing our oceans and that we needed to take some action to reverse it. Of course, space is much larger than our oceans and is not "alive" with plant and animal life as they are. However, if we just look at the last two centuries of human history, we can conclude that the capacity of man to destroy and pollute is infinite.

I'll have to admit that space was on my mind recently when I had occasion to visit with a good friend and former student of mine who heads a company that specializes in cleaning up all sorts of toxic and non-toxic sites. He has offices in several foreign countries. When I asked him if he'd ever thought of starting a "space division," he said that he had not but wanted to know why I would suggest such a thing. I replied, "Well, you know space is getting more and more littered with space junk and several tons of it falls to Earth each year. Much of it burns up during re-entry but some of it strikes the ground. As this junk increases and more and more of it hits the Earth, it's only going to be a matter of time before it starts falling into populated areas. And you've probably read that the space station toilet just stopped up so, again, it's only a matter of time until we've got space full of crap. There's going to be a demand to clean this stuff up and your company could be ahead of the curve on this."

He looked at me a long moment before saying, "I think I'll bring this up at my next Board meeting." I can hardly wait to hear the response.

POLITICS AS USUAL
AND UNUSUAL

Politics are interesting in all sections of our Country but in the South they can be classified as a spectator sport. Some cases in point:

It's probably hard for current, young residents to believe but 50-60 years ago Tennessee was a strongly Democratic State. This story happened in a rural precinct before the era of voting machines. The poll had closed and the poll workers gathered around to count the ballots. One of the first ballots to be drawn from the box was a Republican ballot. All the workers were amazed. Most had never seen a Republican ballot so a discussion ensued about what to do with it. Finally, it was decided to "lay it aside" and figure that out later. Down near the bottom of the box another Republican ballot was discovered. It was "laid aside " with the first.

After the counting was done, they were left with the two uncounted, "laid aside" ballots and the question of what to do about them. One of the senior poll-workers proposed an obvious solution. "Boys," he said, "I think we can all see what's done happened here. Some dirty Republican has done snuck in here and voted twice. I say we just throw both of 'em out." And so they did.

Up in Hancock County in the late 1800s there was a fellow who wanted to be the County Sheriff. He had run for the office two or three times but had not been elected. When the Spanish-American War came along, he hit upon a plan. He would join up, return as a war hero, and be more appealing to voters. He enlisted and was serving with Colonel Teddy Roosevelt's

Rough Riders when they were pinned down at the base of San Juan Hill. Roosevelt rode up and announced, "Boys, the man who leads the charge up this hill can be elected President of the United States."

Our Tennessee Volunteer responded, "You go ahead on, Colonel. I just want to be the Sheriff of Hancock County.

During one campaign Governor Frank Clement was on a swing through East Tennessee, stopping at rallies in small towns. At one stop he mentioned the poor quality of the local roads and promised—or so the crowd thought--a four-lane highway for the area. There was loud cheering on this point. On the way out of town, one of his aides said that he didn't think the Governor should have promised them a four-lane highway. "I didn't," responded Clement. However, the aide persisted, saying that he was sure he'd heard him make that promise. But the Governor cleared that up with, "What I said was, 'the next time I come to this town I'll be riding on a four-lane highway.' What I didn't say was that I'm never coming back to this town." Such are the nature of political promises.

A few years back the Governor of Mississippi was living in a house in Jackson while the Governor's residence was being renovated. It was early afternoon on Christmas Eve. The Governor had sent the house staff and his Highway Patrol officer home to spend the holiday with their families. The Governor and his family were home alone. The doorbell rang. When he opened the door, the Governor was confronted by three very large, rough looking men dressed in overalls, work boots, and John Deere caps. A beat up pick-up sat in the circular drive. The older man held a card in hand and kept looking from it to the Governor who recognized it as one of the Christmas cards he'd sent that year with a picture of his family including the family dog, a beagle. He knew these folks were not on his Christmas card list. The following conversation ensued:

Visitor: "You the Governor?"

Governor: "Yes."

Visitor: "This your card?"

Governor: "Yes it is."

Visitor: "Well, we're the Stooks from Alcorn County. Your picture here shows that you've got our dog and we've come to take him home." (Alcorn in located in the northeast corner of the state about 200 miles from Jackson.)

Governor: "I don't really see how this could be your dog. We've had him for several years."

Visitor: "This picture says he's ours and we've come to get him."

The Governor was feeling especially vulnerable with three rough Stooks on his porch and no police protection. By this time the whole family had gathered at the door. He sent one of the children to get the dog. The elder Stooks examined him from nose to tail, looked at his belly and inside his ears before announcing, "Well Governor, he ain't our dog so you can keep him. Thank you for your trouble." The trio headed for the truck leaving a very relieved First Family with another example of direct democracy at work in the South.

NEW PARTS FOR OLD BODIES

You regular readers will recognize that I seldom go to the hospital for a "regular" procedure and have things turn out that way—"regular" that is. Something unusual always seems to happen. I've had friends accuse me of making the unusual stuff up just so I'll have something to write about. Of course, that's not true at all. I couldn't begin to make that stuff up. Perhaps the only part I play in it is being able to recognize the bizarre and the incongruities when they happen. Well, it just happened again and it happened in spite of the fact that I planned ahead and tried to make preparations which would ensure that this would be a :regular" procedure. But as Robert Burns observed, "The best laid schemes O'mice and men Gang aft a-gley." Mr. Burns surely knew how to call it.

It all started last year when I was told that I needed a knee replacement, that things were not going to get any better, and that I shouldn't wait too long. So, I decided to set it up while I could still call the shots. Fist of all, I decided that mid-February would be a good time. The weather usually isn't very good so being confined indoors wouldn't be so bad and there wouldn't be much pressing yard work to do. Secondly, with that much lead-time, I could get the surgeon I wanted. I close Dr. Craig Ferrell, the founder of The Bone and Joint Clinic. I chose him because he's a great surgeon and also because I've known him since he sat in my European History classes in high school at The Webb School, Bell Buckle. I will not allow some of my former students to get close to me with sharp instruments. However, Dr. Ferrell was as good a history student as he was in science so I know I'd be in good hands.

February 16 was the fateful day. All the pre-op stuff went well. That should have been a warning. I checked into the hospital very early and they soon had me wheeled down to the surgery holding area where I got to visit a few minutes with Mrs. Basia Brock. She's one of the nurses who's been in charge of running that area for several years now. I had both of her sons at BGA and with as many surgeries as I've had, we have run into each other on a regular basis.

Anyway, they soon had an IV in me and both the surgical nurse and Dr. Ferrell had signed their names on my left knee just to make sure they didn't replace the wrong one. The next thing I remember was a voice a long way off saying, "Mr. Boyd, you can wake up now. You're in recovery. We didn't get to do your knee." When the words finally sunk in, I grabbed my knee and it felt the same. In a panic I reached for the other one just to make sure they hadn't gotten turned around. It was normal but my throat was in a lot of pain.

When I finally got awake, they came by and explained what had happened. They were unable to get me intubated. That's a medical term. That was mine for this trip. It's the process of getting a tube down your throat so that you can breath during the surgery. There's not much room to begin with back in there between and behind the vocal cords and they had encountered some soft tissue growing just where they had to make the turn. Poking into it injured it causing it to bleed and swell making the passageway much smaller and more difficult to negotiate. As things went from bad to worse, Dr. Ferrell decided to back off and to try again in a couple of days with another procedure. I spent the rest of the day spitting up blood and trying to get awake enough to go home.

I'd been having trouble for several years with pills getting hung in my throat. Honey had just make fun of me but my throat growth condition proved that it wasn't "just my imagination" as she often said. I felt vindicated.

When I got home, I found that my leg was completely dead. They had blocked the nerve in preparation for the surgery. I could walk on it if I kept it completely straight. Of course, the first thing I did was to let it get out of line and cause me to fall down the three steps into garage. Fortunately, I did not break anything or damage any appliances.

Two days later I got to visit with Mrs. Brock again as my surgery team gave it another try. This time they sprayed my mouth and throat with some vile concoction that tasted like rotten bananas. It deadened everything it touched and they managed to get the tube in place. When I woke up this time, I knew I had a new knee. The pain told me so.

I had been warned that a knee replacement is the most painful of the joint procedures. They were right. It even hurt to think. Praises be for the morphine pump and those white pills. I don't remember this but two of my friends say they came by to see me the second day. They found me in a stupor with the covers pulled up under my chin. When they made their presence know, they say I opened one eye and muttered, "I'm not sure this was such a good idea."

One reason for the pain is that they won't let you find an easy position and stay in it. The new joint needs to be moved so that it doesn't lock up. The second day they brought in a walker and announced that I was to walk. I thought maybe some of my Rotary friends were getting them to play a practical joke on me. But they were serious—and I walked. Within three days I could get myself out of bed and walk to the bathroom.

Many friends came by to see me. A lot brought snacks or insulting get-well cards. None brought flowers. Being the practical person he is, Dick Jordon brought me a can of WD-40 in case I ran low on lubrication. Miles Mennell had come by one day. The phone rang and I asked her to answer it. She did so with, "Luke Boyd's room." There was a pause and you just knew the caller asking is she was my wife to which Miles replied, "Oh, no, I'm the 'other woman.'" It took a while to get that straightened out. I was just thankful it wasn't our pastor calling.

Abby, our little eight-year-old granddaughter, was fascinated with the long row of metal staples that held my incision together. She speculated that they might use a staple remover like the one on my desk to get them out. She was sorry she was in school and couldn't be there for the big removing event.

One day at the rehab center my cute, young therapist was walking me down the hall when Dick Jordon came up behind us. He offered no greeting but just launched right in. "Hey, Luke. Do you know where they got your knee?"

"No, Dick, I don't."

"Well, I have a friend who got one from one of those used joint places—you know like one of those auto salvage yards— and it was not satisfactory. You need to check and make sure you got a good one."

"Thanks, Dick. I'll do that."

"You know I'm getting some new teeth."

"Yes, I knew that."

"Well, I've been checking around and have found out that funeral homes have shoe boxes full that they sell real cheap. And they'll let you try them out. I'm gonna start making the rounds tomorrow."

"That's good, Dick. I hope you find a good set."

About that time we turned into one of the rehab gyms. Dick continued on down the hall as he found someone else to talk to. The look on my therapist's face was priceless.

You meet some interesting people in rehab. There were the two little ladies who always walked the halls together. They kept their walkers and eyes straight ahead seldom responding to a cheerful greeting. Three doors down there was a fellow who sang Broadway show tunes at the top of his lungs for about two hours every morning. He had a pretty good voice.

Even though I'd had good care at Williamson Medical Center and NHC Cool Springs, I was glad to get home. Someone asked about my other knee. Of course, it's doing fine right now but, considering all the pain I've had with this one, if the right one goes bad, it's on its own.

SIDELINE WOMEN

I am for women doing anything they are qualified for and capable of. I think a woman should have equal pay if she performs equal work. I believe women should be deacons and preachers in Baptist Churches. I'm okay with a woman being President of the United States. But, just as there are some places a man shouldn't be, there are places a woman shouldn't be. One of these is the sidelines of a football game—especially at the college and professional level.

It all started with television. When the networks first started televising football games, they did just that—they showed the game. Then, one network began to use long-range lens to zoom in on coaches and players on the sidelines. A rival broadcast team went a step further and actually put a cameraman on the sidelines who began to stick his camera into sideline huddles as well as into the faces of the participants themselves. Not satisfied with just pictures, reporters came to be included with the cameramen to make comments on camera in the midst of all the action.

At first the sideline commentators were men who were not very photogenic and who knew little about the game. Occasional ex-players were the exception but they were few and far between. It didn't take long for some broadcasting executive to get the brilliant idea to replace these male sideline reporters with women. Now, everybody is doing it and the "Sideline Woman" was born. Most have several things in common: (1) They are young. (2) They are very good looking. (3) They have peppy, yuppie names like Brandi, Traci, Kellie, Suzie, and Jill. (4) They know next to nothing about the game of football.

I suppose the purpose of this sideline intrusion is to bring the viewers closer to the game—to make him/her a part of the action, to give the viewer a new perspective on the contest. However, I cringe every time the play-by-play announcer says, "And now down to Jill on the sidelines." And Jill pops up on the screen with all her make up in place and her blowing tresses reflecting the rays of the autumn sun. "Thanks Jack, we just saw quarterback Bill just before this last series and he told me that he has become quite friendly with Bob Superprohero who is the quarterback for the Waco, Texas, Roadrunners. In fact, they talk on the phone every Friday night. You'd think they would talk football." (Jill leans into the camera.) "But, no. They talk about girls, dating, pizza, and guy stuff like that. Back to you Jack." My reaction: Who the heck gives a hoot?

Another example:

"And now here's Brandi on the sidelines:

"Thanks Jerry. I have here with me defensive tackle Tiny Mondelli who stuffed State's fullback on that last play and saved the touchdown."

And standing beside her is a grinning Tiny at 6'5" and 310 pounds with several front teeth missing.

"Tiny tells me he has a lucky T-shirt he's been wearing under his pads since high school. He doesn't feel properly dressed for a game without it. How about letting our viewers see it, Tiny?"

Tiny obligingly pulls up his jersey revealing a tattered and stained T-shirt that looks as if it blew out of a car on the interstate and got run over by other vehicles for about three weeks. Tiny has obviously grown some since high school causing the shirt to be stretched to its limits and only able to cover the upper half of his abdomen. His exposed navel is clogged with bits of turf picked up during the last series.

Even yet another example:

"Now here's Traci on the sidelines."

Traci is standing next to a player who is breathing hard, sweating profusely, and smiling broadly.

"Folks, this is Randy Speeddemon who you just saw make that fantastic, 83-yard run from scrimmage for the TD. Randy, tell our viewers just what you were thinking as you broke past that cornerback into the open with nothing between you and the goal line but green grass and white stripes."

"Yeah, I's thinkin'. I hope dey kant catch me an' I hope I don't fall down. Hi, Mom." (as he waves to the camera)

"Thanks, Randy, and back to you Pete."

These bits of fluff can be ignored but it's hard to discount the things that actually affect the game—like injuries. These Sideline Women jump on an injured player like a duck on a June bug. Apparently, these injury reports have to be quick, up close and personal, and predictive.

Situation: Player is injured, helped off the field, and seated on the bench. Trainer is working his leg to gage how much movement there is in the injured knee. Camera worms its way through sideline personnel and focuses on player's face—eyes clamped shut and contorted in pain. A feminine hand snakes in and pats his shoulder pad. Traci's voice is heard, "Bruno." Bruno opens one eye as a microphone is thrust near his mouth. The question: "How bad does it hurt?"

Situation: It's early in the third quarter. Camera focuses on Kellie standing beside State's star running back. Star running back is in street clothes. He has an ice pack strapped to his injured ankle. He is leaning on crutches. Killie smiles sweetly, holds the mike toward him and asks, " What do you think your chances are of playing this half?"

One of the more recent innovations has been the interview with the opposing coaches at half time. Now, one of the last things a coach wants or needs to do is to go on camera while a game is in progress. But, TV pays big bucks to each school so it calls the shots.

Situation: Siwash U. is down by four touchdowns as the first half ends. Suzie grabs Siwash's coach as he exits the field with his team. Coach's clothes are rumpled, his hat is on crooked, and the look, on his face conveys the message that he's pissed off at everything and everybody. The exchange:

"Coach, you're down by 28 points. What do you have to do in the second half to get back in the game?"

Coach snarls, "Well, obviously we're going to have to score some points plus keep them from scoring any more."

"Do you think you can do that?"

"We can if the defense shows up and if our offensive line opens a hole every now and then to give our backs some running room. Also, they've got to give our quarterback some time to throw the ball."

"Thank you for your insight, coach, and good luck in the second half."

As the teams return to the field, Suzie catches the coach of Enormous State University. He is happier than his counterpart. The exchange:

"Coach, you've got a four touchdown cushion. You must be pretty happy about the play of your team the first half."

"Yes, I am. Of course the four pass interceptions and two fumbles we recovered helped a lot."

"Coach, what did you tell your team at half time?"

"Well, Suzie, I told them we were only half done. That we still have 30 minutes of football left. That a wounded wolf is a dangerous animal. I told them that we had to play just as hard this half."

"Thank you, coach, and best of luck this half." Back to you Bert."

Now, anybody who thinks anyone could learn anything or gain any insight from those exchanges, please raise your hand and I'll put you in contact with a real estate agent selling swampland.

Apparently, the Sideline Women jobs are becoming so sought after that some are willing to go to drastic lengths to advance their careers. <u>Sports</u> <u>Illustrated</u> reports that one CBS Sideline Woman posed mostly nude in a girlie magazine. Question in the article, "Will this hurt her journalistic career?" Answer, "It couldn't. She is not much of a journalist to begin with. And the photos reveal her real talents which probably explains how she got hired in the first place."

Branching out a bit, probably the most useless groups associated with pro football teams are the cheerleaders. They're always on the sidelines. Their only redeeming feature is affording the men something to look at through their binoculars if the game is dull. And you have to be there. They won't show them on TV. Too risqué I suppose.

Anyway, <u>Sports</u> <u>Illustrated</u> reports that at one pro stadium the cheerleaders' dressing room is next to the visiting teams' dressing room. One visiting team created a peephole in the connecting door so that the cheerleaders could be observed running around in their underwear. Of course, word got around the NFL and visiting teams enjoyed making "cheerleader viewing" a part of their pre-game preparation. Eventually the cheerleaders found out about the peephole and filed a several million dollar lawsuit against the team's management for neglecting to discover the hole and thus causing them pain, suffering, and loss of privacy.

Now, the next year's squad, with the lawsuit still pending, came out with a Lingerie Calendar which featured squad members posing in their underwear for each month. <u>Sports</u> <u>Illustrated</u> entitled its story "Thongs for the Memories." When asked if they didn't see incongruity between the lawsuit and the calendar, a spokesperson for the cheerleaders said, "No. The peephole was a crime; the calendar is art." It was not recorded how many blondes there were on the squad.

Even that 80-something year-old journalist, Andy Rooney,

got into the Sideline Women controversy. In an interview he stated, "I'm not a sexist person, but a woman has no business being down there trying to make some comment about a football game." When challenged about this, he apologized— sort of—by saying, "I wish I hadn't included all women covering football, some are quite good. But most of the women are there because they're good looking, not because they know the game."

Actually, Rooney is correct. Some are quite good and should be there for that reason—they've earned it. But what we're seeing with the influx of the "pretty incompetents" is akin to the plight of the spotted owl which is seeing its habitat being destroyed. The sideline incompetents are destroying a man's habitat—a place where a man can spit and scratch and cuss a little when he needs to—a place where a man can survive.

GETTING ABOVE YOUR RAISING

There was an old fellow where I grew up who had this expression he'd use when he saw someone putting on airs or pretending to be something they weren't. He'd say, "They're getting above their raising." We've all known people like that. And it's not only people who are guilty of this sort of thing. Towns can fall victim to the same malady. A couple of cases in point:

There's this town not far from us known for its large, up-scale homes and the snobbish attitude displayed by some of its residents. A few years ago when Home Depot was applying to build a store there some controversy arose. One resident was quoted in an interview saying, "Our homes are so well built that we don't need a Home Depot." Most of the stuff written today about this town reflects its "high-end" attitude but it wasn't always this way. It's not very old as an incorporated place — less than 50 years. It started out as a place just across Nashville's county line where city residents could go to dance, drink, play slot machines, and perhaps engage in a few other popular activities. This aspect of the town's history is not mentioned much in polite circles today. This really irks a friend of mine who grew up there and whose father ran a business there in those early days. He says: "I'm tired of everybody ignoring or not admitting what went on in those days so I'm writing a true history of _____." I hope he gets it published. It may not be popular with some of today's residents but from some of the stories he's told me, it will surely be interesting.

Then, there's this other town in the area. It's an old town

and for most of its history it was just a small, sleepy Southern village. But people moved in, development occurred, and the town grew and prospered. Along with this up-scale prosperity came embarrassment at their humble and often time common beginning. If the town's not careful it's going to lose these stories and this aspect of its history.

For example: For many years within a stone's throw of the courthouse in a run-down business area was a brothel. Its existence was common knowledge. As one long-time resident recalls, "It was mainly patronized by working folk. The businessmen went to Nashville."

The town had its cast of characters found in most Southern towns—the village idiot, the town drunk, etc. The town harlot was a large woman weighing perhaps 250 pounds or so. She plied her trade from a bench in front of the courthouse. Her standard price was two dollars. A number of the town's finer citizens were quite put out when one of the Nashville newspapers did a series on small-town courthouses and the picture of their beautiful structure featured this woman sitting all splay-legged out front. Of course, other people around the State had no idea.

Over on one edge of town near the old cemetery was the residence of a black lady who performed abortions. People came from miles around for her services. You could tell when business was good because she made improvements on her house. After one especially good year, she had it veneered with crab-orchard stone. The stone remains but Roe vs. Wade put her out of business.

There was this attorney in town who was called Judge _____. He had once been a judge and even though he was no longer, the title remained. As he aged, his stomach grew quite large and sagged quite low. Of course, his arms did not grow, leaving him unable to reach one of his important frontal appendages. At home his wife attend to these needs while at the office he employed a young errand boy whose duty it was to assist him when the need arose. One day he was about to be late for court when he headed for the nearest facility with the boy in tow. He kept telling the lad to hurry and succeeded in getting him all flustered which led to his fumbling around and not being able to accomplish the task. Finally, the boy said, "I can't find it." To which the judge replied, "Well, it it's lost, it's your fault. You're the last one that had it."

Rufus was a black entrepreneur who owned a good bit of property and had several business ventures. One of his businesses was a poolroom on one of the main streets. There came a time when the town fathers wanted to beautify the downtown area and a seedy poolroom didn't fit in with their plans. They knew he couldn't be making much money from the pool tables but he could not be induced to leave. Then, one night his building caught fire. It was one of those typical old downtown buildings with a cavernous upper floor. In the putting out of the fire, it was discovered that Rufus was running a brothel on the second floor. This fact never came out in the papers nor was it publicized in any way. The story goes that some of the town's more prominent citizens had been visiting the upper floor and Rufus had kept good records. So the whole thing was kept quiet and he was not charged but he did have to close the poolroom. He went to the outskirts of town and opened a liquor store, lived in the back of it, and kept cats. This business didn't last long. Folks said it always smelled like an unemptied litter box.

Rufus owned some land across the river from town which was then out in the country. It is now an up-scale development. Part of the land was an inaccessible river bottom. Back in the '60s some fellow from up North approached Rufus about growing a crop of marijuana there for which he would be paid. The man would do the harvesting. The agreement was made and things went well until harvest time. The man brought a big truck and a couple of helpers. He also decided he wasn't going to pay Rufus so he got a fellow crook out of Nashville to show up pretending to be a law enforcement agent. He'd told him that he just wanted the pot and that anything he got out of Rufus he could keep. The "agent" let it be known that "for a price" he would let him go. The Northern crooks pretended to give him a substantial bribe. He asked Rufus for $1000. By this time Rufus, who was no dummy, had figured out what was going on so he told the "agent" he only had $100 on him but would bring the rest to a certain street corner in Nashville the next day at a certain time. The "agent" agreed. They all left, and Rufus went to a phone and called the sheriff. The truckload of pot was stopped before it got out of the county and everybody was arrested. To top it off, Rufus took a real agent to Nashville the next day and he arrested the accomplice when he showed up for the rest of his money. Rufus didn't make any profit, but he avoided arrest and was only out $100.

These and other colorful stories like them are a vital part of the histories of most towns and should be preserved—and will be unless folks get too far above their raisings.

Sports Nicknames and Mascots

The advent of nicknames and mascots for sports teams is a relatively new phenomenon in this country. Of course, the reason for that is because there were not any organized sports which lent themselves to competition between schools or communities before baseball and football came upon the scene in the late 1800s. But, in a little over a century we've concocted such a vast array of nicknames and mascots that it has become an industry unto itself.

This was not so in the beginning. Teams were simply known by the city, town, or community they represented. Soon, cities began to have more than one team which produced the Red, White, and Blue Stockings. We still have the Red Sox and White Sox. But items of clothing were limited and teams began to adopt all sorts of names with the appropriate mascots.

Some teams have picked ancient people like the Trojans, Spartans, and Vikings who are noted for their fierce, war-like qualities. The Trojans evoke the picture of a sturdy defense unless a horse gets involved. And who can forget the small, fight-to-the-death group of Spartans at Thermopylae during the Persians wars. Even though the Vikings did a lot of plundering, they were fearless sailors, riding their open boats all over the North Atlantic and even to North America. However, there are some ancient people who have been shunned even though their fierce qualities are not in question. Take the Huns, for example, who were led by Attila. A legend said that no grass would grow on ground touched by the hooves of his horse. And what about the Mongols led by Genghis Khan? Could it be that we just avoid these Asian peoples? It seems to me that "Samurai," the ancient Japanese warriors, would be a good nickname but I've never heard of it being used in this country. Of course, I don't think there's ever been a team called "Vandals" either. They were the fiercest of the German tribes but were so given to wonton destruction that their name has passed into our language with this meaning attached.

Native American names have been very popular. Generic names like Indians or Braves and the names of specific tribes such a Choctaws, Chickasaws, Apaches, or Seminoles are attached to a large number of teams. I've always though that such names were chosen because the choosers admired the positive attributes of these folk. But what I long considered complimentary has come under attached by the PC people. They consider such names demeaning and there's a move afoot to eliminate them all. The NCAA has waded in on this at the college level and set a deadline for compliance a couple of years ago. I'm not sure what the current status is but I do know that the Seminole Tribe has petitioned to allow Florida State to continue using their tribal name. Apparently, there has been a long and healthy relationship between the tribe and the University. Along this line I think the Atlanta Braves have eliminated Chief Knock-a-Homa who resided in a teepee in the outfield bleachers. When a Brave hit a home run, he would emerge and do a war dance around the teepee. It's good he's gone.

By far the most popular team names come from the animal kingdom with land animals leading the pack, so to speak. They are usually selected because they are ferocious beasts whose mere name strikes fear in the heart of any opponent. It's hard to go wrong with lions, tigers, bears/bruins, wildcats/bobcats, cougars, or wolverines. Some teams, mostly colleges, have the real animals or at least they did until the animal rights folks stepped in to protect the wild animals from being cooped up in cages. I remember one year in the early 1950s we were playing The University of Houston Cougars in Houston. They had a cougar in a wheeled cage that they would pull around the field to excite the crowd. We were waiting to go on the field and were right by the cage where his handlers were trying to get the old cat to stand up and look ferocious. One was in the cage cussing the animal because as soon as he got one end up, the other would lay back down. They finally had to give up and wheel him out in the recumbent position.

Some wild animals, however, are just not good mascot material. Who would want to play for or even go see a football team named the sloths? And there doesn't seem to be a big market for possums, zebras, giraffes, hippos, rhinos, jackals or hyenas. It's a shame that these and others always get left out. I suppose it shows that there's prejudice everywhere.

Most mascots were chosen when athletic teams were male. The proliferation of female teams caused some problems in designation. Most of these were solved by just adding "lady" producing Lady Tigers, Lady Bears, Lady Cougars, etc. Of course "Lady Bulls" has a rather odd ring to it. And everyone knows that a Lady Bulldog is a bitch but I've never heard that term used in an "official" or laudatory sense. Some schools handle this a little differently with names like Honey Bears, Tigerbelles, and Viqueens, which is supposed to be a female Viking. Some use Wildkittens for female Wildcats although a kitten can be either sex.

As I stated at the outset, these team names are supposed to evoke a feeling of strength or ferocity. However, some do just the opposite. Probably the mildest one I've heard is attached to the high school teams in a small town in southeast Colorado which is the center of a cantaloupe growing region. They are called the "Meloneers" and their symbol, painted on the outside wall of the gym right next to the highway, is a large cantaloupe with vine attached. I don't know their team colors but I suspect one is cantaloupe orange.

For a number of years, I was associated with a school, The Webb School in Bell Buckle, whose teams carry a very unusual name. It's "Feet" and they are, of course, The Webb Feet. Painted on one end of the gym is a large, dilapidated tennis shoe. The laces are askew, the tongue is hanging out, it's full of holes with a big toe sticking out of one at the end, and a hairy leg rising from its top. At ball games the student body is worked into a frenzy by a student waving a similar shoe affixed to the end of a broomstick. They seem to take a perverse pride in not being normal. And local sports writers find many ways to play on this name with such headlines as: "Feet stink up the court," "Feet stomp Wildcats," "Feet are un-de-Feet-ed so far." It's refreshing to see some schools still having fun with athletics.

TOUCHED BY A GOOBER

When I was at BGA, each spring in a solemn ceremony three new Goobers were named. They were: The Goober (male student), The Gooberette (female student) and The Faculty Goober (or Gooberette). The selections were made by the reigning Goobers of the previous year under the assumption that "it takes a Goober to know a Goober." Goobers are those likable, lovable folk we all know who march just a little off beat to any drummer they hear. They are the ones who start their cars on cold mornings and lock themselves outside with the engine running as they scrape frost off the windows.

They are the ones who show up a day early (or late) when invited to dinner. You get my drift. Probably the best definition of a Goober is "someone who is mildly incompetent but still gets the job done." We've all come across these people on our journey through life. They can be maddening at times but they do make the trip interesting.

A dear friend of mine is a Goober and she knows it. She's smart, talented, and witty but the Goober in her just comes through at times and there's nothing she can do to squelch it. For this piece I'll call her Suzie and say that she was neither a BGA student nor a faculty member. Her dyslexia is probably a contributing factor in her Gooberness but not the sole cause by any means. She admits that she spent some time in a philosophy class in college contemplating the existence of "dog" but managed to get past that state. I first met Suzie about 20 years ago when she was 40 but Gooberism has no age limits. Here are a few of hers.

One morning Suzie was rushing to get to work and had

fixed herself a large bowl of corn flakes with bananas. She decided to take her breakfast with her and eat it at her desk. She sat the bowl on top of her car while she loaded the rest of her stuff and drove away forgetting its location. The bowl rode remarkably well until the first stop sign. At that point inertia took control sending the milk, now soggy flakes, and fruit cascading down her windshield and over the car's hood. The sturdy bowl did not break so she was able to rescue it and the spoon but her breakfast was a total loss. By the time she got to work, both the flakes and bananas were drying and achieving a permanent union with the car. One of her colleagues asked her why she didn't visit a car wash. Suzie replied that she didn't have time right then and would just wait for a good rain to do the job for free. Of course, it was summer and we were in the middle of one of those summer dry spells. It was several weeks before enough rain fell to make a dent in the baked-on breakfast.

On another occasion Suzie was making a quick trip home in the middle of the day to pick up something. As she left the office, she picked up her mail and was checking it on the way to the car. In one letter was a check for her employer. When she got to the car, she threw the mail on top of the dashboard amongst all the other papers that were already up there. It was summer and she had all the car windows down. Now, what are the odds that a cross-draft would blow through the car and carry away only the check and she not notice it? Pretty slim you'd say but that's what happened. Back at the office she was searching everywhere for the check when one of her neighbors brought it in saying he'd found it in his front yard. No harm, no foul.

One cold winter morning Suzie was hosting a large group of visitors who had come in to her workplace for some all-day meetings. She had gotten up early and dressed in the dark. During the first session, she noticed that she had on one brown shoe and one navy shoe. They were the same style so the faux pas wasn't too noticeable unless she got her feet too close together. A comment from one of her colleagues: "For Pete's sake, Suzie, why didn't you turn on a light? You live by yourself." Suzie had no answer.

At a retirement party for a colleague, Suzie brought him two bantam roosters in a cage with the admonition to "set his chickens free." He refused this generous gift and she had to take the birds back home with her. Before she could get them returned to the chicken store, one escaped. It stayed in the neighborhood and was heard crowing most any hour of the day or night, especially at dawn. Her neighbors got upset about "somebody having chickens in the neighborhood" but since no one had seen her with the critters, Suzie played dumb about the matter. In due course the crowing ceased probably because of a marauding nocturnal feline.

Suzie spent most of her career in either public relations or fund raising for several non-profits. Most of these agencies were hard hit by the recent downturn in the economy. Her position was eliminated at one agency. She went to another only to have the same thing happen, leaving her out of a job. A couple of weeks ago a mutual friend told me that Suzie had moved to Denver. I asked at what agency she'd found an opening and was surprised when he answered, "She's with the U. S. Bobsled Team." Considering Suzie, I thought my next question was pretty normal, "What's her position on the sled?" As it turns out, however, she is not roaring down sled runs at 80 MPH but is raising funds to support our sledders as they train and compete in national and international events. So if she sends you a letter about a donation to help our sledders in Olympic competition, send her something. It'll help the team and her career. The one thing I hope she does not do is get on the sled. If she does with her history of gooberocity, there's sure to be an incident of epic proportions. I'm going to be watching the news because I know a goober cannot be changed either by altitude or temperature.

THE QUEEN'S ENGLISH

Winston Churchill was quick to admit that he was not a particularly scholarly schoolboy. His classes were divided into sections called "forms" with the lesser achieving students being placed in the lower forms which concentrated on very basic instruction. However, there can be certain advantages in these "slow" classes as Sir Winston observed. "By being so long in the lowest form (at Harrow) I gained an immense advantage over the cleverer boys....I got into my bones the essential structure of the ordinary British sentence—which is a noble thing."

The English sentence is, indeed, "a noble thing." It can be put together in a myriad of ways and can be used by a skillful writer to evoke any emotion. But even though there are lots of ways to build a sentence, there are certain rules that apply—at least in most cases. One rule says that one should avoid ending a sentence with a preposition. However, in some cases violating this rule is the better alternative. Sir Winston taught this to one of his young assistants while in the process of writing his history of World War II. Churchill had ended a sentence with a preposition which the young fellow had marked. Upon seeing this correction, Churchill changed it back to his original wording and wrote in the margin, "Such impertinence up with which I will not put." Sir Winston was, indeed a master craftsman of our language as the perusal of any of his several volumes will attest.

There are a few little words that some writers have a problem with—"next" for example. A while back Honey and I were attending an event at the Ryman Auditorium. The printed program contained a short history of the Grand Ole Opry. In it was this sentence: "The Opry was moved into a succession of three venues, each larger that the next." I think they meant "last" and I wrote them a note and pointed this out. I'm still waiting for a reply.

Recently, I was at a program given by one of those organizations which train folks to speak better in public. One presenter stated, "We have to make ten speeches and each builds on the next." Quite a feat. This fellow also kept saying that all their speaking programs were led by a mediator. I think he meant a "moderator" unless they were an especially contentious lot. A number of words sound similar but this does not make them interchangeable.

This fact was born out by a fellow I heard being interviewed on the radio the other day. He had just started a new chimney cleaning business and was emphasizing how important it was to maintain a clean chimney. He said, "That smoke residue that collects in there has been burned once but it's still flamboyant."

There is a current ad running on TV touting a Nashville car dealer. It says that it is "where you can have your car serviced all day on Saturday." Now, I don't know about anyone else but I do not want my car subjected to an "all day servicing." I'm not sure my car would appreciate such a lengthy servicing. In fact I don't know of anything, animal, or human who would want to be serviced all day on Saturday or any other day. Why could not the ad writer just say that the business was open all day to service your car?

There is another current TV spot featuring a former NFL quarterback who says "you can ask myself." Whatever happened to "me?' There's a lot of this "affected" pronoun usage going around now. However, the most egregious error in the ad is the use of the objective form of a pronoun as the subject of a sentence. Now, I know the fellow did not write the copy for the ad and he appears to be a nice guy. But why didn't the ad writers catch this?" Why did they have to add him to the stereotypical list of "dumb jocks?"

And some writers continue to have trouble getting modifying phrases in the correct position in the sentence. Two examples: A caption under a photo of a person speaking reads "Tennessee Chief Justice Frank Drowota announces he will retire from the state's Supreme Court during a luncheon at the First Amendment Center." And another caption under a picture of some cars on a highway states, "Vehicles exit off of SR 840 onto Nolensville Road at Triune Wednesday afternoon after the interchange was opened in 2000." The photo was taken in late 2005. Caption writers do seem to have a hard time getting their words in good order.

There are some writers who have trouble with segue. Their grammar may be correct but their sentences are like roller coaster rides, jerking the reader from one idea or concept to another. We were in Halifax, Nova Scotia, this past summer where we visited the only remaining immigration shed through which almost a million people entered the country. In a write-up about this, these immigrants were described as "trembling with fright at the unknown trials they might face." In the next sentence they are described as leaving the shed as "confident new arrivals." Undoubtedly, this was a magic shed. I'm sure they're glad they kept it

Some of the most creative manglers of the Queen's English are students who mangle ideas and facts as well as structure. A classic example is the student writing about Dante who said that "he stood with one foot planted in the Middle Ages and with the other saluted the breaking dawn of the Renaissance." Apparently Dante was a contortionist as well as a good writer.

And while teaching a course in World Civilization at Columbia State, I had a couple of students with some unusual ideas about Napoleon. One stated that Napoleon "wanted nothing less than the success of defeat." Now, there's something to think about. During a lecture on Napoleon, who, as a young, unknown artillery officer, had cannon wheeled into position, dispensed a mob, and saved the government of the Directory, I stated that "Napoleon came upon the pages of history with a "whiff of grapeshot." In his answer to a question about Napoleon on a subsequent test, one student wrote that "Napoleon came on the pages of history with a wrath of grapefruit." I'm going to let you readers analyze that one.

GRANNY SUE'S HOMEGOING

I ran into this fellow I know a while back. This is what he told me.

That's right, I ain't been around for a week or so. I had to go down to one of those states to the South of us for a funeral. Folks there call it a "Homegoing." Sue Ellen Babcock was a great aunt of mine. Ever body in the community knew her and she knew ever body and they all called her "Granny Sue." She was just sorta ever body's granny. She'd lived a long and full life—93 years—and was still doing pretty good. Most all her body parts were working good but alcohol did her in because she just wasn't as spry as she used to be. No, she didn't drink at all, never touched the stuff. She was just crossing the road in front of her house to get to her mail box when a beer truck run her down. I guess he was in a big hurry to make a delivery to that juke joint around the bend from Granny's place. A few years earlier she could have dodged him but, as I said, the years slowed her down too much.

You know, some folks say that something good can come out of ever thing, even a tragedy, and that was surely true here. You see, Budweiser sponsored the funeral. They said it was the least they could do. And talk about a crowd. Folks came from miles around to Granny Sue's "Homegoing." Some said it was because of the Clydesdales but the family wouldn't have none of that. They said it had to be because of Granny Sue and her saintliness. They said some folks was just jealous because it turned out to be much bigger than the one for Billy Ray Thornhead back in '97.

Some of y'all have probably heard of Billy Ray. He was a

local boy who had risen through the ranks to become one of the Grand Dragons in the Klu Klux Klan. And his death was a tragedy just like Granny Sue's was. You see he was having a big rally one night out in Cleve Bodine's pasture. Folks said it was a sight to behold—the flickering light from all those torches reflecting off those while robes and pointed heads. You just don't see sights like that much anymore. Anyway, Billy Ray was up in front of this big burning cross, waving an AK-47 rifle, and working the crowd into a frenzy, when one of the guy wires musta burnt in two. That flaming cross fell rat smack on top of Billy Ray and set his robe on fire. The nearest water was in the stock pond a good piece down the hill but that didn't do 'em no good because they didn't have no buckets. By the time they got the fire beat out and the cross drug off him, Billy Ray was about half burnt up. And some folks say a lot more people woulda come to his funeral if there'd been a casket instead of just that little jar full of ashes. Since he was mostly burnt up anyway, the funeral home gave the family a good deal on a cremation.

But just like I said, something good can come out of a tragedy. Billy Ray's death caused the KKK to see a need and they've formed a Political Action Committee to lobby State Legislatures and Congress to pass laws requiring that all material used in the Klan's robes be fire proof. Y'all probably remember the push a few years ago to get this passed for children's sleep wear. Well, it's no less important for the Klan. These folks are around fire a lot—running around at night with flaming torches, burning crosses in people's yards, fire bombing churches. It's dangerous and we just cannot allow the cream of our Southern leadership to be exposed to these risks without some protection. So far these efforts have not borne fruit but we all know that Atlanta wasn't burned in a day.

But back to Granny Sue. Yes sir. For whatever reason her funeral was bigger. There was people all over the place. The funeral home chapel couldn't begin to hold all of 'em. The parking lot was full of folks standing around amongst the cars. Some were settin' on hoods or in the back of pick-ups. And the road out to Shady Rest Cemetery was lined with folks on both sides. Some had lawn chairs and coolers. And when them horses came by pulling that beer wagon with Granny Sue's coffin and the pall bearers up on top and with that uniformed driver up on the seat waving his whip with that spotted dog settin' beside him, you never heard such cheerin' in all your borned days.

But I thought the best part of the service was at the graveside. The pallbearers, who were all Granny Sue's' grandsons by the way, wore little rose buds on their lapels. It's our custom that before the casket is lowered all the way, the pallbearers take off their flowers and pitch them into the grave. I'm telling you it was touching. Those Clydesdales standing there by the grave stomping their feet and switching the flies away with their tails. That spotted dog settin' there by the front wheel of the beer wagon. And one of Granny Sue's grandsons walks up, takes off his rose, pitches it in, and says, "Granny Sue, this bud's for you."

PART VI

THE HOLIDAYS

EASTER ANIMALS

Our children grew up during the era when it was popular to purchase a colorful baby chick or duck for your child for Easter. Sometime before hatching the eggs were injected with a coloring agent producing babies of many different hues. A whole brooder full of little fuzzy red, blue, green, pink, purple, and orange chicks or ducklings was a sight to behold and had such a high cuteness factor that purchasing was almost impossible to resist.

Of course, this was not a particularly humane industry. The dye killed many of the animals before or shortly after they hatched. The children/owners usually did in most of the others within a week or two by playing with them too roughly. Baby birds are not meant to be played with like toys but a six-year old doesn't understand this. The few that survived became within a few weeks what they really were—scruffy chickens or ducks when feathers replaced the colored fuzz. This loss of cuteness usually meant neglect and death.   Fortunately, the USDA stepped in and outlawed all of this eliminating a lot of pain for chicks, ducklings, children, and parents.

I will have to admit that our family participated in the colored Easter bird industry on more than one occasion. Unfortunately, most of our purchases lived creating even more problems down the road.

One year we got ducklings. The first problem occurred in the car on the way home. We told our kids that they could name their ducklings. Kim proceeded to name hers "Fluffy"—an appropriate name considering its appearance. David, who was into Western heroes at the time, named his "Roy Rogers," causing quite an argument with his sister. Not a good start for the Easter duck business.

For some reason both birds survived. However, we had bought ducks because we had been fearful that this might happen. There was a pond across the road in front of our house. We figured that this would be a good home for the ducks in case they lived. It was only good up to a point.

Fluffy and Roy stayed on or around the pond during the day but when darkness fell, they both came back home to roost by the front door—and to poop all over the porch and steps. Another negative was the large number of turtles in the pond. On the third day Fluffy disappeared. We figured her to be a turtle victim. Roy lived up to his name and avoided this fate.

Even though there was only one left, one-half of the amount of duck poop on the porch was too much. Fortunately, we knew a farmer who agreed to take the duck.

The experience with Roy Rogers and Fluffy was enough to make as swear off of Easter ducks. However, the fading of the duck memory and two children crying and begging before a box of colorful chicks a year later caused us to enter the world of Easter chickens. One was purple as I recall. For some reason they remained nameless.

Anyway, one survived and became a household pet. He would follow us around the yard and would sit with us when we were outside reading. He roosted at night on a big homemade wire clothes-drying rack right by our back door and beside our bedroom window. Upon reaching puberty, he began to crow. Now, crowing is a natural thing for roosters and we didn't mind his crowing at the sunrise, which we felt was normal. But, we lived in town and there were streetlights around. Every time he would open one eye and see a light, he would crow—loudly. With no air-conditioning we had to sleep with the windows open. It was like sleeping in a chicken house.

After several nights of being waked up five or six times, I

devised a tactic to eliminate the noise. At the first crowing, I would get up, grab a broom, step out the back door, and knock the rooster off his perch. Since he could fly, this didn't hurt him. He would flutter to the ground and go off and sleep the rest of the night under a bush where the rays from the streetlights did not penetrate. I suppose he couldn't see how to fly back to his roost in the dark.

This worked well for three or four nights reducing our being disturbed to once each evening. However, I did not figure on the rooster having enough sense to figure out a way to thwart the broom's nightly attack. When his crowing alarm went off about 2:30 the next morning, I got up, grabbed the broom which I was now leaving beside the back door, stepped out, and swatted at the noisy fowl. But this time he was ready. He flapped his wings and rose into the air and as the broom passed beneath him, latched onto the straws with a grip in his feet like the talons of a bald eagle.

It was not a pretty picture. Since it was such a hot night, I was not wearing anything at all. So, there I was, out in the backyard in the middle of the night, naked, waving a broom around with a flapping, squawking rooster on the end of it. I was still mostly asleep so it was a little while before I figured out that I couldn't' shake the rooster off by simply waving the broom around. When I finally woke up enough just to put the broom on the ground, the rooster released his death grip on it and ran off to hide under a nearby shrub.

As far as I know, none of the neighbors witnessed this escapade. At least none ever mentioned it. And I don't think it was captured on film. It's been almost fifty years and nothing as surfaced so far.

The process had been rather long but we had finally learned our lesson: No more Easter animals. The next year the kids found someone selling cute little bunnies but we refused to give in. I could only imagine what havoc two full-grown rabbits might wreak on our household. We shuttered—and did not buy.

WHERE HAVE
THE EGG HUNTS GONE?

It's the day after Easter as I put pen to paper—for me that's literal. As I reflect on the events of the past week, I realize that there are not any "real" Easter egg hunts anymore although there are plenty that are advertised as such. How can I make this dumb statement? It's because most of today's folk apparently do not have a clue what a "real" egg hunt is. Allow me to describe one from "olden times."

* * * * *

First of all, there were no community-wide hunts. Most were private affairs in which several families would be invited to someone's house. Some churches might sponsor one for their children but most churches were small so the number of hunters was not large. One common factor was that everyone (every hunter, that is) brought eggs—6 to 12 real eggs that had been boiled and dyed. This dying operation was a production in and of itself. Some purists made their own dye but most of us went to the ten-cent store (which doesn't exist anymore) and bought a packet containing everything a master dyer needed. It cost less than a quarter. Part of the event was to see who could create the prettiest eggs. The dying was a group project involving the whole family. Usually, by the time all the boiling and decorating was done, all family members and most of the kitchen was dyed. It was a mess but it did make for great memories.

The first activity at the hunt was to admire the artistry of the eggs. Then, while the kids were playing a few games, the parents (usually the fathers) went to an unseen location and hid the eggs.   And they really hid them—in thick grass, under leaves or pieces of bark, in holes in trees, etc.   The finding was based on close observation not how fast you could run around the area.   There was usually a prize for finding the most eggs but the big prize was finding the "Queen's Nest."   It was just that—a nest with a chocolate bunny and other goodies.

From what I read in the papers and see on TV news, these "old fashioned" hunts are now passe'.   Nobody dyes real eggs anymore and the hunt is not a real hunt but a mob scene in which a vast herd of unruly kids bring large containers and race around over an open field scooping up the exposed plastic eggs that have been strewn over the landscape.   The emphasis is on speed and greed.   They should be called "snatchings" and "grabbings" instead of hunts.   One picture showed a bunch of kids running around in an open field picking up plastic eggs "each of which contained a prize," according to the caption.   Of course, in this modern age, _everyone_ must have a prize.   The worst depiction I saw was a large crowd of children behind a rope barricade.   They looked like a miniature version of the start of the Boston Marathon as they waved their containers and strained at the barrier.   They were waiting for the helicopter. Yes, you did read that correctly.   A helicopter came over and dumped thousands of plastic eggs.   I suppose this was something like the dumping of Agent Orange during the Vietnam War.   Then, the rope was dropped and the snatching and grabbing frenzy ensured.   This was the second year of the helicopter dump and the sponsors touted it as "very successful."   However, the article failed to give their definition of "success."

Also making the Easter week news was the fact that two communities had cancelled their egg hunts for this year.   The reason: Last year's hunt had resulted in too many fights among the parents.

What in the world is the world coming to? I don't really know how egg hunts got into the mix but Easter is the most significant observance on the Christian calendar. How has it come down to helicopter egg hunts and fighting parents? I'm not one who wants to go back to the "good old days," which really weren't that good for the most part, but I'll take its spirit over a lot of what goes on now.

THE DREADED HOLIDAY LETTER

With the recent holiday season came stories of some of the unusual holiday letters which have become an integral part of some folks' Christmas greetings. One family reported that, in cleaning out some old cards and letters, they found that some friends had been sending out the same letter for several years, only adding or deleting a line or two each year. Another letter recipient noted that the senders said that their two-year old had developed a terrible odor although he seemed healthy. A visit to the doctor revealed that the smell was emitting from the rotting peas he had pushed up his nose several weeks earlier. My question is "Why would you want to share that?"

Honey and I receive our share of these epistles and, for the most part, look forward to them. During our fifty-seven years of marriage, we've lived in several different places and these letters are a good way to keep up with old friends we rarely see. And I'll have to admit that we have sent out two or three when we've had especially eventful years. Of course, we always get a couple that are just over-the-top.

There's this one family we've known for about thirty years that we can always count on for a holiday letter of extremes. It's written by the wife and she limits herself to one page, front side only. With the children and now grandchildren and new pets and new jobs, you might ask, "How does she do it?" Her answer is to extend the margins and reduce the font. This year she was down to the size found on the labels of cough syrup bottles. If she goes much smaller, she's going to have to include one of those little, square, plastic magnifying things with her letter. We knew her children were perfect because she told us every year. Now, there are the grandchildren. They're perfect to the fourth power. They play so many musical instruments, take dance and martial arts classes, have the lead roles in plays, make the all-star teams in all sports, and produce the top academic work in all their classes. I'm usually so tired from just reading this section that I have to rest before continuing. And the woman writes in exclamation points. I once heard a writing instructor say that all writers should be issued five exclamation points and stopped from using more once these were gone. I think these draconian measures should apply especially to preachers and grandmothers. Anyway, I counted this years' exclamation points. There were forty-nine on the one page. One sentence had five at the end. That's just too much shouting at Christmas time.

What I'd like to see is a requirement that all holiday letters include a "real" version with the spin taken off. Maybe some like this:

> *The letter*:   Greetings, friends.   2007 has been an unforgettable year for the Braggart family.   But through it all we have experience unprecedented personal growth.
>
> *Reality*: We pray to God we'll never have to go through another year like this one.
>
> *The letter*: Early in the year, we became environmentally conscious and decided to "go green" as a family. Our big house in Legend's Ridge with the three story great room was just eating energy so we downsized to a much smaller place.   We were amazed at just how easy it was.   Myrtle now uses solar power in her laundry and since Melvin has taken a new position closer to home, he bikes the two miles to the office each day.

Reality: We got caught in one of those sub-prime loan deals and lost the house. And since they took most of our furniture as well, we had no trouble getting everything into the smaller place. Without a laundry room, Myrtle washes down the street at the Wishy-Washy and hangs the clothes on a line out back. Melvin is thankful he was allowed to resign his old job when they caught him padding his expense account. And he is doubly thankful he found a new one so close since his BMW was repossessed. Fortunately he does not have an expense account with this new job.

The letter: Although Myrtle was enjoying all her volunteer work, she decided to broaden her horizons and re-enter the working world. She was fortunate to land a position in sales with an international company with the prospects of a future position in management.

Reality: With creditors camping on our doorstep, Myrtle got a job as a checker at Wal-Mart. There is hope for advancement.

The letter: In April Melvin developed a medical condition that you only hear about on TV. He spent a hard week in Williamson Medical Center before the doctors got him back to normal. During his stay "Mr. Personality" got to know all the nurses on the third floor and most of the ones on second and fourth who came by each day to check on his condition.

Reality: Myrtle warned him about taking so many of those little blue pills but he wouldn't listen and developed one of those "over four hour" things. Melvin says he'll never be the same and neither will Myrtle.

The letter: Mitch, our eldest and a senior this past school year, got enamoured with academic work in the spring and actually took two courses in the summer before enrolling in UT for the fall. However, we think he may have burned himself out and will take the second semester off to reassess exactly what he wants to do.

Reality: Mitch failed two courses his senior year and had to make them up in summer school to graduate. He didn't fare much better at UT having serious academic and disciplinary problems the whole semester. School officials say that they don't usually let a student go after only one semester but in Mitch's case they're making an exception.

The letter: Mandy started her senior year at D.H.S. but moved to a new school in November. We questioned this late transfer but all her teachers, the principal, and other school officials felt the new school would better fit her needs at this point.

Reality: Mandy is a loyal friend. She insists that she was just holding the large package of assorted drugs found in her school locker for a friend she refuses to name. We all decided that finishing the year at the county's Alternative School would be preferable to Juvenile Court.

The letter: Martin our little "surprise" is in the fourth grade and continues to surprise us. He began band this year and the band teacher already has had him on five different instruments. He may just be a one-man band before he's done. And this year he's tried his hand at basketball, baseball, track, volleyball, tennis, golf, soccer, and football. His broad interests and versatility never cease to amaze us.

Reality: Martin's fourth grade band teacher is working hard to find an instrument he can play. He even tried him on drums but he couldn't seem to find the right beat.   His total lack of hand-eye coordination makes balls hit him more often than he hits or catches them. We hope eventually to find something he can do since schoolwork doesn't seem to be his thing either.

The letter: You will note that our little dog, Mitzi, is not in this year's picture. We lost her late summer as she performed a courageous act. We still have a hard time talking about it. She will forever be our hero.

Reality: We took Mitzi for a romp on The Eastern Flank of the Battlefield late one afternoon. She foolishly attached a pair of coyotes. The last we saw of her she was being dragged across the fourteenth fairway. We still miss her.

The letter: We wish you and yours a wonderful Christmas season and a healthy and prosperous 2008.

Reality: Ditto.

THE FRUITCAKE

Sometimes it began the latter part of October. It was always in full swing by the first days of November. Mama would get the big Sears, Roebuck catalog out and begin surveying the fruitcake section. The selection of the year's holiday fruitcake was too important a decision to be made without a considerable amount of thought and research. And the decision had to be made early so that the cake could be in the house by December 1 to give adequate time for "the soaking."

In the process of making important decisions of this nature, Mama usually talked to herself. While dinner was simmering on the stove, she would get the catalog and pencil and pull her chair over by a window for good light and begin comparing the various ingredients of the several offerings. Sears, Roebuck always had a wide selection which tended to complicate the process.

"Now, let's see, this one has more pecans and other nuts than this one. This one doesn't have any nuts—I don't think we'd want that. And this one has a lot of red and green candied fruit in it. That always makes a pretty cake." These and similar musings would go on for several days as she underlined parts of the descriptions and made notes in the margins with her pencil.

Of course, she never asked my brother or me for an opinion. As far as I was concerned, they could leave out all those red and green chunks. I usually managed to pick most of these out of my servings. However, if Daddy happened to venture too near the chair of anguish, he usually got included. "Luke, what do you think about our fruitcake for Christmas?" His reply was the same every year, "Bill, you know I don't care."

My mother's nickname was "Bill." I never knew why even though I asked on several occasions. I was always told, "That's just what it is." My family was unusual in some other ways, also.

At times, neighbors would be included in the process. Mama would meet some lady she knew in town on Saturday and ask, "Y'all gonna have a fruitcake this year?"

"Sure are. Always do."

"You gonna order from Sears?"

"I'm sure I will. They have about the best around."

"Have you looked at them yet? What do you think about that one with all the candied fruit in it?"

"No, I haven't started looking yet. I'll probably just order one at the last minute like I always do."

The neighbors usually were not of much help.

But, somehow, a choice would be made which brought up the next dilemma: the three or the five pounder. This was usually fairly easily resolved and depended upon how many folk we were expecting during the holidays. Some years uncertain plans prolonged the poundage decision but weight was never a real stumbling block.

Shape was never an issue. Mama always ordered the round loaf with the hole in the middle because "they always soak so much better."

With all the critical decisions made, the order would be dispatched via the Postal Service which would, in turn, deliver the prize in about ten days or so.

I always enjoyed the unveiling. Mama would unpack the round tin, open it, and plop out the cellophane wrapped delicacy. She would then remove the cellophane and place the cake on clean cloths made from flour or meal sacks. I always begged for a piece but always got the same reply. "It wouldn't be good now. Too dry. It's got to be soaked."

The soaking was done with spirits distilled either from the vine or the stalk. And these were not easy to come by since Mississippi was a dry state. Some years Daddy would bring in a half croker sack of wild muscadines which would be turned into wine for this purpose. Other years he would have to resort to one of the local bootleggers or elicit a favor from a friend who was making a trip to Memphis. Daddy's role was to produce the moisture by which Mama would turn the round fruit desert (or dessert) into a verdant oasis.

Mama would distribute one ounce of the spirit-of-the-year evenly over the top of the cake before swaddling it in the cloths and placing it back in its tin. She gave as much attention to the wrapping as the ancient Egyptians had to their mummies. "It's gotta be tight to keep the moisture in," she'd say.

From then until Christmas Day, the soaking became a daily ritual. After supper Mama would unwrap the cake for its daily dose of moisture. My brother, Gene, and I would crowd in closely so we could smell it. I imagine it was comparable to the yearly unfolding of the Shroud of Turin.

The cake was not cut until Christmas dinner when it was usually served with a cup of homemade boiled custard or eggnog. After that it was fair game. Everybody that came to the house or even near the house was offered a piece. Even with such heavy demand, a five-pounder could last almost through February.

One year Daddy procured a bottle of bourbon (I don't recall the brand.) as the moistening agent. I was so taken by its smell when Mama opened it each evening until I suggested that we just drink some of it. Mama was horrified. She gave me a good lecture on the evils of drink and all the terrible results of its consumption. I could not really see the difference in drinking it and pouring it over a cake and then eating the cake. I supposed it was just one of those things like girls which I was told I'd "understand later when I grew up." I'm still waiting on that one.

Anyway, in the "year of the bourbon," Mama somehow lost her sense of perspective as to how much liquid there was in an ounce. On that Christmas Day when she cut it, she had to dip it onto the dessert plates. I discovered that if I held my plate up between a light and me, I could see little distorted waves rising not unlike looking down a long stretch of concrete highway in mid-July. My cake was floating around the small plate like pieces of land trying to form a new continent. Gene was eating his with his spoon. Daddy, knowing how Mama got her feelings hurt when her culinary efforts were not well received, only made one comment, "I'll say one thing, Bill, you really know how to soak a fruitcake."

When word got around the community about Mama's fruitcake, it barely lasted through New Year's Day.

ANOTHER STAR

This story is not original. It comes out of World War II. I think I read it in _Reader's Digest_ when I was eleven or twelve. Obviously, it made a lasting impression on me because I have never forgotten it. The names of the people and military units involved long ago escaped my memory, but the story has remained. This year we have troops overseas at Christmas just as we had in the early 40s. This makes the story appropriate.

The setting is the China-Burma Theater. Most of the personnel who served in this Theater were assigned the task of getting supplies into Western China to the Chinese army led by Chiang Kai-shek. The land route was the famous Burma Road out of Burma. Supplies were also flown in from airfields in India. This particular operation was called "flying the hump" with the "hump" being the Himalayan Mountains. Although these airmen seldom had to face Japanese fighter planes or anti-aircraft fire, their missions were fraught with danger from the mountains themselves and the weather they produced. This is the account of one of those flights.

The squadron caught a mission on Christmas Eve. War took no holidays and the planes had to fly when there was a break in the weather. They were to take a load of supplies in on 24 December and return on Christmas Day.

The mission was routine at first but beyond the point of no return, one plane developed engine trouble and had to drop out of formation. The pilot hoped to nurse it on to its destination but the rest of the squadron had to fly on.

Things did not go well with the crippled plane. First, it was caught by darkness and then, worse than that, by an unexpected snowstorm which blew it off course. The pilot was having trouble maintaining altitude even before the storm. Soon he was fighting a losing battle as ice began to form on the wings. He ordered the crew to jettison cargo but the ice continued to win. When his instruments told him that he was flying lower than some of the peaks in the area, he knew it was only a matter of time until they hit one.

Although not unexpected, the crash was startling when it came. All of a sudden it felt as if the plane were riding on rough waters. The pilot quickly cut the engines. After a few seconds the plane began to break apart and, then, all was quiet.

As they were to learn later, they had not flown head-on into a mountain. Instead, they had pancaked onto a shelf above the tree line. The deep snow slowed their momentum so that as they skidded down into the forest, the trees completed the braking process without totally destroying the plane.

By some miracle they were all still alive, even though a couple of the crew were injured. The pilot got them all huddled together in the largest unbroken section of fuselage. There they waited out the storm and the night. Some even slept.

When dawn came, the pilot began to assess their situation. Things did not look good. The radio was beyond repair. Snow was waist deep and had covered the wreckage making it impossible to spot from the air. They could probably find enough debris to pile up for a signal fire in case a plane flew over. But a plane coming their way was highly unlikely since the pilot figured they'd been blown quite a distance from their normal supply routes.

The pilot knew that there were villages in some of the mountain valleys. But he had no idea where one might be. There could be one directly down the mountain or twenty miles away. Anyway, heading out in snow that deep in sub-zero temperatures would be suicide.

It seemed to the pilot that they had been spared the quick

death of hitting a mountain head-on only to be given a slow death of cold and starvation. They could last for a while with the shelter and the few rations they could salvage from the wreckage. But it would only be a matter of time. Although it was not spoken, the faces of his crew told the pilot that they had come to the same conclusion.

Nevertheless, they busied themselves with sorting through the wreckage for items that might be of use. They also plugged up all the holes they could in the piece of fuselage they were using to live in. This was tiring but necessary work.

Sometime up in the day, they were huddled together in the fuselage trying to warm up from their outside labors when they heard voices. No one believed they were real at first. The pilot thought that fatigue, the cold, and stress were affecting their minds. But they seemed too real not to be real. The pilot threw back the cover they had rigged over one end of the fuselage and could not believe his eyes. The voices came from a rescue party from the village in the valley below.

Fortunately, one of the villagers could speak a little broken English. After the initial excitement of being found had subsided, the pilot began to try to figure out just how they'd been located. It took a lot of arm waving and other gestures plus words. The villagers had heard the plane and the crash in the night and had set out at dawn to look for survivors. They had obviously come directly to the crash site and the pilot kept trying to find out, with all the other mountains around, how they knew which one to climb. Finally, he understood the villager to say, "We followed the star."

"They followed the star?" It sounded so biblical. What star?

Seeing the puzzled look on the pilot's face, the villager turned and pointed up the mountain. There, wedged into the top of the tallest tree was the tip of one of the plane's wings with its U.S. star insignia sparkling in the sunlight.

It was then that the pilot realized that it was Christmas Day.

'TIS THE SEASON

In late Medieval times, the various art forms that began to emerge in the Western world were centered on religion. The Church had the resources to commission painters and sculptors whose work not only beautified drab buildings but was also used as teaching tools. The largely illiterate population got much of their knowledge of the Bible from Church art. Even today in our literate world, we get a lot of our scriptural "knowledge" from sources other than the Bible which may explain why, as Mark Twain observed, "We know so much that ain't so." Take Christmas for example.

As Christianity developed, the Church neutralized pagan festivals by placing Christian observances on those dates. The pagan festival marking the winter solstice was designated by the Church as "Christ's mass" (later Christmas) to celebrate the birth of Jesus. Biblical scholars do not think Jesus was born during the winter because shepherds were in the fields with their flocks at night which would only have occurred during warm weather. Actually, there is no way to know the date or Jesus' birth.

As one moves about during the Christmas season, nativity scenes depicting the stable birth are quite common. They always have a star. The scriptural account mentions no star at this point. It simply says that an angel appeared to a bunch of shepherds (persons of very low social rank) and told them what had just happened. Then a large group of heavenly hosts appeared, singing and praising God. When all this was over the shepherds said, "Let's go see for ourselves." They did so and found the Babe just as the angel had said. But no star led them.

Some nativity scenes depict quite a variety of animals in attendance. If it was the stable of the inn which had no room for Mary and Joseph, it probably housed mostly the donkeys its guests had ridden to Bethlehem. But modern depicters like a wide variety. A few years ago one church advertised a very large nativity display with live people and animals, which included donkeys, goats, sheep, a camel, and a zebra. For Pete's sake, Jesus was not born in a zoo. We have to take something that was beautiful in its simplicity and "Hollywood" it up because it makes a better visual display. And observers tend to think, "that's the way it was."

Now to the star. Nativity scenes always show three wise men with their camels squatting nearby. They were not there. The magi could have arrived as much as two years later because Herod commanded the killing of all male infants in the area aged two and under. Scriptural accounts say that the star led them to the place or house where the child or young boy was. No stable. And we don't know that they came on camels or that there were three—just more than one. We infer that there were three because there were three gifts.

Many nativity scenes have angels about and there are many depictions of angels during the Christmas season. They are usually shown in long white robes wearing a halo and with a large set of wings attached to their shoulder blades. Angels are messengers from God who bring a message or a command to humans. They do not have wings. Nowhere in scripture are angels presented as having wings. Apparently, they appear as an ordinary person like the one who was sent to Gideon. The angel sat under an oak tree for a spell and then spoke with Gideon and no one noticed anything unusual about his appearance.

There are heavenly beings with wings, however. At the time of his call from God, Isaiah saw seraphim each with three pairs (six) of wings.

Then where do the angel's wings come from? They first appeared in Medieval times with the surge of religious art. These artists reasoned that God's messengers had to have some way to get around, so wings appeared. And they have been with us ever since in paintings, on statuary, in song and story and movies. This year's Macy's Thanksgiving Day Parade featured one group of children dressed as angels with their little gossamer wings flapping in the breeze.

Now, does all this mean we should look at Christmas with a jaundiced eye? I think not. Just because people can't get it right doesn't mean that God didn't. It's message was simple, plain, and straightforward. Over the centuries in order to make it "play better in Peoria," people have obfuscated this plain message with bright lights, tinsel, shopping, and all sorts of "knowledge" from the wrong sources. It's only from the "real source" that we learn the Season's true meaning.

Coon Dogs and Outhouses
Volume I
Tall Tales From The Old South

This first collection of his stories is part remembrance of a culture that is gradually fading, part recollection of lessons learned over a lifetime. Luke Boyd's matter-of fact style and clarity of detail are cut from the cloth of the oral tradition, which flourished in the rural South of his upbringing. He deftly places the hilarious story of chain saw-toting Phinos Ledbetter and his botched baptism at the East Fork Southern Missionary Baptist Church alongside the powerful memory of an uncle known by the poor tenant farmhands he served only as "The Jesus Doctor."

The author's characters are depicted so clearly and accurately as to leave the reader guessing which stories are fact and which are imagined. And whether the teachers in these tales are smudged with the dust of chalk or caked with the mud of the field, their lives and lessons are faithfully recorded here in the straightforward prose of Luke Boyd.

- ➤ Author:　　Lucas G. Boyd
- ➤ Publisher　TotalRecall Publications, Inc.
- ➤ Publication Date:　9/1/2008
- ➤ ISBN Paper Back:　978-1-59095-837-7
- ➤ ISBN eBook:　　978-1-59095-838-4
- ➤ Distribution arrangements:
  Ingram, Baker Taylor, Amazon.com, Barnes and Noble, etc.
- ➤ Publicity contact information:
  Bruce Moran, 281-992-3131

Coon Dogs and Outhouses
Volume 2
Tall Tales From The Mississippi Delta

It was the Depression and very few areas were as economically depressed as the rural South. The road in front of our house was dirt (mud when it rained) and with no electric lights and no plumbing, we lived a bare and stark existence. There was no money to purchase entertainment so we made our own. Whether rocking on the front porch before bedtime or sitting around the kitchen table after supper, it was story time. Daddy was a storyteller and had a number of tales he told on a regular basis.

Stories flew thick and fast when visitors were in the house. With my uncles it was tales about the family or about people they grew up with. With neighbors I learned who had been caught making moonshine and who was stepping out on his wife. Much of my early education came from sitting on the floor off to the side during these sessions. I not only learned the stories, I also learned how to tell one.

- ➤ Author: Lucas G. Boyd
- ➤ Publisher   TotalRecall Publications, Inc.
- ➤ Publication Date: 10/16/2008
- ➤ ISBN Paper Back: 978-1-59095-839-1
- ➤ ISBN eBook: 978-1-59095-840-7
- ➤ Distribution arrangements:
  Ingram, Baker Taylor, Amazon.com, Barnes and Noble, etc.
- ➤ Publicity contact information:
  Bruce Moran, 281-992-3131